CONTEMPT

RENZO + LUCIA, BOOK 3

BETHANY-KRIS

Published by Bethany-Kris

www.bethanykris.com

ISBN 13: 978-1-988197-82-1

Cover Art © London Miller

Editor: Elizabeth Peters

For the littlest loves of my life, my boys.

CONTENTS

PROLOGUE

Compassion is contempt with a human face.
—John McCarthy

I miss New York.

It was the first thing that drifted through Lucia Marcello's mind as she strolled through The Annex for the first time in almost a year. She'd visited the market shortly before heading out to California the year before, but that was only to grab a few jars of her favorite homemade loose tea. She wouldn't be able to get it anywhere but here.

California was ... exactly what Lucia needed. It gave her space from her family, and allowed the bitterness and contempt she constantly felt for them to stay hidden, for the most part. Oh, sure, it was still there. Festering and living well, but it just didn't show itself nearly as much when she didn't have to face people like her father or brother day in and day out.

Except ... California wasn't *one thing.*

That one thing being home.

New York was always going to be home to Lucia.

Maybe that's why she felt so goddamn nostalgic as she took in the many vendor tents, and the new faces filling up The Annex. It had always been a melting pot of races, religions, and cultures. There was something for everyone here. That's part of the reason why she loved it so much.

Despite the way she wanted to enjoy being *here* when she hadn't been here in so long, Lucia couldn't settle into that comfort as easily as she wished. She might have been able to blame it on the fact this was her first trip home in almost a year, but that wasn't it at all.

More like the man walking a few paces behind her. Her brother—John. Sure, he'd kept quiet as Lucia became acquainted with the woman he simply explained that he *loved.* He'd said it so surely, so honestly, that Lucia had no choice but to believe her brother when he introduced her to Siena Calabrese. She didn't think she had ever heard her brother sound so entirely sure about anything before.

Not like he had when he told Lucia about Siena.

So, maybe it made her feel a little sick to her fucking stomach that her brother was happy in a way. That he'd found someone to love; someone he wanted to protect and adore for the rest of his life; someone he needed as much as he needed air. Because that was all the things John dared to explain to Lucia when he brought Siena along for their trip out—one her mother

1

had all but demanded she take. *To let John apologize; to fix the burned bridges*, her mother offered like Lucia gave a single damn.

She wasn't sure if she did.

Lucia *did* know that the fact John had found someone he loved felt like a gut punch for her. Why was he allowed to have someone he wanted and loved when he had practically ripped that very same thing out of her arms?

He'd helped to take her love away.

He'd done that.

And she was supposed to be happy for him right now? God knew she tried—over the last year, she'd tried damn hard to forgive her brother for all the shit that had gone down with Renzo.

That was the thing about feeling such a strong contempt for the people you also loved, Lucia had found. It was relentless, and vicious. It didn't just draw lines in the sand, no. It *painted* them with the blood of memories from happier times, ruined and stained. It was like a damn poison, slowing taking over a person's body.

Because that's how it worked. It killed a person while they waited for it to kill someone else. Despite knowing all of this, Lucia couldn't let it go. She was infected with it—dying from it slowly.

Being angry was easier.

She didn't know how to be anything else now.

It was funny.

Sickening, too.

A year could change so fucking much for everyone else. But a year changed *nothing* for her. She was still just as raw as she had been. Still just as hurt, and angry. Everyone else's world continued to turn, and hers was stuck in this standstill she couldn't seem to escape.

Lucia wasn't sure if she wanted to escape it, honestly. Again … easier.

John continued to stay far enough behind them to give Lucia some breathing room even as they headed further into The Annex. She was grateful he made the effort,, but John had always been the type to give people their space when he got the impression they needed it. Mostly because he wanted people to afford him the same thing.

Despite being slightly uncomfortable because of her brother's constant presence that day, Lucia couldn't deny the fact that there was something … sweet about Siena Calabrese. Lucia had taken to her almost the second she said hello with a bright smile. Like she had heard all about Lucia—the woman probably had, knowing John—and couldn't wait to make friends.

It was kind of hard to be angry with a woman who just wanted to like you. Plus, Siena didn't have *anything* to do with the whole Renzo episode a year earlier. Lucia found herself surprised at how easily she wanted to make friends with Siena, too. Like maybe she was in desperate need of another friend in her life.

She had so few of those.

It sucked.

"I think he's lonely back there," Siena said to Lucia. "John never does well as the third wheel, does he?"

She gave a little laugh. "He's going to be fine."

Siena bumped Lucia gently with her hip. "He loves you so much. Talks about you all the time, Lucia. He's had a rough time this last year. I think you have, too. It might help you both if you just tried—"

"Probably not," Lucia muttered under her breath.

Instead of trying to argue with her further, Siena gave her a look and then shrugged her shoulder when Lucia refused to break her cold, calm mask. "All right, don't say I didn't give you the chance to make the first step without help, you know."

What in the hell did that mean?

Lucia would soon find out.

It seemed it wasn't only her mother—her father had all but given up on trying to close the distance between the two of them—who was willing to play the Devil's advocate for Lucia and her brother. Siena seemed ready to jump into the fray, too.

Great.

"John, you're out of that jam you like, right?" Siena asked, looking over her shoulder.

Lucia's gaze drifted to John, too, but the second he looked back at her, the coldness slipped into her heart once more to freeze it all over. Just like that, she went from feeling fire and fury to *nothing*. Nothing at all. Sometimes, she hated that emotion played tricks with her now. Like she was feeling entirely too much one second, and then the next, she couldn't feel anything at all. She wished it would just pick one goddamn thing or the other and stop giving her whiplash.

She quickly tore her stare away from her brother, refusing to give him more of her attention right then. She didn't like the way it left her empty, and feeling more alone than ever.

John sighed behind her.

Siena looked Lucia's way like she wanted to grab her attention. Lucia even refused to look at her.

"We can grab some of the jam on the way out," John said. "Don't worry about it, *bella*."

Siena was quick to reply, "No, I can make a trip around. I need to grab something else that way, too. You and Lucia keep going. She wants to grab—what is that, again?"

Lucia didn't look back at her brother as she muttered, "Some loose tea."

Kind of wishing I didn't want it at all, now. I wouldn't have to be here to begin with.

Hell, even her thoughts were a particular brand of nasty today.

3

"Yeah, so take her," Siena said, dropping Lucia's arm and giving John a pointed look. "And I will meet you at the entrance on the way out of the market."

It further proved what she believed—the woman was going to attempt to force Lucia to make nice with her brother by not giving her a choice when she left her alone with him. That was laughable. Lucia could sit in a room with *anyone* and say absolutely nothing. They could be looking her right in the eye, and she could keep her expression blank, and her mouth firmly fucking shut.

Out of the corner of her eye, Lucia watched Siena drop a quick kiss to John's lips and murmured something she couldn't hear. Whatever it was, it made her brother pout. Like a fucking little boy. It was almost amusing.

"I will meet you at the entrance," John grumbled when Siena stepped away from him.

"Good," she replied.

Siena patted his cheek with a soft hand, and then just as fast, headed into the crowd, back the way they first came. Lucia didn't miss how one of two enforcers that were following them for the day headed after her without a word. She didn't think to ask her brother why he had enforcers trailing this close to them, but she didn't need to, either.

They were mafia kids.

Well, even if they weren't kids anymore.

Something dangerous was always following close behind. The next attempt on someone's life was always right around the corner. Not to mention, Lucia didn't know all the details about the past year as she hadn't thought to ask, but she did hear whispers. Her brother had taken over a rival family—people were unhappy.

That meant bad things.

Probably another reason for the enforcers.

With Siena gone, that left John and Lucia.

Alone.

Shit.

Lucia sighed, wanting to get this done and over with. At least with the buffer of Siena between them, she didn't feel so out of place with her brother. Waving a hand at her brother and heading into the crowd, Lucia said, "Well, come on, then. It's cold, and I don't want to freeze out here for too long."

John chuckled, and his footsteps followed behind. "You didn't mind five minutes ago when Siena was here."

Lucia stiffened.

Asshole.

He would have to say that, wouldn't he? She wished he just wouldn't start to begin with. Make this easy on her, and all that shit. Nothing could ever be that simple in Lucia's life. It was never simple.

"Yeah, well ..."

What else could she say?

Apparently, she didn't need to say anything because John had all sorts of things to say. *Fucking perfect.*

"What do you need me to say, Lucia?" John asked quietly from behind her. She still refused to turn around and face him even as he spoke. Maybe it was rude, but it was better than him seeing the hatred shining back in her eyes. She didn't want to hear anything he said, but here they were, it seemed. Just her luck, too. "Tell me what to say so that we can move on, and I will do that. Sorry isn't going to be good enough—I get that. So what will do it for you?"

For a second, she stopped walking. Her heart stuttered—playing tricks on her again, as the emotions blew all around her like the people still swarming The Annex. The tension between her and John still felt thick and loaded with all the things she had said to him before this—things she knew hurt him because *God*, she just needed him to understand and feel the way he made her feel—and things they had yet to say to one another.

Did he really want to know?

Did he honestly want to know what would make this better?

Because she didn't think *anything* would.

Slowly, Lucia turned to stare at her brother. The familiar prickling behind her eyes said the tears were coming, and she bet John could see the water shining back at him, but she held it all at bay. She *would not* cry. Not then.

"You're right," Lucia said, "sorry *won't* be good enough, John."

"But I am sorry."

She believed him for no other reason than the truth staring back in his gaze, and the way he dropped every pretense he'd been holding onto before this moment. She heard the truth in his voice, and how it colored his tone thickly with emotion she understood all too well.

Regret.

Pain.

She knew that well because she felt it constantly.

So, yeah, she believed that he was sorry.

Lucia nodded. "*Now.*"

"The day it happened. The day I found you. The day Renzo was taken away. That very second, Lucia, I was *sorry*," her brother muttered, his tone aching. "That was not what was supposed to happen."

Oh, God.

There was so much she wanted to say to him. So many words that wanted to snap out of her tightening jaw just because she could. It would be easy, and it had become habit for her to cut her brother or father with her words to hurt them instead of trying to listen to them. She tried something different, and not for John, but because she was goddamn tired.

Way too tired to be angry right then.

"Did you know he hated me?" she asked softly.

John's brow dipped. "Who?"

"Renzo," Lucia said. "At first, he thought I was just some little rich bitch with an air-filled head, and a pretty face. I didn't know what it was like to be poor, or to struggle. I didn't know the streets, or how hard they are on people like him. I didn't know what it was like to come where he comes from, or how to survive without a trust fund."

"Lucia—"

Lucia shrugged, feeling the bitter laugher rising in her throat, though she managed to hold it back somehow. "He was right, too. And maybe I should have thanked him for making that obvious to me, you know? He woke me up. It took thirty days to change my life, and *seconds* to make it worse all over again."

John dragged his hand down over his jaw, and looked away from her. Lucia didn't know what to expect from her brother, then. She wanted him to understand how different her life had become because Renzo stepped into it, and then how irrevocably worse it had changed yet again because her brother and father took him away from her. If he could know those things, and understand what it meant for Lucia, then maybe … God, maybe, she could work on this wall between them.

He had to understand, though.

That had to come first.

John slipped a hand into his pocket, and without a word, pulled out a piece of folded up paper. He held it out to Lucia like he wanted her to take it, but she stared at it, unmoving.

"Here," John said.

Lucia didn't move a muscle. "What is it?"

"A better apology."

What?

Lucia took the paper from his outstretched hand, but didn't take her eyes off him. She didn't have a reason to distrust her brother at this moment, but he'd given her one in the past. She didn't know what she might find when she opened that damn paper up, and she was not willing to find more pain and heartache in whatever he was giving to her.

Simple as that.

Lucia unfolded the paper, and felt the air catch painfully in her chest as she read over the information that had been scribbled down in her brother's familiar, messy handwriting. To someone else, this information might be nothing. To her, though, it was fucking *everything*.

And more.

Renzo Zulla, it read at the top. And then right below, an address had been written down. She could tell it was just a PO box, and nothing more. Not an actual address to a home or … something. Not even a prison address with an inmate number.

She'd searched for him in the system. Tried to find him time and time again. No one seemed to know where Renzo had been moved after New York. It was like he vanished into thin air. Lucia was mad—too mad to ask her father what in the hell was happening with Renzo, but she didn't think Lucian would be honest with her even if she did ask him for the truth. But she *knew* … something wasn't right. Something had happened with Renzo.

But what?

Where was he?

Here, apparently. This fucking *PO box*. In Nevada?

Lucia's fingers tightened around the paper, and crumpled the edges. She glanced up at her brother to see the firmness in John's gaze as he stared back at her. She had so many more questions than she had answers as she looked between her brother and the paper.

Where is he?

What happened to him?

Can I see him?

All she found staring back from John was a silent request to *not ask a damn thing*. Sometimes, that's how their life went. Sometimes, she couldn't ask questions. None of them could. Sometimes, it was just better not to know.

Even if all of her was *begging* to know.

Hadn't a year been long enough?

She just wanted Renzo back.

"You don't have to say anything," John told her, finally breaking the silence between them. "Not thank you, or fuck you, or anything, Lucia."

She didn't know what to say.

Well, except one thing …

"Does Dad know you got this for me?" she asked.

"Nope," he said, shaking his head. "It's also not about Dad. It's about us. Sometimes, I think Dad just worries too much about us. He wants us to be safe, and happy, and fulfilled. In the process, his protective nature sometimes smothers us, too. And that's just Dad—he is who he is, and we have to love him regardless, Lucia."

"I do love Daddy, but—"

"You're angry with him, too."

Finally, those tears she'd been holding back decided to make themselves known whether she wanted them to or not. A single tear slipped down her cheek, but she didn't wipe it away. For the first time in a long time, that tear felt *good*. "So fucking mad, John."

"It's cliché, kiddo, but what's meant to be, will be, and fuck the rest." John pointed at the paper in her hand, saying, "There's your lifeline, Lucia. You want to talk to Renzo—you want to *know*? He's right there. I'm sorry it's not more."

Lucia clenched the paper between her fingertips again, and stared at her brother. She didn't know what this paper or the address on it was going to lead to—but it was something. A first step. An option for her to take. Maybe it would give her everything she had been searching for this last year. Maybe it would fill the emptiness she constantly felt now.

She wouldn't know unless she used it, right?

"This is perfect, John."

Her brother smiled. "That's all I wanted to—"

John never got to finish his sentence. It was drowned out by the screams of people in The Annex, and the sudden swell of a crowd rushing their way when in the background, she heard, "*She's got a gun!*"

Maybe it was the look in John's eye—the fear staring back from her brother—that told Lucia ... this wasn't random. So was their life, it seemed. Even hiding herself away in California couldn't keep her safe and untouched by the mafia. Nothing would ever keep her safe from it all.

Lucia had been right, too. It was about them ... or rather, her brother and Siena.

Later in the evening, while she sat in a hard plastic chair of an emergency room as Siena Calabrese fought for her life ... Lucia managed to convince a nurse to find her a pad of paper and a pen.

She wrote her first letter to Renzo as her family paced in the waiting area. She watched the clock, counting the minutes of a surgery that took longer than normal on Siena for her brother who was barely able to breathe. She heard her father demand someone get Lucia a ticket *as soon as fucking possible* back to California just in case.

To keep her safe.

Like it would ever make a difference.

Lucia penned that letter, then.

Renzo, it started. And then, right below, she wrote, *Do you feel like this, too? Alone all the time? Empty, too? That's me without you.*

ONE

"Fair warning."

The man walking in stride with Renzo down the dark corridor grinned. It was almost a creepy sight, if Renzo was the type to let that sort of shit bother him. A sly smile that curved a little too much at the edges, and in the darkness, all he could see was the man's white teeth and his eyeballs glowing under the black lights.

Why did they need black lights in the hallway anyway? Except at the far end of the corridor without doors, he could see a red light flashing over top of what looked like the only door. A stark, black door. What did that lead into?

They'd covered his head for a portion of time—most of the fucking time. He didn't know what kind of a building they were in, or even where in the country considering they'd driven for what felt like days. They covered his head, then, too.

Hell, he still wasn't sure if he should even ask where he was. It didn't seem like the right time. The team of people walking behind him and the man beside him didn't seem up for conversation.

They walked in rows of three—there were nine of them in total—shoulder to shoulder, and the only thing visible beneath the bandanas wrapped around their faces were their eyes. And not one of them would look at him. They didn't meet his gaze, and they didn't speak a word. Maybe they weren't allowed, or maybe they couldn't. Renzo wasn't sure.

What had Lucian Marcello gotten him into now?

What was this deal?

Lucian hadn't said anything like this was going to happen when the man visited him in the prison. Sure, he hadn't said this wouldn't happen, either. In fact, he hadn't given Renzo a lot of details about this stupid deal. Just his freedom for five years of his life. That was it, that was all. Renzo was starting to think he should have demanded a hell of a lot more info.

"What's that warning?" Renzo asked, rubbing his raw wrists while he had the chance. They'd cut the broken cuffs off him from the prison after snatching him during a transfer, and they weren't easy about it by any means. "Is it going to help me?"

The man laughed.

Renzo didn't even know his name.

Or the others' names, either.

"This place, New York, is gonna break you." The man nodded, his smile gone in a blink. "It's gonna break you—that's inevitable. You'll come out better for it, that's how it works. Just accept it now. Better to learn to enjoy it instead of waste energy hating it. Let it go now."

Christ.

He'd been told that before. The whole let it go thing. It never did make much of a difference for him. It never helped to get rid of the bitterness and contempt bred deep into

9

his sinew for the shitty hand life had dealt him in some ways. No, he'd never let it go, but he had handled it.

It was basically the same, right?

All too soon, the end of the hallway was right in front of Renzo. He finally realized what that blinking red light was for when the guy who had been walking with him, looked upward, raised a hand, and nodded. Renzo followed his gaze to find the gleam of a lens trained right on them.

A security camera.

Fuck.

What was this place?

Renzo was sure he was going to be asking that question a lot for the next while. Who knew for how long, because he sure as hell didn't know a thing.

"You're going to enter this door," the man beside him said, "and everything is going to change. That's all I can tell you."

The white skull design on the man's bandana hanging loosely around his neck—he was the only one in the team of ten that came for him who pulled his face covering down—lit up a funny purple color under the blacklights.

"Can't even tell me your name?" Renzo asked.

"Not yet," the man returned.

A loud ring echoed throughout the hallway. It was distracting enough that Renzo almost wanted to cover his ears. It took his attention away from the guy for just long enough that he didn't see him pull his bandana back up, never mind the rest of the nine people behind them who quickly closed the distance to come closer.

The door opened.

Renzo turned back around.

It felt, sort of, like he was staring into hell for a second. Like he turned around to see faceless people dressed in all black, their bodies strapped with weapons, and he was the intended target.

"You can fight if you want," the guy murmured behind his skull bandana. "It's still gonna happen, New York."

What would happen?

Renzo didn't ask that.

He had a different question.

"Where in the hell am I?"

The man's eyes gleamed—amused, Renzo thought. He looked amused. "The League."

• • •

Renzo blinked out of the memory, and knew exactly why it had been pulled forward in his mind and so quickly yanked him out of the present. The red lights surrounding him were far too bright. Even when Renzo closed his eyes, he was still seeing a shine of red behind his eyelids. It certainly wasn't the blinking red light over the black door that changed his life that night, but it was the thing he remembered first before anything else.

Everything else was ... difficult.

His gaze scanned the room he was currently in just because he could, and this was what he had been taught to do. Renzo knew better than to move, or make some kind of scene. It didn't matter that he was mostly naked—in nothing but boxer-briefs—and standing on a raised platform of sorts while facing a wall of mirrors that weren't mirrors at all. He knew they weren't *just* mirrors—more like windows for the people behind them to watch him.

To *appraise* him.

The windows continued all the way around the room in sections of eight-feet wide by ten-feet tall. Except for one off to the left—another black door. The League loved their black doors. He always felt those black doors were a warning, of sorts. A way to tell people ... *you don't belong here; do not pass.*

Over each section of windows, a red light rested behind metal cages. For now, they were all lit up and unblinking. Just stark, red lights shining down on him. Overhead, far brighter, white lights gleamed down on his body. The heat from those lights was more than enough to keep him warm, but that didn't mean he was fucking comfortable.

No, those were two entirely different things.

"Six feet, three inches," came a distorted voice ringing throughout the room. Renzo didn't know where in the hell the speakers were, but he stiffened in place as the voice continued on with listing his physical stats. Everything from the length of his arms, to the width of his shoulders. How much he could bench, the distance and speed at which he could run, and finally, they finished it off with, "One hundred ninety-two pounds."

Renzo blinked.

How in the hell did *they* know his weight, and he didn't even know that? Oh, sure, The *fucking* League certainly kept up with all of that when they brought him in twice a week to be weighed and checked over, but *damn*.

He maybe weighed one-seventy-five when he came to this damn place. That weight gain spoke to the intensity the last year had been for him. One year—that's all it took from the time he stepped into the compound run by The League to the point he now stood *here*.

On a platform.
Being appraised.
Soon to be sold.
Like cattle.

• • •

Fuck, fuck, fuck!

Renzo blinked awake with fuck as his only thought as the rattling overhead started up again. His warning that the chains attached to the harness that was connected to the straight jacket he wore was about to start lowering him.

Again.

Into that tank of water.

Again.

How long had he been in here again? This black room … it felt dead, he thought. Dead, and cold. No life, no light, and no sound. At least, not that he had ever seen.

The darkness and silence wouldn't be so bad if it weren't for the fact that it was just one of those things or the other. But when both of them were put together, it made a hell of a combination. It was enough to make a man's mind play tricks on him. Renzo often thought he was seeing or hearing things that didn't exist in the space. And it didn't matter how much shouting and fighting he did, he was not *getting out of that straight jacket.*

Oh, sure, occasionally someone came in, pulled him down from the harness, and let him out of his restraints. He'd tried fighting back once—quickly learned that wasn't going to change a thing. It was one *person who came in, and the man beat the shit out of Renzo himself before putting him back in the straightjacket, and hooking him back up to the harness. He didn't get to eat or relieve himself that day—or night; he didn't even know what time it had been.*

For the most part, Renzo was alone.

He thought … it had to be a few days, now. A few days he had been doing this same thing over and over and over—

He didn't get to finish his thought before he was plunged into freezing cold water. If the rattling of the chains overhead hadn't properly woken him up and reminded him of the hell that was his current life, the fucking water sure did it.

Because he couldn't breathe.

He'd learned the first time the hoist let him fall into the water that as soon as he was dropped down, a cover on some kind of automatic arm flipped on the tank to close it up tight. *Or as tight as it could get, anyway. Tight enough that he couldn't open it.*

Basically, he was dropped in the tank of water, the lid closed him in, and then for several minutes, he was under water with no way to breathe while being entirely bound by a straightjacket. He basically had no sense of what was up or down while he was in the tank because he couldn't see anything. He was rarely able to get to the top where he might find a small pocket of air to breathe in, and he mostly just focused on trying to stay alive.

Fun, right?

Yeah.

The panic didn't swell as hard this time. Sure, he gulped in a mouthful of water, and choked on it because he'd been distracted when he fell in. Too distracted to prepare himself for another round of this goddamn game of torture.

Shame on him.

Renzo had gotten used to counting the seconds when he was in the tank. Even as his body twisted to find the spot to come up, and even as he kicked and struggled because that was human instinct to try and save one's self, he still counted the seconds.

Usually, around the three minute mark ... he knew he was going to be coming back up soon. Except this time, three minutes passed.

That panic he hadn't been feeling before started to rise hot and heavy in his throat. He became acutely aware of his heartbeat as his lungs started to scream with the need for air. With his eyes wide, though he couldn't see a damn thing, he felt his shoulder hit something hard. *The wall of the tank, likely. It wasn't that big. A six foot by six foot box, maybe.*

At the four minute mark, he was damn sure he was going to die. He didn't even think about it when he opened his mouth, and let out a shout. Instinct again, maybe. Who knew? All that caused was for water to rush into his mouth, and he swallowed it down.

Ever vomit under water?

Renzo did.

Yep.

His back hit the wall again, and again. He managed to get some kind of leverage with his foot in the corner, and he pushed his weight against the top—or what he thought was the top—of the tank, and the side wall. His gaze started to blacken, and the constant swell of fear and panic became a background noise to the humming in his ears.

Well, not so much a humming as a white noise.

Constant, and low.

Death was on the way.

Just as his eyes started to close without his permission, his body finally giving up the fight, he felt the pressure release. It wasn't the hoist pulling him up this time, though. No, instead of going up with the hoist, he dropped fast. Like a sack of rocks being released from six feet high. He heard the rushing sounds fill his ears, and felt his body skim across something hard as more water rushed over his face.

He didn't know when he came to a stop. He didn't know why it was so bright when he opened his eyes. He didn't know the faceless people who now stood above him in a tight circle—each holding a long, rod in their hands.

It looked like bamboo.

Maybe?

Renzo choked and coughed, his lungs aching with every breath he sucked in. And with every exhale, he vomited more *water. Humiliation filled Renzo in a way he'd never felt before. He probably looked like a fucking idiot. Rolling over to his knees, he finally figured out what happened as his gaze landed on what used to be the box he suspected they were using as his fucking torture chamber.*

All four walls of plexiglass had collapsed. Because of him, or because it was time to let him out, Renzo didn't know.

Water fell from his face in droplets as he breathed heavily and tried to calm his racing thoughts. The anger was most present—rage so strong it was thick in his throat. But there was a darkness there, too. Like the darkness he'd been kept in for so long felt like an old friend who now made a home inside his mind.

It wasn't about to leave anytime soon, either.

"Almost too late, Cree," someone murmured above him. "Another ten seconds, and—"

"He looks fine," came a feminine reply. "He was strong-willed. He needed that, didn't he, Cree?"

"Mmm, we'll see. Get up to your fucking feet," someone else—Cree?—barked. The voice sounded familiar to him. It was the same voice belonging to the man who walked him to this hell with the skull bandana hanging around his neck. "Time for something different, New York."

Renzo didn't move.

The first strike of the bamboo rod came down across his back. *He shuddered, and shook. Still didn't stand, though.*

"Maybe that extra ten seconds would have been good for him, then," the first voice muttered.

"Remember what I told you?" The familiar voice—Cree, if Renzo was to believe the people around him talking—came close as a man bent down beside him. Sure enough, when Renzo tipped his head to the side, he recognized the man's eyes. "Do you remember what I said about this place, New York?"

Renzo swallowed hard. "It's gonna break me."

Cree nodded. "Yeah, just let it happen. It's easier. Renzo Zulla, that person who walked in here a few days ago, he doesn't exist anymore. You get to be whoever you wanna fucking be here, all right? Just let it happen, man."

He stood, then, despite the fact he didn't want to. Not that it mattered. The second he was up on his feet, someone knocked him to his back when they hit him across the chest with a bamboo rod. He found the cement almost welcoming, if it wasn't so goddamn cold.

Letting out a bitter, breathless laugh from the pain, Renzo said, "Jesus, at least let me be dry for this, or something.*"*

"Learn to enjoy being in a state of discomfort, and it will never be used against you," Cree murmured from up above him. "Comfort is for the weak."

Well, then …

"All right," Renzo muttered.

"Stand again."

He did.

Only to get knocked the hell down again.

More fun.

● ● ●

"Scores," came the voice again through the speakers to drag Renzo from his thoughts once more. "Ten out of ten—hand to hand combat; excellent.

Seven out of ten—hacking; moderate. Ten out of ten—weapons, in both practical and applied; excellent."

The distorted voice continued on describing skills that had been, for the most part, either beaten into Renzo during his first year at The League, or ones he already had that were picked up on and honed. Everything from his understanding of vehicles, to his ability to survive.

The scores went on for at least ten minutes before the man moved onto something else. They'd already described the tattoos on his body that the people behind the mirrored glass might not be able to see fully—he'd been told once not to mark up his skin when he was first allowed a bit of freedom from The League. He went ahead and did it anyway.

Suffered for it, too.

It was worth it.

Renzo kept going until he had one whole fucking sleeve of tattoos. Memories he didn't want to forget because it seemed like with every passing day that he spent here, he forgot something else. Like the way his little brother sounded first thing in the morning when he got his favorite breakfast. He started to forget the color of his sister's hair, too. Or how Lucia's eyes glinted with her slyness when she knew something he didn't.

He was so controlled—constantly. No phones, no access to the outside without someone else right there. A chip implanted into his arm to keep track of him nonstop. Which lead him to believe, yes, they knew every single time he went in for more ink, and while they could have stopped him, they didn't.

They never stepped in.

They punished him *after*.

Worth it.

He was here.

This was his life for the next … well, four years now.

That was the fucking deal.

Right?

He wasn't gonna forget while he was here.

Simple as that.

"Excelled specialty for The League—explosives," the distorted voice drawled on, bringing Renzo back to the present. "Bidding will begin at one-point-three million."

Instantly, those red lights over the windows started flickering.

Renzo blinked.

Bids, he realized.

It had begun.

His life was now up for sale.

• • •

"What the fuck are you doing?"

Renzo didn't move his gaze away from the ceiling of his room. His one space in The League's compound that was just his. So much so, as were the rules set out for the trained assassins who lived within these walls, that Cree didn't inch past the threshold of the doorway. That's why Renzo liked it in here—outside of his room, anybody above him could make sure he knew he was the lowest fucker on the totem pole. Inside here, nobody could say a damn thing.

"What do you want?" Renzo asked.

His trainer—for all purposes—let out a grunt. He eyed the Native from the corner of his eye, and watched the man shift from foot to foot. His slick, black hair had been braided over his shoulder today, and his dark russet eyes narrowed. A good sign of his impatience.

Mostly, Renzo liked Cree. He kept Renzo in line, and gave him a wide berth of space when he needed it. Cree was also the only one who thought to give Renzo a heads up about what The League was going to be like. No need to fill his head full of bullshit, after all. He respected that. It didn't mean he always liked Cree, though.

Cree was usually the one meting out the punishment when Renzo deserved it. He was the one pushing and pushing when Renzo just wanted someone to back off. Cree was the one beating the hell out of him in hand-to-hand combat and bringing in others when the training became more intensive.

This man woke him up and allowed him to sleep.

This man told him when to eat and shit.

This man drove him fucking crazy.

Renzo figured Cree was a higher up in The League because of his closeness to the man running the place. Except he also worked alongside the assassins. He was one in a team of ten. Although, according to Cree, his team varied. They could do a rescue, a retrieval, or even take something or someone out. They weren't picky as long as they were paid, and on time.

And whether Cree was higher on the totem pole at The League, it didn't matter. Most were treated the same. The League gave new recruits—as few and far in between as those were—to assassins who had already earned their stripes, so to speak. It reminded those who were already well-established in The League that they still had a responsibility, and if they failed ... if they failed for any reason, well it wouldn't end well for them.

That was the thing about Cree.

If Renzo failed, then so did Cree.

"I know you were supposed to be in basics an hour ago," Cree said, "so you wanna explain to me why you're sitting in here playing with your fucking cock?"

Renzo glanced over at the man. "Do you see my dick, or ...?"

"Don't be a smartass, New York."

"Could you use my name?"

"No, it helps me to disassociate."

Renzo blinked.

Huh.

That was the first time Cree ever admitted that.

It made sense.

"I'm not going anywhere today. I'm not doing anything.*"*

Cree grunted under his breath again—a sign he was quickly losing his patience. *"Why?"*

"Because for the six months I have been here, I haven't had one single day to—"

"You think anyone gives a fuck about what you want?" Cree interjected sharply. "We don't, Renzo. What we care is that you're capable. That if, by chance, you're put on a team, we can trust you. That you know what you're doing. That's what we care about. Stop being a selfish child, and get to basics."

Renzo didn't move. "When will I be able to leave?"

"Not for a long while."

"That tells me nothing."

"Ask specific questions, then," Cree uttered.

Well, he did ask.

"I want to walk outside. And not with the rest of you. I want a cheeseburger from In-and-Out. I want to call my little brother, or my sister." Lucia, too. God, he wanted her more than anybody else could possibly ever know. "I want—"

"You're back to thinking I give a fuck what you want, and I don't."

Renzo's jaw tightened.

Asshole.

"Other people here have outside contact," Renzo said, trying to keep his tone level. *"Why can't I?"*

Cree folded his thick arms over his chest, and leaned against the doorjamb of Renzo's room. "Here's what I haven't explained to you yet, Renzo. At one year here, you're going to be put in front of buyers. Whoever wins your bid will take over your contract from The League for the next four years, at which point, as long as you are still alive …"

The man trailed off before sighing, and adding, "You will be able to decide whether you want to go through the auction again to contract yourself out, whether you want to leave The League entirely, or if you want to remain as an independent contractor. But do you know what happens when you're fucking useless because you've spent too much time whining in your room about people you want to see instead of doing what you should be doing?"

"Not particularly," Renzo muttered.

"Well, nothing. If you can't sell—if you can't be the tool someone needs to add to their organization, or team … or whatever, then you are useless to The League. And they will cut their losses. You making it to the end of your contract is dependent on being useful, Renzo."

Well, then.

Cree had delivered all of that with a cold flatness that rang heavily in Renzo's mind long after the man was done speaking.

"They auction off my remaining term?" Renzo said.

"They spend the money to train you—to make you into ... well, you see what we are. And in your case, you owe a debt to The League. You killed a trainee, Renzo."

No, he had not. Lucia did that. Renzo was never going to tell them that, though.

"Which means," Cree continued, "that your debt is even higher. Five years with this organization is what you owe—any money you make under the contract of your buyer, if you get a buyer, will go back to paying your debt. But if you're going to be useless, they will cut their losses."

Which meant death.

No Diego.

No Rose.

No Lucia.

No freedom.

Renzo swallowed the lump forming in his throat. "So—"

"You want privileges," Cree interjected, not letting Renzo speak at all, "like contact with people outside, or the ability to get out of here once in a while, then you better fucking *earn it. That's how you get those things. Not by sitting in here doing fuck all, and wasting my time."*

Yeah, he got it.

"What's my debt total to The League?"

"Twenty million—that's the average one makes between the auction, and a four year contract with a buyer. So, they've rounded it out for you."

Shit.

"What happens if after the five years, it's not all paid back?"

Cree arched a brow. "I imagine, you'll go under contract again."

Nope.

That wasn't going to happen.

Renzo sat up on the bed, and swung his legs over the side. His combat boots hit the cement with a hard smack, and then he was standing up straight. "So, all I have to do is make sure my buyer pays more than that at the auction, right?"

Cree laughed. "New York, at the rate you're going, you'll be lucky to get anything at all. Useless, remember? Typical purchase is ten million—fifteen if you've got a specialty worth taking a second look at. You're six months into this and causing more trouble than you're worth. Don't get in over your head. You'll drown."

Maybe so.

"What's basics for today?" Renzo asked, switching the conversation altogether.

"Explosives. Bombs."

"That sounds fun."

Cree gave him a look. "Earn what you want, Renzo."

He would.

He'd have to.

• • •

A loud chime rang through the room filled with red lights and wall-to-wall mirrors. He knew, somewhere behind one of those windows, Cree was watching his trainee. Probably behind the only mirror without a light overhead to his right, but Renzo didn't know.

And then, the distorted voice came over the speakers again to say, "Sold—twenty-five-point-three million. R.Z., please step down from the platform, and return to the door."

Renzo felt like a robot.

That number was still ringing in the back of his mind even as he was shuffled in the opened door that he had also been brought in through, and found familiar faces waiting behind it. Cree … others who came from Cree's team. One of the handlers for The League—Renzo would call the man an owner, but he barely spoke to any of them, and he seemed cold whenever he was around—stood in the corner with a red phone pressed to his ear as he fixed a button on his three-piece suit.

"That's a fucking record," he heard Cree say.

A hand slapped his back.

His debt was paid with that bid, but he still had four more fucking years here. Four years owed to The League, and whoever now owned his contract.

Four years without the people he wanted the most.

But who was his buyer?

"Tell *M* the product will be ready for the first job whenever he needs him to be sent out … as soon as the money is transferred," the man in the corner with the red phone said. "Transfer must be done within twenty-four hours."

Renzo almost wanted to scoff. He'd spent the last year of his life being molded into … a machine, frankly. Unfeeling. Indifferent. A killer. And he was reduced to being called a *product*.

And M?

M.

Well, who the hell was that?

TWO

Three and a half years later ...

April showers bring May flowers.

The thought passed Lucia's mind with a sing-song flair as she stepped out of her apartment. That was probably the thing she missed about New York the most ... *rain*. At least, rain in the spring. In all her twenty-three years on earth, she thought there was nothing like a good rain in the springtime. There was a certain smell that followed a good spring rain. Fresh, clean, and earthy, if it were possible.

California wasn't quite the same. Constantly dry, they were usually begging for a little rain here. There was a whole damn season for wild fires, even. For a small portion of the year, the air would have a slight taste of smoke every time someone breathed.

But ... Cali was where Lucia needed to be. That didn't mean she always wanted to be here, but it was where she knew she needed to be. It made all the difference when her traitorous heart dared to make her consider going back home.

After she finished her art degree six months earlier, she settled in Los Angeles. An offer came up from someone her aunt, Kim, knew that owned a gallery. A *paid* year-long internship in a major art gallery with some of the best up and coming names in the art world under the head curator.

Lucia didn't dare say no.

Besides, it gave her another reason to avoid the discussion with her mother—or God forbid—her father, about why she wasn't coming home yet. From the day she graduated, they asked her when she was coming back.

New York is your home.

Your family is here, Lucia.

We miss you.

They weren't wrong; they weren't entirely right, either. New York *had* been home, once. And yes, her family was back there while she was here. The fact still remained the same for her ... going back only made her angry. Maybe she'd been trying for almost five years now to let go of that anger. Yet, with every short trip back to New York, Lucia found it was like ripping a scab off an almost-healed wound.

She'd be hurt again.

Bleeding again.

Raw again.

New York was full of memories that stung like needles poking into her heart constantly. It felt like an apology that never came from her father, and an emptiness in her chest that she couldn't escape from no matter how hard she tried to do exactly that.

New York felt like Renzo.

It felt like what her life was like without him, now.

Lucia didn't think heartbreak was supposed to be like this—although, was it heartbreak if there had never been a proper end between them? If they were never able to truly say goodbye to one another, was it losing her first love?

She didn't know.

It still felt like it.

Maybe that's why it was made worse. Because there hadn't been a proper goodbye. There had been no closure, at least, not for her. Despite the fact that she tried to find him, wrote letter after letter that was never answered, and hoped for something that clearly wasn't going to happen, well, she was stuck. Suspended between the things she wanted, and a reality that just killed her every time she had to face it all over again.

And fuck her stupid heart because no matter how hard she tried to just get better, feel better or something ... he was still there. In her dreams and thoughts. Absent in her heart where she wanted to feel him the most.

Gone, like her soul.

He'd taken that.

Wherever he was.

Her trips home became more and more infrequent over the years to the point she hadn't been back home in almost ... well, over a year now. The longest she'd gone back for was a two-week stay during that trip three and a half years ago, a year after she moved to Cali. Not that it stopped her family from asking her to come back more often.

She didn't.

It wasn't about them—even if her anger was caused by the things her father had done. Sure, she'd mostly forgiven her brother over the years, but not her dad. It wasn't Lucian's fault for that, either.

It was Lucia's.

He would try, if only she would let him. That was the thing, though ... maybe she was too damn stubborn for her own good. Maybe she was like every good Marcello who knew how to hold a grudge like nobody's business. Who cared what the reason was?

Lucia wasn't ready to forgive.

She certainly couldn't *forget*.

Distance and time should have helped. That's why she came to California in the first place, but here it was ... almost five years *after* Renzo had been taken from her, and she was still raw. It couldn't be normal, but this contempt she lived with constantly felt like an old friend, now. A friend she wasn't willing to give up because it was the only thing that left her with any sort of comfort, even if it was a cold one.

The Uber she had called earlier was already waiting at the entrance of her apartment building when she exited. She slipped into the backseat, and rattled off the address for the gallery as the phone in her bag started to vibrate with a call. She pulled it out to answer the call as the guy driving pulled out onto the road.

Lucia didn't even bother to check the caller ID. "Hello?"

"Lucia."

She smiled at her mother's sweet tone.

"Hey, Ma."

"Thought if I didn't call you now, I'd probably miss you later," Jordyn teased. "I never seem to get the time difference right."

That … or the truth was more like Lucia often ignored calls that came from her parents' home. There was a good chance it might be her father calling, and she didn't want to have a conversation with him. She would rather ignore the call, and if it was her mother, Jordyn always left a message. She called her mother's cell phone, then.

Simple.

Honestly, it was exhausting.

Whatever.

"You got me for a few minutes," Lucia said, buckling up in the backseat when the driver gave her a look in the rearview mirror. "I'm heading over to the gallery for my shift this afternoon."

"Yes, Kim said you were enjoying working there."

Lucia heard the edge to her mother's words. It wasn't like Lucia called her aunt more than she called her mother, but considering that the curator Lucia worked under was also her aunt's friend … well, it would make sense that the woman kept her aunt informed.

"It's nice," Lucia said. "Fits me, you know?"

"You always did have a healthy appreciation for art." Jordyn cleared her throat, asking, "Have you given any thought to when you might be coming home again?"

"I—"

"I was hoping it would be soon," her mother interjected before she could figure out some kind of excuse. "We would really like to see you, Lucia."

By *we* her mother meant her father, too. But Jordyn was getting smarter about these conversations with Lucia. The less she brought Lucian up directly to her daughter, the more likely Lucia was to stay on the phone.

Damn her for being quick.

"I've only been at the gallery for six months, Ma," Lucia said. "I don't think I could get time off right now if I tried. Maybe in the summer, okay?"

Jordyn sighed.

If she knew her daughter was lying, she didn't seem willing to call Lucia out on it. Truth was, the curator she was interning for had already told her that she could take up to a month's worth of vacation, if she needed. And they were always willing to make arrangements if something came up like an emergency in case she needed to take more time. The gallery was a dream.

New York was the fucking nightmare.

"Okay," Jordyn said softly. "Um, your father might call later."

Lucia stared out the window at the passing buildings. A coldness settled in her heart as she replied, "Tell him not to bother, Ma."

"Please don't do that, Lucia."

"Ma—"

"He loves you."

And she loved him, too.

That changed nothing.

"I gotta go, Ma," Lucia said.

She didn't wait for her mother to say *goodbye* or even her familiar *I love you* before she hung up the phone. So was her life, now.

This was easier.

• • •

For such a short, tiny woman, Kelly Campbell had a big personality, and an even bigger presence. Often, people assumed gallery curators—and even the owners—all came from the same stuffy, stuck-up stock. Pant suits for the women, and slicked back hair for the men.

Kelly was not like that.

At all.

Kelly was light-hearted, and free-spirited. She didn't take anything too seriously, and she wasn't afraid to tell a client where they could shove their attitude and money when it was needed. It was one of the many reasons why Lucia adored her boss.

Today, she was wearing a flimsy summer dress that looked like she had needed to tape the plunging neckline to her chest lest she show off more than she was willing to. Her pale pink, cropped hair stuck out around her ears where she had tucked the strands back, so it would stay out of her eyes as she surveyed the print resting on an illuminated table.

"Lucia, come here and look at this, will you?"

Dropping the file she had been surveying for another client, Lucia crossed the room and took the magnifying glasses Kelly held out for her.

Slipping them over her eyes when the woman waved at her, she was quick to lean over the table, too.

"What do you see on this print?" Kelly asked, pointing at one section of the abstract face of an unknown man. His chin, actually. A bright blue compared to the black of his mouth.

Lucia took in the specks and ink spots on the print through the magnifying glasses. Some of the ink was a little smudged where maybe the press hadn't come down perfectly, and left a bit of paper beneath uncolored. All typical of art prints done with the usual press. Nothing stood out to her that Kelly would want her to see, anyway. Pulling the glasses off her face, she glanced up at her boss.

"It all looks normal."

Kelly pursed her lips, and nodded. "Try the other one—same spot."

Lucia did as she was told, and surveyed the second print on the table of the same abstract profile. Except this time, she couldn't help but notice there were more spots on the ink that were missing color, and less perfection. She was sure if she took the measurements of the first print to the second print, parts of the profile would be slightly off, too.

Also, not uncommon.

With hand-pressed ink prints done in productions of a hundred—typical, give or take a couple of dozen—then each print couldn't exactly replicate the one that came before it. It was part of what made each piece unique in the row.

Lucia pulled the glasses off again, and carefully rested her elbow along the edge of the table as she peered up at her boss. "It looks standard."

"Doesn't it?" Kelly mused.

Something was wrong with it, though. Lucia could tell just by the tone her boss used as she folded her arms over her chest, and glanced between the two prints.

"Can you guess how much this piece is worth?" Kelly asked. "The second, not the first. The first belongs to a friend—I had him bring it in today for me to compare because it was the thirtieth printed in the production."

Lucia knew the artist well—not personally, simply by name and his work. She liked his abstracts and his methods of printing using ink-covered, smoothed down wooden blocks pressed against paper. The man was edging closer to his seventies, now, and it hadn't been more than a few years ago when his art blew up in the art world.

"A *Blackmouth* went for two-hundred thousand at an auction you took me to last month," Lucia said, referring to the print they were currently overlooking. Only fifty had been printed of this particular piece. The artist had the original, and the first print. "So, in that range, I would say."

"Even if it were one of the first ten printed?" Kelly asked.

Lucia blinked.

Then, she quickly went back to the prints. She didn't miss how the first print had the usual *30* scribbled on the bottom of the print with the artist's name directly beside it. But the second print? It had *8* alongside the artist's name.

"It's a fake," Lucia murmured.

She found Kelly grinning at her. "And how do you know that?"

"Eight comes before thirty," Lucia said, shaking her head. "There's no way the eighth print would be less perfect than the thirtieth. It has more area where ink hasn't properly covered, and the jaw area of the profile is slightly off centered from the bottom lip."

"*And?*"

Lucia laughed. "I mean, usually we don't see that in hand-pressed prints until around the fiftieth print when they reset the blocks."

Kelly nodded. "Well done."

"It's a good fake, though. I mean, if the number was different, maybe higher, then I would have overlooked it. Especially if it was in a print run with more than a hundred copies."

"The eighth print in this edition has been missing for years."

Ah.

Makes sense why someone would choose that number, then.

"Do you think the owner is trying to sell it knowing it's a fake?" Lucia asked.

Kelly shook her head, and carefully picked up the first print which belonged to her friend. "Not at all. Christian Savino brought it in after his art dealer in Italy bought it to add to his *profile*, as he said. He trusted the dealer to know what he was doing. Afterward, he apparently had reason to believe the print was a forgery, and contacts of his put him in contact with us because I have access to one of the first fifty prints in this edition."

"He's not going to be happy when you send that back to him with the truth—"

"Oh, he's here," Kelly said, slyly. "Brought the print along with him for a trip, apparently." Her boss checked the watch on her wrist, and then gave Lucia a smile. "He'll be here in a few minutes, if he isn't already. The man is punctual to a fault, but he isn't all that bad to look at. Care to join me in delivering the news?"

Lucia shrugged. "Yeah, why not."

Kelly wasn't wrong, in fact, the owner of the fake print was already waiting in her office by the time the two had crossed to the other side of the gallery where the glass-walled offices were situated. All Lucia could see of the tall man—he was easily over six feet—was the expanse of his broad shoulders that faced them when they entered the office. With his hands shoved loosely into the pockets of his suit, he continued watching the street from the window of the office.

"Mr. Savino," Kelly started.

"Christian," the man said smoothly. "I have told you ten times now, it is just *Christian*."

The Italian lilt to his words shouldn't have shocked Lucia, but it did a little bit. Sure, Kelly had said an art dealer in Italy, but … she didn't know any Italians outside of those who were still waiting for her to come back home to New York.

Then, Christian turned around. His wide smile welcomed them both, and his dark brown eyes drifted over Kelly before passing to Lucia just as quickly.

"Ah, this must be the apprentice you were telling me about, *sì?*" Christian's charming smile widened a bit as Lucia stepped close enough to take his outstretched hand. She shook his hand, noting his tanned skin, and the gold rings adorning three of his fingers. She thought he had to be in his later twenties, but not older than thirty-five, at the most. As handsome as he was, and God knew Lucia had been put in front of enough handsome men over the last few years, she didn't feel a flicker of any interest staring at this man's face. Nothing. It was like she was dead inside. Soon, she dropped his hand, and stepped back to stand beside Kelly. "I hope you're soaking in everything Kelly is teaching you. I hear she is the best of the very best."

Kelly laughed. "Keep your charm to yourself, we have business to discuss. This print of yours, I mean."

With that said, she tossed the tube holding Christian's print of *Blackmouth* to the desk. He didn't move to pick it up.

"Bad news, then?" he asked.

Kelly gave Lucia a look.

Lucia shrugged. "Well, it's not great."

Christian scowled. "It never is when I want it to be. Go on then, tell me."

"It's a fake," Kelly said.

"Of course, it is."

"I know you said the dealer bought it for your profile, but if you're looking for an actual *Blackmouth*, I might be able to find you one," Kelly suggested.

That did make Christian's attention perk. "Could you?"

"It might take a while."

The man chuckled. "I have time."

• • •

"John?" Lucia's older brother gave her a wide smile as she opened the door to her apartment. At the sight of him waiting in the hallway, she almost *blinked*. "What are you doing here?"

John laughed. "Business."

"You didn't think to call before showing up?"

"Do I have to call when I want to see my sister?"

Well … not really, but *still*.

"Since when do you have business in California?" Lucia asked.

John shrugged one shoulder. "That's not for you to worry about, Lucy. Are you going to let me in, or what?"

She bristled at the nickname, but stepped back to let John enter her apartment. Once he had his blazer and shoes put away, she directed her brother into the small kitchen. He stayed silent as she prepped him a cup of tea—she was trying to cut down on coffee, so the best way was to keep it out of her place altogether.

"You know," John said after Lucia had passed his cup over the island, "had you let Dad call you back last week when Ma called you, then maybe you would have known I was coming out this way, Lucia."

Lucia gave her brother a look. "Please tell me you didn't come all the way to Cali just to scold me for not talking to Daddy on the phone, John."

"No, I did have business."

"Good."

"But I wasn't planning on coming to see you for another couple of days. Then, you went and acted like a brat to Ma, so I decided to speed that up."

Dammit.

"John, listen—"

"No, I think it's time for you to listen," her brother interjected calmly, his familiar hazel eyes locking onto hers with an intensity that quieted her instantly. "There's shit going on that you don't know, Lucia. Stuff with Dad, all right. And maybe Ma's been trying to get you to come home *because* of that, but without telling you all the details. Problem is, you're so stuck in your feelings that you won't even let her *talk*."

"I let Ma talk."

"Not about Dad."

Lucia's shoulders straightened. "So? I don't have to talk about him or to him, not if I don't want to, John."

She had forgiven her brother. It took time, and more than one apology. It took her brother making an actual effort to understand the way he hurt her that day in San Francisco, and owning what he did. It took things her father had yet to *attempt* to do for her. It certainly didn't help that her heart just wasn't ready to let go of its bitterness and contempt, either.

John let out a sigh, and turned to peer out the kitchen window. "Are you going to keep being like this, or can you shut up and listen for five minutes?"

"Are we going to talk about him, or—"

"Dad's sick, Lucia. He's been sick. Stage two renal cancer. He's been handling it privately—it's just Ma, me, Cella, and Liliana that know. He had surgery a while back for it. Lied and told everyone else it was for kidney stones, I guess. The surgery didn't work because the bloodwork didn't come back clean. He's been doing treatments for a month, now. Three times a week."

Lucia's heart stopped.

She was sure of it.

It *ached.*

"What?" she asked.

John's gaze drifted back to her. "The doctors say he's gonna be okay, we do know that now, but he's been sick for a while. And I'm fucking sorry that you're not over your pity party yet, but it's time to swallow it for a while, Lucia. Time to go home for a bit, and see him. If you want to be selfish on your own time, then you go ahead and do that. I'll be the first person to tell you to go on and do it, but it's not your time right now. It's Dad's."

Lucia had a million and one things she wanted to ask, but mostly, the pain squeezing around her heart like a fist kept her quiet. Up until that moment, every single time someone mentioned her father, the first thing she felt was anger. Ever-present, and stronger than ever. Shockingly so. Violently, even.

Except right then … she just felt pain.

She didn't think about the man who took away the person she loved and wanted the most. No, she saw the man who had tucked her into bed, read her dozens of stories whenever she asked, and let her hold his pinky finger when they crossed the road.

She thought about her dad.

Lucia wasn't sure how long she stayed quiet, stuck in memories that flooded her mind and heart with a nostalgia she had been ignoring for five fucking years. Too long, anyway. Long enough for her brother to just about finish his tea entirely.

John cleared his throat, and stood from the stool before downing the rest of the tea left in his mug. "Ma needs you, too. They both do, but they're not going to say it because they know you *need your fucking time.* But fuck your time, Lucia … I'm here to tell you that. Fuck your time. You've had enough of it."

Apparently so.

THREE

It took two years of constant supervision from The League before Renzo was finally allowed the privilege of having his own place outside of their compound—a large building in the middle of the desolate Nevada land that his companions at The League had not-so-affectionately dubbed the *complex*.

The nickname seemed appropriate considering it was as huge as what someone would consider a complex. They all had some sort of feeling about the complex—good or bad. It was the place where each one of them had been brought in, irrevocably changed, and then in most cases, sold to the highest bidder for their skills and talents. There wasn't much affection in that, was there?

At first, having his own place was strange to Renzo for a number of reasons. The top one being the fact that he had never ... lived on his own before. *Ever.* He needed privacy, and space. He needed the idea that The League wasn't controlling literally every moment of his waking days, even if he knew they still would own his ass whether he lived on his own, and off their property, or not.

At the time, he'd been twenty-two when The League let him find a place *they* approved and could monitor. They tried to say it was so they could make sure he was safe, but Renzo wasn't a goddamn idiot. It was so that they could watch him, and make sure he didn't break one of their many rules, or run. Not that it would make much of a difference. They would still come for him, if he did think to run.

That was two and a half years ago, and here he was ... twenty-fucking-five, and it still felt strange to come home to a quiet apartment where no one was waiting to ask him a million and one questions, or take away what little space he managed to make for himself. He'd thought he would like having the time alone to himself, but more often than not, he didn't like it at all.

It left him alone with his thoughts, and that was never a good thing when it came to Renzo. As if his life hadn't already taught him that, he got to be reminded of it night in and night out. A joy.

It was like his damn mind wouldn't let go of the years he'd spent cramped in tiny apartments with his brother and sister. Even his mother, despite the fact he didn't miss that bitch at all. Nonetheless, it felt strange to be alone.

Once, Renzo made the mistake of mentioning it to Cree—offhandedly, mostly, when the man asked how he was liking his space and time outside of The League. Cree told him to, "Learn to like being alone, Renzo."

Cree always did have a fucking way with words.

The asshole.

Tonight was one of those nights, unfortunately. Renzo had been left to play alone in his big apartment with nothing but his goddamn thoughts to keep him company. Nothing good ever came from him being restless, and he wasn't the only person to notice that fact, either. The League often tried to keep him busy by moving him from one job to the next so that he was never by himself for very long, and his hands always had something to do.

It'd been almost a month since they had given him a job—either solo, or with one of the teams. He checked in daily, as he was supposed to do. He went to the complex daily for briefs, though none of them were for him. And lately, he came home alone because everyone else at The League were on assignments or had other things to handle; wives ... families.

People who needed them.

Renzo, on the other hand, was alone.

He tried walking the halls of his place—it did nothing but let his footsteps echo. That just reminded him, despite how he tried to fill the spaces with things he enjoyed looking at, the apartment was empty except for his sorry ass.

It left him with far too much time to think.

Again, that was a problem.

Renzo opted for the familiar comfort of an empty bathtub, and him resting inside it. He lined the edges of the clawfoot bathtub with all the items he could pull out of his pockets in a neat row. He blamed that on The League, too. It wasn't just a certain sort of skills that had been beaten into him over the course of a year during their training, but a certain way of living, too.

If it was possible to have OCD tendencies beaten into you, The League did that to him. But it wasn't something he wanted to get into, at the moment.

Something else was on his mind.

It wouldn't leave.

Renzo's gaze drifted to the folder that was carefully balancing on the edge of the bathtub. Despite the many rules that The League placed on him, and the amount of control they had over his entire life for the next ... six months, anyway ... there were still people within the walls of the organization that would lend a hand, and stay quiet about it. Members of The League who weren't as controlled as he was because they had earned their place and spot, and were now considered independent contractors to the organization.

One of them—or rather, two, now—just happened to be the Guzzi twins. Christopher and Corrado Guzzi, two members of the team Cree usually worked with when he did jobs that required more than one person.

The twins had come into The League willingly, for reasons Renzo never thought to ask, and had a hell of a lot more freedom than anyone else that he knew inside the organization.

And for the most part, he'd made friends with the twins.

As difficult as they were …

The folder was a favor from them to him, as was the contents inside. Something he'd asked them to do a while back—a few months ago when he knew his term and contract with The League was almost up, and finally coming to a real end—but that they only now got back to him.

Swallowing the lump forming in his throat, he brought the joint to his lips, and sucked on the tip. The heady smoke filled his lungs, and made his mind looser than ever. God knew he needed something for *this*.

Before he could think better of it, Renzo reached out and snatched the folder. He stubbed his smoke into the ashtray, so he would have two hands free to do what he needed. He ignored the way his fingers trembled at the tips as he flipped open the cover to find what the first page would be when he laid eyes on it.

Her picture.

A recent one, likely. He knew it had to be recent because her hair had changed slightly. More highlights of reds and blondes mixed in with a chocolate brown layered style. Soft waves falling over her shoulder as she turned to look at something behind her—or maybe someone had called her name. The shot had clearly been taken from outside of *somewhere*. He only knew that because he could see the slight glare of glass, and the reflection of a street on the window.

He went back to the woman in the photo. Her hazel eyes, and soft smile. Those eyes of hers were still the same. Full of life, and ready to explore.

Renzo took in the background around her—the artwork on the walls, and the sculpture resting on a raised stand. An art gallery, maybe?

The next page in the folder confirmed that idea. It seemed she was doing an internship for a gallery in California, and had graduated not too long ago. He wasn't even surprised that she went after her dream where the art world was concerned. Maybe she couldn't paint or draw or create to save her life, but *damn*, she loved art.

Renzo flipped through the last few pages in the file. It wasn't anything important. Simple details about her current status and life. Nothing that concerned him, or made him worry. He went back to the first page.

Her picture.

Lucia's smile stared back at him.

Renzo found that lump in his throat was back.

She was off limits.

Entirely.

The League made that clear, and it was almost fucking creepy how much they knew about his relationship with Lucia Marcello before he was brought to their organization. He should have expected that, if only because Lucia's father had been the one to make the deal with The League. Five years of his fucking life to repay the debt of killing one of their members.

Five years without her.

Five years was almost up.

Renzo wouldn't wait one second longer once he was done. He'd waited long enough, and not once in five years had this woman left his thoughts. She was always there in the background ... constantly.

Something he couldn't let go of. Someone he couldn't forget, even if he had thought to try. He didn't know about *her*, though. And that was the thing that probably fucked with his head the most.

Had she moved on?

Was she done?

Those were questions he didn't have answers to.

Renzo didn't like questions.

It left too much unknown.

The League had taught him to work on only *absolutes*. Nothing more, and nothing less. Anything else was dangerous, and trouble. This time, it wouldn't be his fucking life on the line, but something far more important.

His heart.

His soul.

Except ... he didn't have a choice, did he?

There were no absolutes here.

Not with Lucia.

Not after five years.

Flipping his arm up, he checked the watch on his wrist. The digital calendar in the background of the face told him the date, and without even thinking about it, he already knew the number of days left before his contract was up.

Until he could find her ...

That wasn't today, though.

The phone on the edge of the tub rang—the device given to him by The League. Constantly monitored and scrubbed, when needed, it was just another way for them to control him. Should he be found with any electronic device not given to him or approved by them, then it wouldn't end well for Renzo.

He put Lucia to the back of his mind for the moment.

Work called.

• • •

Renzo hung back near the doorway to one of the many rooms inside the complex. This one in particular was setup like a personal gym, but with everything and anything one of the members of The League might want or need to stay in shape, and ready to go to battle. Including an entire wall of weapons—fake and real—to use when sparring.

And a boxing ring right in the middle.

Speaking of which …

The hard smack of tape-wrapped fists connecting to hard flesh brought Renzo back to the present, and put his attention on the three men in the room. Corrado Guzzi was going head-to-head with Cree in the ring, and *getting his ass beat.*

It was almost funny.

Not that Corrado wasn't a good fighter because he *was.* But nobody was Cree, either. The man took the whole *float like a butterfly* thing to a new fucking level. Cree always seemed cool and calm—usually—but especially when he was fighting. So much so, that it could be creepy. And then he waited until he could find your weakness, the opening for him to use against you, and he struck.

If you gave him that opening—and you would; everyone did—he was going to lay you out.

Renzo had only managed to make Cree tap out once, and it was after a particularly hellish week where his mind was constantly racing. He was too unpredictable, and just needed an outlet for his craziness. Cree took him into the ring, but because he was so wild, never managed to find that opening.

Which let Renzo in on Cree's weakness, in a way.

"Fucking *hell*," Christopher—though, he preferred Chris—said, leaning over the top rope of the ring. Corrado's back hit the mat of the ring hard enough to take his breath away, and he didn't move. "Stay down, you stupid *fuck.*"

"*Hate you*," Corrado snarled at his brother.

"You know Alessio and Ginevra don't want to deal with your concussed ass again. The last time was enough."

Renzo chuckled under his breath at that. So, maybe this wasn't the first time Corrado had tried to go head-to-head with Cree, like he thought each time was going to make a difference. The man's spouse—Ginevra—and his … other spouse, Alessio … yeah, Renzo didn't understand how that whole relationship came to be with two men and one woman between them, but he knew enough to know it wasn't his fucking business to ask.

Simple as that.

Nonetheless, the man's spouses didn't enjoy taking care of Corrado after he tried to take on Cree for another round. It probably didn't help that Alessio, the third person in the whole relationship, was also a free-range member of The League, too. So, he knew what Cree was like, and that this would always be pointless to try.

On the other side of the ring, Cree leaned against the ropes, and stretched his neck back and forth as he let the twins shout at one another. Still cool and calm. Still entirely unbothered, and looking like he hadn't even broken a sweat.

Then, all at once, Cree's gaze drifted to the doorway and landed on Renzo. The dark-eyed man didn't look the least bit surprised to find Renzo standing there. It was as if he had known the entire time that Renzo was watching the entire fight play out.

He probably did.

Cree was strange that way.

"Finally got a call, did you?" Cree asked.

That drew in the attention of the Guzzi twins as well. Chris nodded to Renzo, and he returned the gesture. Corrado, on the other hand, waved one tapped up fist in a silent hello, but offered nothing more. Renzo didn't blame the man. He knew what it felt like to be on the mat after getting the air beat out of you from Cree.

It wasn't a fun experience.

"Guess so," Renzo replied in response to Cree's question. "About time, too."

"What's it for?"

Renzo shrugged. "I wasn't told."

It could be anything. Even though Renzo's remaining contract had been sold to someone who went by *M* when he asked for a job to be done, M was also known to allow The League to negotiate the use of Renzo's skills in other jobs and for teams, too. M didn't care—as long as he still had his tool to use when the time called for it, and he needed Renzo.

Odd as it was ...

"Ah." Cree nodded at the doorway. "Get going, then. You don't need to be making him wait when he calls. Likely knows you're already in the building and pissing around, too, instead of being where you should be."

He gave the man a look. "You know, for being my handler, you'd think you would loosen up my leash every now and then."

Cree laughed. "No can do, New York."

Renzo bristled at the nickname.

Cree still used it when he wanted to differentiate between friends, and the man he was responsible for because of The League.

"Abused dogs never forget where they come from," Cree said from the corner of his mouth, never taking his gaze off Corrado who was still lying on the mat. "And just when you think they've learned enough to listen, and you give them a bit of freedom, they never miss the chance to bite you when they believe they can."

"Did you just call me a dog?"

Although, Cree wasn't wrong. Renzo was waiting for his moment—for the second they loosened the chains around his neck, and let him go free again. He was going to bite back, and bite hard. It might be just the fact that he never came back to The League, or it might be something different.

Not that it mattered.

Cree was still right.

The man knew it, too.

Cree looked his way again. "Why are you still standing there?"

Asshole.

• • •

"*Is that another fucking tattoo?*"

Renzo looked away from the window—which only faced another fucking steel wall of the warehouse across the way—in Dare's office to see the man glaring at him from the doorway. He didn't need to ask what Dare was going on about now. He knew.

The intricate start of a tattoo on the back of his neck—all black, beginning with a large rose right above his neckline, and surrounded by different shapes to create a design that disappeared up into the high fade of his hairstyle. The rose was the new part on his back—Dare had made Cree lock Renzo in the *quiet room* for a week after he'd gotten the bit up under his hairline.

The quiet room being a black room with no light, no noise, and … nothing.

Like that fucking bothered Renzo, now.

It didn't.

Mostly, he tried to keep his tattoos where people couldn't see them—the design up the back of his neck, double guns pointed down, with two doves holding a ribbon that wrapped a heart, was the first one where he hadn't done that. And Dare had not been impressed, clearly. He had one sleeve done on one arm, and his other was entirely bare. Besides his back, he kept his tattoos mostly to one side of his body.

"It looked kind of stupid with a big spot there," Renzo pointed out.

Dare's gaze narrowed. "You …"

He didn't know Dare's real name, except that Dare wasn't it. That was about all he was told. They all called the asshole *Dare*. A last name wasn't even in the equation for them to know.

Turning to face the man fully, Renzo shrugged. "It's there now, so …"

Which was the same thing he always told Dare whenever he added something new to his body without permission. They had to know when he went in for another ink session. They had a tracker *in his body*. He always took his phone, and he knew that fucking thing was tracked, too. They could stop him, if they wanted. They never did. That told him one thing— they either enjoyed punishing him, or they knew it would be pointless to try and stop Renzo from doing this simple thing.

A rebellious thing, sure. But it was a constant need he had since he'd been here. It never left him. He blamed *them*. They controlled everything about his life—sure, they loosened up a bit over the last year, letting him take trips out alone, and call his sister on occasion, but it was still an illusion. He was not making those choices because he *could*. He made them because they allowed him to. And this was the one way they seemed to allow him to rebel, even if he did suffer for it.

The need was never going to leave him.

Not while he was here, anyway.

Dare scowled, but shook his head. "And you still have that nose ring in, I see?"

Renzo chewed on the piece of mint gum in his mouth, unbothered by the dangerous edge to Dare's tone. "Yeah, it's healed now. Nice, huh?"

The gold ring in his left nostril had been another split-second decision. Not that he had any particular reason why he had it done during his second to last tattoo session, but it was in there now. Unless someone wanted to rip it out of his face, he wasn't removing it.

Renzo could tell he was pushing Dare's very thin patience to the limit, but that was just fine, too. He needed to do something back to this man for all the hell he put Renzo through daily. Dare, one of the main owners of The League, rivaled Cree for the biggest asshole in the building regularly.

Dare also thought Renzo was too … difficult.

Stubborn.

Wild.

Insubordinate.

The man also wasn't wrong.

Ren just didn't care.

God knew he had to keep a bit of pride—The League had stripped the rest of it away in different ways.

"You got a job for me, or what?" Renzo asked.

Dare's jaw muscles tightened, but he nodded. Probably happy that they were now onto an entirely different conversation. Nobody said dealing with Renzo when he was in one of his moods was particularly easy.

Even he knew that about himself.

"Folder on the desk—black strip across the front," Dare murmured.

Ah, great.

A black strip on the folder meant the job came directly from M. It was the only way Dare chose to differentiate from the jobs he negotiated for Renzo, and the ones that came specifically from M for him to do.

Crossing the office, Renzo picked up the folder, and flipped it open. He found the picture of a tanned-skinned man with short, black cropped hair and brown eyes attached to a sheet of details with a simple paper clip. He gave the picture about five seconds of his attention before lifting it up to read the bit of details it covered.

Christian Savino.

32.

Born: Sienna, Italy.

Known drug trafficker.

Renzo took in the rest of the details about the man before quickly closing the folder, and giving Dare his attention again. The man still hadn't come further into his office, instead opting to stand in the doorway.

"So the job is what, kill him?"

Because the file didn't say.

Dare shook his head. "M wants you to keep an eye on the man, apparently. He doesn't come over to this side very often—most of his business stays on his side of the world, I suppose. Except, he's here for a span of time. Could be a couple of weeks, could be a lot more. For whatever reason, your boss has reason to believe that while he's here, he could cause trouble. So yes, keep an eye on him. Report back to me once a week, and I will relay whatever information you give to M. He will decide what to do from there."

Renzo blinked.

Like a fucking *idiot.*

"You want me to *babysit* some fucking Italian because he came to America?"

All the skills Renzo had ... the shit he could do, and they wanted him to *babysit* somebody?

"That's a joke, right?" Renzo asked.

Dare glanced at the folder. "That's a folder from M, Ren. Do you think that's a joke?"

Jesus Christ.

"Fine, where is this ... *Savino* now?"

"Apparently, California," Dare replied, "but it's possible he's doing work across the states, too. You might have to follow him."

Renzo heard a lot in Dare's statement, but only one thing registered to him.

California.

Lucia.

He knew better—he needed to stay away until the five-year term was up. The rebel in him was fucking *dancing,* though.

"Yeah, all right," Renzo said. "Cali first, then."

"Follow him wherever he goes."

Renzo nodded. "No worries."

Mostly.

FOUR

The second a plane's wheels hit the runway was always the most nerve-wracking moment for Lucia during a flight. Just the way the plane jerked and jumped was enough to make her clutch at the armrests of the seats, and suck in a quick breath.

Maybe throw up a prayer to God.

Anything helped.

Thankfully, those few seconds never lasted long, and the plane had taxied into the gate at LaGuardia. Lucia didn't bother to rush like all the other passengers did once they were allowed to deplane. She was already a mixture of emotions that she didn't know how to deal with, so she figured prolonging the need to face it head-on would be in her best interests.

Or that was the lie she was going to tell herself.

Whatever worked.

All too soon, she had deplaned, and was heading down the escalator for arrivals when she first spotted her brother. It wasn't like she could miss John, honestly. He tended to stick out in a crowd considering he towered over six feet, always wore a three-piece suit, and practically refused to meet the gaze of anyone who looked his way.

Besides, he wasn't looking for anyone but her, anyway. His gaze was already locked on her form as she started to come down the escalator. Like he knew somehow that she was going to be the next person coming down.

Lucia still felt the occasional flare of annoyance and anger whenever she saw her brother, but it wasn't nearly as bad as it used to be. The fact that John didn't try to make excuses for the things that had happened almost five years ago helped that along.

Right now, she wasn't sure *what*—if anything—she felt about her brother. She had been trying to avoid New York as much as possible, and yet, all it took was a single visit and a conversation with her brother to basically put her on a flight less than a week later.

And here she was.

In *New York*.

Fuck.

"Hey," John greeted, arms already open.

Lucia took her brother's hug, and then passed her carry-on luggage over when he offered to take it, too. "Hey, John."

"Do you have any more luggage?"

"A small bag."

John arched a brow. "That's all?"

Lucia didn't want to say it out loud, but the truth was, she didn't know how much stuff to bring, or if it would be a smart idea. Hell, if she took a weekend trip to somewhere for work, she would pack a large suitcase full of shit just because she liked to have options. Problem was, if she did that *now*, it might give her father the idea that she was going to stay for longer than was good for her.

She needed to see him.

Wanted to, even.

That didn't mean she could stay after it was said and done. Lucia brought enough stuff to get her through a few days, but nothing more. And if she did, for some reason, opt to stay longer than what she prepared for, well she would handle that, too.

She couldn't do much else.

Lucia offered her brother a shrug, but said nothing. John only nodded like he understood, and then draped an arm around her shoulders as he said, "Let's go get your luggage then, kiddo."

She couldn't help it.

Lucia *laughed*.

"You know I'm twenty—"

"I know how old you are," her brother muttered. "Still my kid sister. Even when you hate my guts."

Damn.

Yeah, that was the thing, right? Even when she had been terrible to John—it didn't matter how much awful shit she said to him, or the distance she forced between the two of them—he was still there loving her.

That's just what he did.

It's what *family* did.

Lucia still didn't know how to handle it.

"I don't hate you, John," she said.

John's arm tightened around her shoulders. "Not *now*, maybe."

"Not even back then."

It was almost sickening how Lucia didn't want to verbalize the worst time in her life. She didn't like to say Renzo's name out loud. It felt like a fucking echo every time she dared to let it slip past her lips. One that continued to bounce around and come back to her time and time again like a slap she couldn't dodge no matter how many times she tried. So, she just avoided it altogether. It was easier on her heart.

"You certainly said it enough times back then," John muttered.

That was true.

"Because I didn't know how to deal," she said lamely.

Also, the truth.

John chose not to push, instead saying, "Well, what matters is while you're here, that you let it *go*. Or try, Lucia. Be good for him—Dad, I mean. He could use that right now."

Lucia knew that.

She didn't need to be told.

"I know, John."

That didn't mean this felt good, or that she wasn't wary about what might come out of this trip because she *was*. All of it. The unknown left Lucia feeling a little out of control, and she didn't like that feeling at all.

It didn't matter.

Her brother was right.

It wasn't about her.

"Let's get your bags," John said.

Yes, and then what?

Lucia didn't need to be told.

She knew.

Her dad.

• • •

"Aren't you coming in?" Lucia asked.

John shook his head. "You'll be fine … besides, they don't like more than one support person in the room when he's having his chemo."

Lucia flinched.

Chemo.

Just the word made her stomach clench.

John didn't say anything if he saw her reaction, though. Checking his watch, he added, "He should be finishing up, anyway. It'll be good for him to see you. Maybe it'll make him feel better—chemo isn't easy, you know."

Jesus.

Her brother was putting this on *thick*.

"Where are you going to be?" Lucia asked.

John waved the phone in his hand. "Siena and the kids; she had something today, so I need to check in."

Lucia nodded. "All right."

She still didn't move.

Neither did her brother.

"Lucia," John murmured.

Her gaze lifted to meet her brother's. "Yeah?"

"He does miss you. I promise … *that is all* he cares about. That he misses and loves you, nothing else. And if for right now, that's what you can focus on, too, then that's all that matters, okay? Nothing else has to come into play."

41

Easy for John to say.

Not so much for her.

"Yeah, okay," Lucia whispered.

John nodded toward the door at the end of the hospital hallway, and didn't move a muscle until Lucia started walking that way. She passed a look over her shoulder just before she came to the doorway, only to watch her brother disappear around the corner.

She took a deep breath, and passed the hospital room a look.

Now or never …

She knew Lucian loved her.

That was the problem.

He loved her *too* much, maybe.

Lucia put those thoughts in the back of her mind, and headed inside the hospital room in just enough time to watch the nurse take the cap her father offered. His hair stuck up in all different directions, but he was quick to smooth the strands back down once his hands were free of the white, jelly-looking cap.

"It's been helping, then?" the nurse asked.

"Seems so," her father replied, tiredly. "No hair loss."

"Good, Mr. Marcello."

Lucia stayed quiet in the doorway as the nurse removed the IV from the port that had been inserted in the right side of her father's chest. Lucian glanced away from the nurse as she worked quickly and quietly to clean up the area, and then allowed him to button up his shirt.

"You know," she said, "we could bandage down the IV port differently, if you—"

"This is fine; allows me to keep it out of sight."

Lucia frowned.

John had said their father was keeping this a secret, hadn't he?

But *why?*

It didn't make sense when she knew her father was close to his brothers. She had no doubt that if her uncles knew her father was undergoing chemo treatments for renal cancer, that they would be here *every single treatment*. Or at least, one of them.

Lucia didn't get the chance to think on it for too long. Her father stood from the chair, and reached for the blazer that had been tossed to a table nearby. As he did so, his attention finally landed on her.

He froze for a split second.

She smiled.

"Hey, Daddy," Lucia said, waving a hand.

There was a flash of something in his eyes—some emotion she couldn't place, but maybe that was because it was a mixture of a lot of things. And then, just as quickly, a small smile stretched his lips.

"Lucia," he murmured.

The nurse was quick to pack up the rest of the things, and then she left them to have some privacy without saying a word. Lucia was grateful.

She came further into the room, and closed the door behind her. She waited her father out as he *slowly* put on his jacket, and with careful hands, buttoned up the first two buttons. She took that chance to look him over—to check for the changes she might have missed since the last time she had come home to visit.

Lucia didn't know what she expected to see—she didn't want to see him frail, and sick. That was one of the things she had been *most* sure of when she decided to come home. That wasn't the man she knew to be her father. He wasn't weak, and he wouldn't show weakness. She didn't want him to *look* weak, either.

Thankfully, he didn't.

Mostly.

He did look like he had lost a bit of weight, and his movements were slower than they would usually be, considering. Still, his skin color was the same golden tan it had always been, and his eyes didn't seem dimmed. He looked tired, sure, but she bet chemo was fucking tiring. It likely made him sick, and exhausted. According to John, their father was doing three rounds a week because this was an aggressive attack on the sickness after surgery hadn't corrected it like they thought it would.

"Do I get a hug?" her father asked.

Lucia looked up from his hands—she'd been focused on the way his fingers deftly worked the buttons into the holes of his jacket. "Of course, Daddy."

She crossed the room without hesitation, and found warmth in her father's embrace. For a moment, the time and distance spent apart slipped away. All it took was the tightening of his arms around her shoulders for Lucia to remember every single little thing that she loved and adored about her dad.

"Missed you," Lucian murmured into her hair.

"I know, me too."

He cleared his throat, and loosened his hold just enough for Lucia to look up at him. "You look good, you know."

Lucian laughed. "Lots of medication, nothing more."

Yeah, she bet.

How much of it made him sick, too?

"John said you haven't told anyone outside of mom and—"

"And I don't plan on telling anyone until it's all done," Lucian interjected quickly. "It's not hard to keep it quiet when at this age, I don't have to *be* anywhere. No one is controlling my work or life. Jordyn helps, and tells people I'm … busy with something else, should they call."

Lucia frowned openly. "But why?"

"I just want to focus on getting better right now."

That didn't make sense to Lucia.

She also wasn't the one with *cancer*.

Lucian tucked a strand of her hair behind her ear, and his fingertips slid down her cheek with a soft touch. It was strange to her because just a couple of weeks ago, the thought of being in the same room as her father would have sent her rage spiraling again. And yet, here she stood, hugging him, and wishing she could make him better.

God, she wanted him to be better.

"Don't cry," her dad whispered.

Was she?

"I'm sorry," Lucia said quickly, wiping away the tears that had escaped. "I don't want to upset you, or anything."

Lucian laughed. "You're here, Lucia. You can't upset me."

But she had.

Before.

Purposely.

"What did it, anyway?" her dad asked.

"Huh?"

"Guilt from your brother, or ...?"

Oh.

He thought she came here because John emotionally blackmailed her into it. That was so far from the truth, it wasn't even funny. Sure, she might not have known that their father was sick had John not let her in on the secret, but she came home because of something else her brother had said.

She had enough time.

It was *enough*.

"I came because I wanted to come," Lucia said, smiling a little. "That's all, Daddy."

"I'm going to be fine, Lucia."

"I know."

She was sure he would.

He was her dad.

How could he *not?*

"But while you *are* here," her father said, "maybe we could work on ... well, us."

She blinked.

Yeah, there it was.

"Maybe," she whispered.

"You still can't forgive me, then?"

"I forgive you."

The lie came out easily.

Maybe *that* was the guilt.

Lucian laughed under his breath, and hugged her a little tighter. "You don't, and I know it. You might look like your mother, Lucia, but God knows you are *just like me*."

Yeah.

She really was.

"Okay, then I *want* to forgive you," she said. "Or get to that point."

That was not a lie.

She didn't want to live forever in a constant hurricane of contempt and pain that she had created by forcing distance between her and Lucian. She didn't want to feel like she hated him whenever he crossed her mind.

She loved her dad.

That's *all* she wanted to do.

He hugged her again. "How long are you staying?"

"We'll see. I was due a visit, so it could be a while. All depends."

"Good enough for me, *dolcezza*."

Yeah, her too.

• • •

The one thing Lucia didn't want to do during her visit to New York? Stay at her parents' home. She knew her old bedroom would be waiting there to comfort her if she felt the need to use it, and her parents would jump at the chance to have her there with them … but she still needed a bit of space.

That was all.

Sitting on the edge of the bed, Lucia toyed with the cell phone in her hands as she peered out the double doors leading to the hotel room's veranda. Overlooking a bustling Manhattan street, she certainly felt *at home* sitting there.

That's what New York was for her, even if it was also painful. She was starting to think the pain might not entirely be owned by her father, either. It was here that she met him—*Renzo*. It was in this city that she fell in love. He wasn't taken from her while they were here, sure, but it still kind of felt like it, in a way.

The clenching ache in her heart was more than enough to make Lucia want to do something—anything—different. She was sick and tired of constantly feeling like her heart was broken, and empty.

Even if that *something else* was nothing more than a distraction, she didn't care.

Turning the phone on, she dialed a familiar number, and put it to her ear. On the third ring, a familiar voice picked up with a sweet, "Hello?"

"Hey, Kelly," Lucia replied.

Her boss hadn't even *blinked* when Lucia said she had a family emergency that she needed to deal with. Sure, Kelly had asked for a little bit of details, but Lucia thought that was normal, all things considered. She tried to explain what was going on without giving away all of her father's personal issues, but it was enough.

Kelly gave her time off, just like that.

"How're things in New York—your dad?" Kelly asked.

"Pretty good. As much as can be expected, you know."

"I bet. It's been a while since you've been back home, right?"

"Yeah, it's been … a long time."

"Well, try to enjoy it."

Yeah, she didn't exactly know how possible that was going to be, but she was going to make the best of it.

"So, I just wanted to check," Lucia said, "but we're still good if I need a couple of months?"

"I *hope* it doesn't take that long, but yes, I will figure something out, Lucia. You don't have to worry about that, I promise. Besides, you know what I think of you, don't you?"

Lucia laughed. "I mean, not really."

"You are too talented to waste it—I will be waiting whenever you are ready to come back. All right?"

That was good enough for her.

"Yeah, okay. Thank you again. I can't tell you enough."

Kelly made a noise under her breath. "No thanks needed. Oh, and guess who came to the gallery today and asked about you?"

Lucia blinked. "Uh … who?"

"Christian Savino. Well, to be fair, he had to come in to overlook the contract and take a copy for his lawyers for me to acquire the piece of art he wants, but while he was here, he happened to *notice* you weren't here, too."

"Oh."

Lucia was still trying to figure out why she should care about that, honestly.

"Anyway, he asked where you were," Kelly continued on, clearly missing the confusion in Lucia's tone, "and I thought he seemed … interested in you, so to speak. I hope you don't mind, but I mentioned you had flown home to New York for a family thing. I didn't give details, but yeah."

Fuck.

Well, yeah, Lucia did kind of mind a little. She had no interest at all in Christian Savino. Not that the man wasn't good-looking—he was. And sure, he seemed interesting enough. He'd certainly been charming, but most men were when they cleaned up well and put on a three-piece suit. Hell, she'd grown up around all kinds of men like that. Their charm didn't particularly work on her.

Still, Lucia could put this issue out of her mind, for the time being, anyway. Christian could have all the interest he wanted, but she didn't plan on answering it back. Besides, he was in California dealing with Kelly, and Lucia was here … in New York. A whole fucking country away.

That was fine with her.

"That was okay, right? I mean … I thought it was sweet that he remembered you, and thought to ask."

Ugh.

"Yeah, no worries," she told Kelly. "I'm going to head to my parents' place for dinner. I'll give you an update soon, okay?"

"You better."

But maybe not.

Especially not if Kelly thought she was going to try playing matchmaker with Lucia and some strange Italian that she didn't know from a hole in the ground. Lucia had better things to be doing than worrying about dating, or *love.*

Besides, she felt love.

She was still *in* love.

She just didn't have the man she loved.

FIVE

Tucked inside the entrance of a damp alleyway, Renzo brought the filter of a lit Marlboro to his lips, and took a heavy drag. The thick smoke filled his lungs, and he refused to exhale, instead letting it burn and ache in his lungs until he didn't have a choice. The smoke came out in a steady stream, lifting higher in spiraling streaks of gray.

He'd made a choice—one he might regret, sure, but it was too late to back out now. There was something familiar about the dampness in the air, and the way the city smelled polluted and yet wet at the same time that felt comforting to him. There was a chill in the air, despite it being spring, and he reveled in the feeling even through his leather jacket, and dark-wash jeans.

God.

Renzo sucked in a breath of air, no smoke this time.

He was finally home.

New York never looked better.

Oh, sure, Dare was going to kill him when he got back to Nevada. There was no doubt about it. He'd have Renzo's ass on a silver platter for this, but it would be fucking worth it, too. How could it not be?

The last time he was in New York was two and a half years ago for a job that involved breaking into the home of a Senator, and busting open the man's safe. Given the fact the safe was underground, and built into a concrete wall, Cree's team had needed his skills with explosives to get it done quick, easy, and mostly clean, too. He hadn't known what they were looking for in the safe, but it hadn't mattered to him, either.

As fast as they were in New York back then, they'd taken him away from it, too. He hadn't been able to visit his sister, or brother. Shit, he barely left the hotel room, and he couldn't even get a piece of roadside pizza, for fuck's sake.

Well, he was going to do *all* of that now.

He had time, after all.

Renzo would deal with the consequences later, especially those that came from Nevada, and The League. Besides, they *had* to know where he was right now. He'd not tried to hide what he did after spending *two weeks* following that stupid fucking Italian around California and to neighboring states.

The man didn't do a lot of shit. Dinner meets, and phone calls. Christian Savino kept his head down, and didn't cause problems. Or at least, that's what it seemed like to Renzo. He visited a lot of art galleries, for whatever reason. One of them happened to be the one Renzo knew Lucia worked at—if the information he had on her was to be trusted, anyway, but that was probably just circumstance.

He'd not seen *her*, either.

He looked, though.

Fuck yeah, he looked.

Five years.

That was the deal.

Nonetheless, The League had to know what Renzo had done. They could locate him with his phone, and the chip in his arm. He wasn't hiding this—they were welcome to come get him, if they wanted to. But until then, he had other business to handle.

Finishing off the last bit of his cigarette, he eyed the cherry red tip before cocking his boot up over his knee to stub the smoke. Then, he stuffed the ruined cigarette into the pocket of his leather jacket, tucking it safely away. That way, he left nothing behind to say he had been standing in this alleyway for almost an hour now trying to convince himself just to walk across the goddamn street and say hello. Force of habit, maybe—The League liked to think of them all as ghosts, and the first thing they learned was how to behave like one.

Now that the cigarette was gone, Renzo had no choice but to stare across the road again. The small shop with the pretty sign above the large bay windows overlooking the inside didn't seem like much, maybe. A small place, but he bet his sister loved it like nothing else.

It was hers.

Her shop—or gallery … studio, whatever.

Renzo didn't know what Rose considered the place. Maybe a mixture of all three things. She had rented the place out for two years, now. She used it to work, display, and sell her many pieces of art. It was all hers.

Like he wanted, she'd done something. Made something of herself, and took care of Diego all the while. Some of it, after a while, had been with his help from afar. He called maybe once a month after the first two years of being with The League, but those phone calls were contingent on a lot of things.

One, that he never talked about business.

Two, that he *behaved*.

Three, that it never lasted more than ten minutes.

Four, she could never talk about *him* to anyone.

God knew he fucking *wanted* those phone calls. He craved them like nothing else. His sister was his one contact with the outside world, and honestly, his *past*. Before The League had happened, and all of the rest of it. Rose was his one connection—so fuck yeah, he didn't talk about where he was, or what happened, regardless of how many times his sister begged; he didn't step out of line, mostly, and he kept to the time limit they demanded when he called. He wanted those calls to Rose, so he did what they told him to.

Simple as that.

As for whether or not Rose kept up her end of the bargain ... well, he didn't know. He suspected she did if only because he explained how important it was that she follow the rules, so he could keep calling.

Anyway, contact with Rose allowed him the ability to help her. At first, she hadn't wanted to take any money from him—some shit never changed. Still, she took it when he didn't give her a choice. The one thing he wanted the most from their conversations was the chance to speak to Diego again.

It'd yet to happen.

Rose offered, and Diego always refused quietly in the background. It killed Renzo—like a knife right into his heart, but what could he do?

It was what it was.

He'd just worked up the nerve to head across the street to his sister's shop when the phone in his pocket started to vibrate.

Fuck.

Renzo knew better than to ignore a call, but especially because the only people who ever called him were those from The League. Pulling the phone out, he swiped his thumb across the screen to answer it, and put the device to his ear.

He didn't even say hello.

He didn't have to.

"*What are you doing?*"

Yeah, Cree sounded *pissed.*

"Currently—watching a white car drive in front of my position," Renzo replied dryly.

"Don't you fuck with me, New York."

"Nice to hear from you, too, Cree."

Sarcasm was his best defense when he didn't want to deal with one of Cree's moods, to be honest. Plus, it just irritated the man even more when Renzo refused to feed into his attitude. A win-win, truly.

"You're in New York?"

"How long did that take you to figure out?" Renzo asked. "I've been here for a couple of hours, now."

"That wasn't approved," Cree spat.

"Listen, I told Dare I wasn't a fucking babysitter. I'm not following that Italian everywhere day in and day out. Besides, I've got beads on him. I know where he is, and what he's doing. The same shit he was doing for the last two goddamn weeks—*nothing.*"

"You have a job."

"Yeah, I'll get back to it."

"*Renzo!*"

Ouch.

Full first name.

Cree was at his limit.

"Listen, I have something personal to handle, all right," Renzo muttered, leaning against the brick wall as he eyed the shop across the way. "And then I'll get back to the fucking Italian. It won't be for long, and he is being watched. I've got people who keep me updated regularly. A day or two isn't going to hurt, is it?"

"I have Dare on my ass right now about this," Cree returned. "Calling me every five fucking minutes because you're not where you're supposed to be. I haven't picked up yet, but trust that he's left a voicemail each goddamn time."

"So, lie."

Cree said nothing.

Renzo almost chuckled.

"Why would I lie for you?" Cree asked, deathly calm.

That one seemed obvious, didn't it?

"Because what I do is always reflected back on *you*, right?" Renzo did let out a bitter laugh, then, adding, "Wouldn't want him to think I'm running wild when you're the one who'll have to answer for it, would you?"

Cree made a grunt. "You're a fucking—"

"It's not going to be for long," Renzo repeated.

Although, he couldn't say that was the truth. What he did know was that his five years were almost up—he was *itching* for it. This little side trip was just a taste of what was yet to come for him, and he planned on soaking every second of it up.

"Make sure your stupid ass is back on the job *ASAP*."

"Yeah, yeah."

Renzo hung up the phone without a proper goodbye, and stepped out of the alleyway into the bright sunlight of the spring day. His first step toward his sister—practice, maybe, for what was yet to come.

Who knew?

• • •

Rose hadn't changed a bit. At least, not in Renzo's eyes. Sure, she was five years older than she had been the last time he laid eyes on her. Gone was that teenaged girl who seemed to behave and talk like every other teenage girl. In her place was a young woman with her hair pulled back into a neat braid, carefully applied makeup, and an artist's smock covering a tasteful black dress that fell to her knees.

She was still his kid sister.

He looked at her from across the shop—he was going to fix the bell above the door that didn't ding when he entered like it should have—and still saw the little girl who he had taken care of for almost his entire life.

He saw the paintbrush in her hand as she carefully worked on adding the details to the pottery vase in front of her, and remembered the girl he'd lifted packages of paintbrushes for so she could get her stroke *just right*. He saw the way she tilted her head to the right in her concentration, and remembered how she used to bend over a canvas on their living room floor for hours despite the ache in her back just so she could finish something because he couldn't afford to buy her a proper fucking easel.

No, she wasn't the same girl.

Yet, she was to him.

"Rose," Renzo said quietly.

Instantly, his sister looked up from her work, that heavy concentration written across her brow flitting away. It took her no time at all to find him standing just beyond the doorway of her shop—her gaze widened, and her mouth fell open.

The paintbrush fell from her fingertips.

It took her a second.

Then, two.

She blinked like she was trying to convince herself what she was seeing was something that existed. It took her entirely too long to reply to him like she believed he was standing right there, but that was okay, too. Renzo didn't mind waiting; he didn't doubt this had been a surprise to her.

But he figured … when would be a good time to do this?

He didn't know.

"Ren?" Rose whispered, her tone thick with emotions.

Renzo grinned. "Hey, Rose."

"Oh, my God, *Ren?*"

"Yeah, that's still my name."

At least, his first name. His surname depended on whatever document he was using at the time provided to him from The League. Not that it mattered right now.

All at once, Rose seemed to snap out of her daze. Renzo barely had time to open his arms to catch his sister as she flew at him. Her hug felt like bars locking around his neck—so fucking tight, he couldn't breathe properly.

Renzo didn't even care.

He held her just as tight.

"I missed you so fucking much," he muttered into her hair.

Rose's laughter mixed with the sounds of her crying. "Me, too."

He wasn't sure how long the two of them stayed like that, but it didn't matter, either. It was perfect—just him and his sister. The rest of the world stopped existing for a time. It was perfect. A reunion he had been wanting forever.

One of many, honestly.

Rose pulled away a little bit, but Renzo still kept a hold of her. "You couldn't call and let me know you were going to be around, or what?"

He shrugged. "Last minute decision."

That wasn't a lie.

She laughed, still crying. He wiped the tears from her face without saying a word about them. She let him.

"Just … where have you been?" she demanded.

Renzo arched a brow. "Rules still apply, Rose."

Don't ask.

Don't know.

Don't tell.

Simple.

Rose let out a shaky breath. "But why?"

Well, he wasn't sure if that fell into the category of the rules, or not. Sometimes, it was better to play it safe, but he figured … his sister had waited all this time, and he did owe her *something*.

"Someone made a deal for me," he said, knowing he couldn't give much more than that without explaining The League. That was most certainly off the table entirely. "Stuff you wouldn't believe was true even if I told you it was, Rose. But there's rules—okay? As long as we follow them, then it's good."

"But if you don't follow them?"

Renzo smiled crookedly. "Let's not find out, yeah?"

God knew he pushed the line enough.

"Okay," she whispered, her hands fluttering across his chest before patting him quickly. "How long are you in the city? Could you come for dinner tonight? I'm sure Diego would love to see you, and you must want to see him. I mean, if you can and you don't mind but—"

"Rose, relax."

His sister let out a hard breath, and sniffled. "It's been a *long* time, Ren."

He hated that water in her eyes.

Hated the tears that escaped.

Mostly, because he knew that he was the cause.

"I know, I'm sorry."

It was the best he could offer.

"Diego would like to see you, though," Rose murmured.

"Even though he never wants to talk to me when I call?"

"Because he's scared. He knows you're going to have to hang up again … he doesn't want to say goodbye a second time, Ren. He's almost nine years old, but he's not stupid, and he hasn't forgotten everything that happened. Keep that in mind."

Well, then …

Fuck.

"I'll come over for dinner," he promised.

"Tonight?"

"Yeah, whenever you want. Also, I'll give you the number to my hotel room. If you're free tomorrow, give me a call and we'll work something out for that, too."

He still couldn't give her the cell number he used—The League let him call his siblings, they weren't allowed the same, unfortunately.

Rose smiled brilliantly. "Yeah, okay."

• • •

As easily as it had been for Renzo to agree to dinner with Rose and Diego, his nerves decided to make an appearance as soon as he was standing outside of his sister's place later in the day. He couldn't place *why*, exactly, but it was there.

Maybe because it had been so long.

Maybe for Diego …

Maybe because this was the universe's way of reminding Renzo that no matter who or what he was now, he was still fucking human. And the universe had come around to kick him in the ass with something like anxiety just because it needed a good laugh.

Who fucking knew?

He wanted to see his brother, though. He greatly wanted to spend more time with Rose because honestly, he didn't know how long this trip was going to last. Who knew, Cree might just get pissed off enough that he would come after Renzo to bring him back, or put him back to work. Or shit, he might send someone else to do the job.

Either way, how long he was able to stay here was contingent on a lot of things that he had absolutely no control over. If he didn't go up there tonight—whether he was fucking nervous or not—then he didn't know *when* he would get another chance.

When his contract was up, sure … if he stayed alive that long.

Christ.

His thoughts were morbid tonight.

Renzo finished the smoke he'd been using as a way to take the edge off, and stubbed it before dropping it into his pocket. *Now or never* … He hadn't thought to call up and let Rose know he was downstairs, but that was mostly because he was trying to stay off the phone when it came to his sister. At least, then, the fuckers back at The League wouldn't think his family was the one and only reason he headed to New York when he should have been working. Sure, he could have used a payphone but fuck it.

Next time …

Coming around the corner of his sister's building, he headed for the front entrance. He planned on just getting Rose to buzz him in, but as he came up to the front door, something made him hesitate.

Something made him *stop*.

Maybe it was the buzz that drifted over his skin.

Or the way his fine hairs stood up on end.

Like his nerves just *knew*.

Knew to stop.

Knew to look.

Knew she was *there*.

Renzo glanced over his shoulder as a cab pulled up on the other side of the street, and sure enough, he watched Lucia step out of the back of the yellow car. *Holy fucking shit*—his heart probably stopped right then and there, he couldn't be sure. It was like the whole fucking world tilted, and put itself on the correct axis again.

Oh, sure, he'd known for a long time that he was living the wrong way—that everything about life just felt *off*. He knew it was because he was without her, but he'd become comfortable in this, sort of. He'd gotten used to feeling this way, and the sudden shift set him off balance. It took him entirely too long to blink out of it.

He wasn't surprised that she was at his sister's place—he knew Lucia kept in contact with Rose and Diego, when she could. Rose filled him in on that, but she promised to *never* mention him to Lucia. Not that she talked to him about Lucia, or anything else.

She couldn't.

Those fucking *rules* …

Fucking hell.

God.

She looked beautiful.

Just the same.

And yet, wonderfully new and different. That picture in the file had not done her justice.

Renzo didn't even have the time to appreciate seeing Lucia for the first time in almost five years. Not when she looked up, and all at once, her gaze connected with his across the street. Her eyes didn't widen, and she didn't act like she was seeing him. It was as though, for a brief moment, she was staring past him.

Or … like maybe she was seeing a ghost.

Her mouth opened like she might say something, and her brow dipped. She started to raise a single hand toward him when all of the sudden, the cab she had stepped out of pulled off into the street, taking her attention away. She looked that way to watch the cab drive off, and Renzo fucking *panicked*.

Rules.

Those goddamn rules had been beaten into him—five years, that was the damn deal. She wasn't even supposed to be *in* New York! Why was she here?

Before he could think better of it, he slipped back around the building. By the time Lucia looked his way again, he was already gone. He watched her shoulders drop, but he couldn't think on it for long.

His panic was far more relevant.

What would The League do if *this* was the rule he broke? God knew he broke every other one they set out for him, or at the very least, bent the rules enough to earn himself a punishment. But this one? *Her?* That was the line they drew in the sand, and made sure he understood it *well*.

Fuck.

Fucking fuck.

His soul was screaming.

It wanted to go back—to her.

His brain was louder.

He headed down the street.

Away from her, and his family.

Just ... away.

SIX

Lucia couldn't breathe.

Oh, God.

She couldn't fucking *breathe.*

She felt frozen on the side of the road. Standing just beyond the sidewalk, people blew behind her going in all directions. She could see people walking on the other side of the street, too. Going to somewhere, or coming from something. She didn't know, but they all seemed to be moving in slow motion.

Her world had slowed.

Almost *stopped.*

Like her heart.

She was sure her manicured fingernails were digging crescent marks into her palms, but fuck, she couldn't feel *anything.* Nothing but the beats of her heart. A *thump-thump-thumping* beat that felt like it was about to pulse its way right out of her chest, if it were possible.

She couldn't hear anything, either. The city had seemed so loud to her that day. Almost two weeks in New York, and for whatever reason, the city came alive more than ever. And just like that, with a split second, it turned into nothing. No noise; nothing. There was only a rushing in her ears—her blood, she knew.

She had seen him.

Didn't she?

She saw *Renzo.*

He was different, sure. Gone was the young man, and in his place was someone else who looked like him and stood like he used to. Gone was that leather jacket that he told her once he had won in a bare-knuckle boxing match. In its place was a new leather jacket full of zippers and opened so she could see the barest hint of ink peeking out at his throat. Strong features dusted with dark facial hair, and eyes so fucking *expressive.*

Those eyes hadn't changed.

Even from all the way across the street, it had been his eyes that she noticed first.

Hadn't it been him?

It *had to be him.*

Where had he gone?

Lucia felt like she had suddenly walked into the Twilight Zone, and absolutely nothing felt right or made sense. She knew that she probably looked like an idiot standing there on the side of the street staring across as though a ghost had just crossed her line of vision.

But that's exactly what it felt like, too.

He was the fucking ghost.

A ghost from her past.

Sort of.

Renzo couldn't be from her past when he had never left her mind, right? He still felt like a constant presence in her life every single day. He was never far from her thoughts. He was *always* in her heart, even though it felt empty, too.

God.

She couldn't date because this man had ruined everything for her. Sex, men … love. All of it. She didn't even *try.*

Her mind screamed *move.*

Her body didn't.

She closed her eyes, and opened them again, looking away from the passing cab to stare across the street, only to find it was empty. Coming to visit Rose had been a last-minute decision—she kept in contact with Renzo's younger sister just because she felt like it was the right thing to do. Sometimes, she didn't call as often as she wanted to, and she certainly didn't get to visit as much as she should, but Rose had never said anything one way or another.

And Diego …

That kid couldn't wait to get on the phone with her. He could chat for *hours* about the most mundane things, but Lucia didn't care. She would sit there and listen to him go on and on as long as he wanted her to listen.

She figured that since she was in the city, the least she could do was stop by. Especially as she still wasn't sure when she was going back to Cali.

But she had not been expecting to see …

Well, had she even seen him?

It felt like her mind and heart had played a trick on her. It was as though she stepped out of that car, and saw what she *wanted* to see, and maybe … not what was there. Was that even possible?

Lucia didn't know.

It felt like it.

Jesus.

But in her heart?

Her gut?

Her *lungs*?

That lost soul of hers?

It all said the same thing … she'd seen him.

She knew.

The parts of her that mattered—they knew.

• • •

"I thought you weren't coming. What took you so long? I told Diego you were here, and he freaked—"

Rose Zulla's words instantly came to a stop when her gaze fell on Lucia. Standing on the other side of the apartment's front door staring at Renzo's sister, that was when Lucia knew without question that it had been Renzo outside. Rose was talking like she *knew* someone was coming over. As though she was certain she knew who it was, and that it was someone Diego would be crazy happy to see.

Someone like Renzo.

And instead, she opened the door to find Lucia standing behind it, and not the person she expected. That was probably why when she buzzed the apartment to be let in, Rose didn't even come on the speaker to ask who it was downstairs. She just believed it was going to be someone else because that's what was supposed to happen.

It shouldn't have been Lucia standing there.

It should have been him.

Renzo.

Yeah, that's when Lucia knew for sure.

"Lucia," Rose said quietly.

Lucia felt the way her jaw tensed in an effort to hide the fact that her bottom lip trembled. Why she felt like crying, she didn't know. She couldn't explain the heaviness in her heart, either, or the tightening in her chest.

Like a panic attack was coming.

The *breakdown.*

She'd been holding it together for so damn long. Pretending was a game she had become good at playing alone. Everyone else thought she was okay, and she was so great at making them believe it, that she could trick herself into thinking the same thing.

Nothing was wrong.

Everything was just fine.

Fuck.

She was such a liar.

Nothing was fine.

It hadn't been for a long time.

Rose stilled in the doorway, her fingers tightening around the edge of the door like she didn't know what to do. There was concern shining back in her eyes even as she looked beyond Lucia like she expected someone else to be standing there, or maybe even coming around the corner. No one was; it was just Lucia in the hallway.

Still, it was another sign.

"I wanted to stop by while I was in the city," Lucia whispered.

Rose's gaze came back to her. "You're always welcome here."

Yeah, sure.

Lucia nodded. "He's back, isn't he?"

She stopped asking Rose about Renzo a long time ago. Every time she did ask, Rose didn't have very much to tell. It almost seemed like the young woman had given up on her brother, or at least, that's how it felt to Lucia. She didn't know if it hurt Rose to talk about him, but she was sure it caused Diego pain because the kid didn't hide it. So yeah, she stopped asking.

Now, she wondered if Rose didn't talk about him because ... she had a reason to.

"He is back, then," Lucia said quieter.

Rose sucked in a breath, and drummed her fingers against the edge of the door. "Lucia—"

"Just tell me. I thought I saw him outside, but then I thought my mind was playing tricks on me ... but it couldn't have been. I fucking *felt* him, Rose. He's back, isn't he?"

"He's ... in the city."

Oh, my God.

Her heart screamed.

Lucia didn't know what to say.

Rose saved her from saying anything at all when she added, "I don't know for how long, and I can't say much, but—"

"How long have you ... known where he was, or ... anything?"

She didn't want to put a guilt trip on Rose. She certainly didn't want to make the woman feel badly for making a choice to exclude Lucia from the details about Renzo's life, freedom, or whatever was going on with him.

But it was hard.

Damn, it was *hard*.

"Two years, or so," Rose said, glancing away. "I couldn't tell you, Lucia. He told me I couldn't because of their ru—"

"Okay," Lucia murmured.

That was all she needed to know.

She didn't need details.

"Did he happen to see you, too?" Rose asked.

"I think so."

Rose met her stare again, and stepped back a little to open the door. "Okay, well then I don't think he's coming, so do you want to come in and have dinner with me and Diego? He's going to be disappointed that Renzo isn't coming like he thought, and you will help with that, I bet."

Lucia should have said no.

She wasn't in the mood to eat. She certainly wasn't in the right state to entertain. She needed to go back to her hotel, and breakdown privately where no one could see her.

She was a *mess*.

Still, Lucia nodded. "Yeah, sure. Dinner sounds good."

SEVEN

Fuck.

Renzo swore way too much as it was—he used fuck like the interchangeable word it was in his thoughts and everyday conversations. It could be anything and everything he needed when he used it. An adjective, verb ... noun. A compliment, or insult.

It didn't matter.

Right now, though?

Fuck was the only thing his mind was screaming. It was the only word that seemed to accurately describe the screw up that was this goddamn day. He knew it wasn't that big of a deal, in a way. He could head out of the city, and pretend like Lucia *hadn't* seen him. If he didn't entertain it, then it didn't happen.

Yeah, shit.

He could pretend.

Not that he wanted to.

God.

More than anything, he wanted to go find her. Right now. Five minutes ago. Hell, if he had the ability to turn time back, then he would have walked right across the street as soon as he saw her step out of that cab.

Except ... he couldn't.

The League and their stupid fucking *rules*. Lucia was the one line in the sand he didn't even attempt to cross. He didn't even toe it, for Christ's sake. It wasn't because he was unwilling to push their limits—because clearly, he would—but Lucia was the one thing he wanted so very badly.

She was the one thing that, after all these years, he still didn't have back in one way or another. He was able to speak to his sister, and get updates about his brother. He wasn't followed twenty-four-seven anymore. He could live on his own, and do work without someone constantly looking over his shoulder.

But her?

Lucia?

She was the only thing he didn't have.

And whether or not The League allowed him contact with her before the five-year contract was up meant *nothing* once it was over. Still, he followed that rule. He stayed in line when it came to her, and their demands.

He did what he was supposed to do because *Christ*, he wanted her. He had to make it to the end of those five years, so he could get her.

Simple as that.

Renzo threw open the door to his hotel room, and slammed it shut far harder than was necessary. He wasn't even thinking. Mostly, he felt like he was currently running on autopilot for the most part.

He'd hoped his stay in New York would be a couple of days longer than this—at least long enough for him to spend some time with his sister and brother. Maybe take a walk on his old streets, and get that familiar comfort running through his veins.

He was going to have to cut his time here short, but that couldn't be helped. He knew exactly what would happen in this city if he stayed knowing Lucia was here, too. Now that he'd laid eyes on her, and felt her near?

Oh, yeah.

He fucking knew what he would do.

Run.

Right to her.

He'd not felt this way when he was following that stupid Italian fuck around California. Even knowing she was there—somewhere nearby—he'd not purposely tried to seek her out. He knew better; knew what it would mean for himself. He thought New York was going to be safe; he figured it would be fine because she wasn't even *here*.

Clearly, he'd been wrong.

Renzo was weaker than he thought.

Fuck him for it, too.

Yanking the small, navy blue duffle bag out from under the bed, Renzo tossed it to the sheets. He didn't even bother to prop it open before he was coming back to the bag with an armful of shit that he basically just grabbed up from the table where he had set it after arriving in the city, and checking in to the room.

Clothes and other things he had brought along for this short trip. Certainly nothing he gave much of a damn about, but he was going to need it when he headed back to work. The Savino job was still very much on the table.

Renzo didn't think he was in the right frame of mind to be working right now, but at least it would keep him focused on something else instead of the thing he wanted to do the most. He wasn't very good at denying himself something he wanted, and so, he was going to have to put his attention somewhere else for as long as he possibly could.

He'd been willing to argue about being some fucker's babysitter before, but screw that, now. They wanted him to babysit? Fine, that's what he would do. Whatever got him out of this city, and kept him as far away from it as was possible.

Renzo zipped up the duffle bag, and slung it over his shoulder at the same time the phone on the bedside table started to ring. He glared at it—

knowing who it probably was, and wishing he could just ignore it. He'd only given the room's phone number to one person. His fucking sister. It would be far easier for him to apologize to Rose at a later date, over the phone instead of face to face, let her rage at him, and then she'd be over it.

Yeah, easier.

But he wasn't a damn coward, either.

At least, he could say that.

Even if was stupid.

Before he could go ahead and prove himself wrong on the coward thing, Renzo leaned over the bed, and grabbed the ringing phone. He put it to his ear, already cringing because he knew what was about to come his way from Rose.

"Yeah, it's Ren here," he said calmly.

"What happened?" Rose demanded almost instantly. "Did you even consider what you did today, Ren?"

No *hello*.

No *you're late*.

Nope.

"Avoided a problem?" he asked.

Not that he expected his sister to understand what he meant by that, but he understood. That was more than enough for him. It's what counted.

"I told Diego you were coming, Ren!"

The level of her shout was enough for him to yank the phone away from his ear to try and save his eardrums. Jesus, Rose could get loud when she wanted to. Not that he was able to ignore the words she said because he couldn't.

They were still ringing in the back of his mind—knives stabbing into his heart, honestly. *Fuck.* Yet another thing for Diego to add to his list of things Renzo failed him on. Something else to add to an already huge pile of issues he was probably never going to be able to fix where his kid brother was concerned.

Life was a joke.

Or … it liked playing jokes on him.

"Rose," Renzo tried to say.

"No, you *listen*," his sister snapped back just as fast. "I was *so happy*. And I thought … you were here, so it was safe for me to let him know. He'd be okay because he would get to see you. And do you know what? He was *excited*. He wanted to get out of school to come right home when I called in, and got them to bring him into the office."

"Yeah, but I didn't—"

Nope, his sister didn't even let him try to talk.

"He loves you, Ren. He misses you all the time," she practically hissed. "And yeah, I know he won't get on the phone to talk when you call, but that's because out of all the fucking things you taught him—you forgot to teach him that it was okay to say goodbye because it doesn't always mean you won't be back when you say it."

Shit.

Rose wasn't pulling any punches here. Each one that she threw out hit Renzo like a ton of bricks right to the gut. Whether or not she knew that, he couldn't say, but they did. It hurt like a motherfucker.

"And I'm the one who has to deal with that. I am the only one tonight who will be here picking up the pieces of a little boy when he breaks all apart again. Fuck you for making me do that to him again."

The phone line went so quiet after Rose finished her rant that Renzo almost thought she might have hung up the phone on him. After a couple of seconds, he didn't hear the dial tone, so he figured she hadn't hung up, and maybe it was safe to speak again.

Well, he tried to speak.

His voice failed.

What could he say?

Renzo blinked at the wall.

He'd ... messed up.

Badly.

"Rose, I'm sorry."

His sister let out a shaky breath. "God, I thought this was going to be a changing point, or something, Ren. I know you didn't say that when you came to my shop earlier, but you were there ... and I just assumed things were going to be different if you—"

"I'm sorry."

It was the best he could do.

It was the only appropriate thing to say.

"I shouldn't have come around yet," Renzo muttered. "It wasn't the right time. I just ... acted rashly. I know better than that. Will you tell Diego I'm sorry?"

"No, you can do that when you see him."

"I'm not staying in the city, Rose. I'm leaving before the night is out."

"But you'll be back *someday*, right?"

Her question came out more like a demand than anything else, and it almost made Renzo chuckle. It was like he could hear the threat in her tone—she didn't try to tamper it. There was only one appropriate answer, and his sister wasn't going to accept anything else.

"Someday," he echoed.

"Good, then *someday*," Rose said firmly, "you can apologize yourself. She saw you, by the way. She knew it was you."

Renzo stilled in place.

So ... then Rose *did* know.

Lucia had been going to visit.

Huh.

"Did she?" he asked.

Stupid man.

He knew better than to put himself in this position; knew better than to ask about her, or the conversation she might have had with Rose after he took off like an idiot. Not only would it be punishing for him personally, but it would also feel like a dangling treat on the end of the rope. One he was all too likely to chase, especially when catching the treat meant getting Lucia.

God.

He was *fucked.*

"I told her you were back in the city for a bit," Rose added.

Great.

That meant a lot of things—none of them good. If his sister had confirmed to Lucia that he was well and good, plus around … well, what did that mean?

"And?" he asked.

"That woman, Ren …"

"Yeah?"

He didn't want to know, except he did.

He shouldn't ask, but he had.

"That woman still loves you, but it's messed her up … you know what I mean?"

Yeah, he did.

Because he was the same.

"I gotta go, Rose," Renzo muttered.

He waited just long enough to hear the goodbye and *I love you* his sister mumbled into the phone before he hung up. Readjusting the bag over his shoulder, and leaning back over the bed to hang up the hotel phone, he straightened up with a sigh.

He had to leave. He couldn't chase a dream he wasn't allowed to have. He had to get out of New York.

Now.

Renzo was just stepping out of the hotel room, and readying to go downstairs to check out when the cell phone in his pocket rang. He didn't even think about it, simply fished in his pocket as he headed down the hallway, and answered the call.

"Ren here," he muttered, balancing the phone between his cheek and shoulder. "What's up?"

"Got news on your subject."

Renzo's walk came to a stop.

He knew that voice on the phone—one of the contacts he was using to keep him informed on the whereabouts and movements of Christian Savino.

Fuck.

What now?

"What's happening?" Renzo asked.

"Your guy is hitting a flight tonight. Thought you might wanna know because this is where my watch ends if he's headed out of Cali."

That was fine with Renzo. He would follow after Christian Savino, and take over the watch he was supposed to be doing, anyway.

As long as it took him out of—

"He's going to New York," the guy said, interrupting his thoughts. "After layovers, and all, it looks like he'll land at about five in the morning."

Of course.

Because this was his life now.

A fucking *joke.*

• • •

Renzo pulled the black rental to the side of the street a good eight car lengths down from where Christian Savino's driver parked. He took note of the busy, popular club across the street—he suspected it had to be popular considering the line of people that went halfway down the block.

Damn.

How long had it been since he enjoyed a club?

Too long, likely.

Renzo put his attention back where it needed to be which was on his current subject. Christian didn't step out of his vehicle until the driver who had been accompanying him during his entire stay in New York—a week, so far, though it felt like a million fucking years to Renzo—came around to the back of the vehicle, and opened his door.

The man liked his respect, Renzo noticed. He didn't open his own doors, and hell, he wouldn't even clear an empty dish away from himself lest it seem like he was a servant. The man never left his hotel unless he was impeccably dressed, and usually, with a man or two following behind. Always one, at the very least.

Christian went nowhere alone.

Renzo was still trying to figure out why he was following this fucker. If he went by the information provided to him in the file—which, honestly, didn't mean much when M could easily not include relevant details about Christian—then it might have something to do with Christian's involvement in the drug trafficking trade. Maybe this Italian was

67

encroaching on M's business in a way, but he needed to know it for sure before he acted on it.

It could be a lot of things.

None of them mattered right now.

Renzo had to move as Christian was now standing on the side of the road, and looked as though he was going to head for that club. Business or pleasure? He didn't know, but it seemed like he was going to get to see the inside of a club for the first time in God knew how long.

Thankfully, Christian hadn't noticed Renzo tailing him for the week he'd been in New York, but that was kind of the point. He suspected the man regularly had paranoia about being followed anyway, so he took extra precautions when it came to the Italian just to be safe.

Like now.

Renzo waited until Christian had crossed the street with his driver, and then disappeared into the club before he too got out of his vehicle. There was no way he was going to get past the idiot at the front manning the doors and deciding who could get in or out of the business. Instead, he slipped into an alleyway beside the club, and looked for … there it was.

An exit door.

And it had a lock on the outside, too.

A pickable lock.

Renzo grinned, bent down a little, and pulled the tool from the back of his jeans that had served him well over the years. Even before he was brought into The League, he'd been damn good at picking a lock. It got him out of some tough situations.

This was *cake*.

Before long, Renzo was standing in the middle of the club's dance floor. In the swell of moving people, he was able to blend in better as he searched the tables and booths for Christian. Apparently, he had been looking in the wrong place.

Renzo found the man in the VIP section.

Maybe that wasn't surprising.

But the fact he was sitting across the table from Johnathan Marcello certainly was fucking surprising, and *confusing*.

It had been years since Renzo last laid eyes on Lucia's older brother. The last time, the man had been dragging her out of an apartment in San Francisco after letting his men beat the shit out of Renzo. He might have been pissed to see John again after all this time, if not for the fact that Renzo was starting to feel like something wasn't right here.

Christian had been in Cali, too.

Near Lucia.

And here he was in New York, talking to her brother?

What was going on?

Nothing good, he suspected.

• • •

"John, you still working that Capo job for your family, or have you gotten yourself something better since the last time we met up?"

Johnathan Marcello's head snapped up at the sound of Renzo's voice. Renzo grinned, and stepped out of the alleyway, the cigarette on his lips bouncing with his chuckles. The Marcello man's gaze landed on him, and for a second, he looked as though he didn't believe what he was seeing.

He'd just stepped out of his club—yeah, Renzo heard someone talking; the place was John's—about thirty minutes after Christian left. He'd managed to get close enough to their meeting that he heard some of the details. Drugs, imports ... Lucia came up once, which made his blood boil because apparently Christian had taken a liking to her.

John didn't seem to notice.

Renzo did.

"Ren," John murmured.

The man held up a single hand, and the two men close to his back instantly moved further away whereas they had looked as though they might try to take Renzo on.

They were welcome to try it.

He might get some anger out breaking their faces.

Who knew?

"You're looking well," John said, "and yes, to your question ... I have moved elsewhere."

Renzo arched a brow, and took a drag from his smoke. "Doing what, because I heard Andino is heading the Marcellos now, right?"

"I control the old Calabrese faction in the city."

He nodded. "Nice."

"Suits me well."

"I imagine."

"How's The League?" John asked.

Renzo stiffened, and the smoke drifted from his lips in curling tendrils toward the sky. "How the fuck do you know—"

"I have always known."

Huh.

"It breaks you," Renzo offered, saying nothing else.

"Yeah, I bet." John cleared his throat. "Something you want, or what? Because as far as I know, you've still got a contract with The League, don't you? Pretty sure you're not supposed to be around this area unless it's for a job."

Renzo laughed. "Ah, and it is. Right you are."

He was also concerned how or *why* John seemed to know so much about his business with The League, but that was a conversation for another day. He would deal with it later.

"Christian Savino," Renzo said.

John tipped his chin up. "What about him?"

"Do you wanna tell me why you're having meetings with a man I've been delegated to babysit from afar while he's on this continent?"

"I—"

"Or why I heard him mention Lucia's name when I know he's also been at her place of work in California, too?"

John's lips flattened into a grim line. "My business with Savino is just that—*business*. As far as Lucia, I know he brought over an art print that he needed validated, but the only one capable here was the same gallery where Lucia interns. Circumstance and coincidence, that's all. Probably not something you should worry about, Ren."

Yeah, but that was the thing.

Renzo didn't believe in coincidences.

"Why the hell am I following him, then?"

John gave Renzo a shrug. "Well, I have no fucking idea. Ask your boss—whoever that is."

"I would," Renzo said, "if I knew my boss."

"Shitty luck for you, then, I suppose."

Maybe.

Renzo grinned. "You know, I still owe you a punch in the mouth for that shit in San Francisco five years ago."

John cleared his throat. "But not tonight, huh?"

He sighed. "No, but someday."

That was a promise.

He liked to keep those.

"I don't doubt it, Ren," John murmured. "I've been waiting for it, honestly."

Good.

He liked when people saw him coming.

EIGHT

"Miss, your breakfast …" The server slid the plate of waffles in front of Lucia, and offered her a bright smile. "Enjoy."

"*Grazie.*"

The girl gave her a nod. "If there's anything else I can do, don't hesitate to let me know."

"Will do."

Once the server was gone, Lucia went back to her breakfast. Usually, she would take her meals right in her hotel room, but this morning, she decided to try something different. Her short stay in New York had turned into three weeks, now. Not something she had expected, but … well, she wasn't ready to leave.

Plus, her father wasn't quite finished his treatments. Almost, though, which was one good thing. Nonetheless, she wasn't ready to head back to Cali until she thought it was the right time. Lucia didn't have any idea when the right time was, but she knew it wasn't now.

Add in the Renzo thing a week earlier, and … yeah.

Maybe she kept looking over her shoulder, expecting him to be standing there again. Watching her, but unmoving like a statue. Yet, with eyes still so expressive and full of a soul she hadn't felt in far too long.

She wanted to find him standing there.

He wasn't.

Lucia wasn't ready to give up, though.

Taking a sip of the orange juice in the crystal glass next to her plate of food, Lucia's gaze drifted to her cell phone on the table just as it started to buzz with a text. She quickly picked it up, and unlocked the screen to see what the text said.

It was her mom.

Your father sent a driver to the hotel whenever you're ready, Jordyn had wrote.

Lucia smiled. *Thanks*, she wrote back.

I love you, quickly came the next message.

You too, Ma, she typed, ending the conversation.

Her mother wasn't going to say it, sure, but Jordyn was ecstatic that Lucia was making an effort where her father was concerned. It was all her mother wanted. Lucia wasn't willing to explain to her mother that, no, she hadn't exactly forgiven her father, but she was putting it aside for the moment.

It was something she would come back to later, and then she and Lucian could hash out everything that had happened in the past.

Now was not the right time.

Lucian had a treatment today at the hospital, and since Jordyn had something else she needed to take care of, that meant her father would have to go it alone. Lucia didn't like the thought of that, and while sometimes, the treatments made her father sick and moody, she would rather be there to give him someone to talk to while he did the chemo.

Hence, the waiting driver outside.

Probably a Marcello enforcer.

It would have to be someone she recognized—they wouldn't send someone random. Once she finished her breakfast, she would go out and meet the driver, then, head to the hospital to sit with her father during his treatment.

Lucia was half done with the waffles when a familiar voice had her lifting her head. Instantly, her gaze landed on the tall, handsome man walking her way. He grinned at the sight of her—showing off perfect rows of white teeth with an easy, charming smile. His three-piece suit looked tailored to his fit form, and covered his broad shoulders well. His cropped hair had been slicked back, and his brown eyes lit up with his happiness.

She, on the other hand, froze.

Christian Savino.

"Lucia, *dolcezza*, what are the chances you would be at this hotel, too?" he asked, coming closer to her table with every single word. His stride was easy, and confident. If he noticed her discomfort at seeing him there—in New York, at the *same* hotel as her like it had to be a coincidence—then he didn't show it. "The Astoria does have the best of the best, doesn't it?"

She took entirely too long to respond, which was a fucking mistake. Mostly because her hesitance gave Christian more than enough time to get to her table, and sit down across from her. You know, without being invited to do so.

Sitting across from her, he let out a laugh, and reached over to pick up her hand. He brought her knuckles to his lips, and pressed a quick kiss to her skin. She resisted the urge to tug her hand back, but only because she didn't want to purposely be rude to this man. Sure, she didn't share the interest he seemed to have in her, but that didn't mean she needed to kick his ego while she was at it, too.

That seemed like a bit much.

Besides, Italians always did want to get *close*. That was how they expressed *everything* in life. Quite literally. From their anger, to their joy, or love. It was all expressed through physical actions. Like a kiss to the cheek, or a smack to the back of the head.

Or even a kiss to someone's knuckles. It didn't have to *mean* something specific—it just was. Except … she knew this man had an interest in her, so she was inclined to believe that for him, it meant more than just a sweet gesture.

"Christian," Lucia said, keeping her tone pleasant. "I'm surprised to see you here."

Not a lie.

Had he just come to New York because that's where Kelly told him Lucia had gone? Because if so, that was a little creepy.

Christian smiled, and waved a hand. Finally, he let go of her hand, too, and she took the chance to hide her hand under the table where she wiped off the feeling of his lips on her knuckles against the skirt of her spring dress.

"Business," he said. "The deal I was trying to make with someone in Cali—separate from the art print I brought along with me—almost fell through, and I figured coming right to his home territory might ... well, change things. Or that's my hope."

Huh.

"And what is your business?" Lucia asked.

Christian shrugged. "A little of this, and a little of that. I import and export, essentially. Someone needs something specific, and I have the means to get it to them."

She didn't think he was telling her the entire truth considering the sly smile he sported, but Lucia opted not to press. She had learned over her life not to ask too many questions about someone's business because like her family ... well, it might not be all legal. She didn't need the details.

"But lucky me," Christian said, "because I get to see you again. I would like to do that more often, Lucia. See you, I mean."

She blinked.

Wow.

That was ... forward.

She gave him points for his confidence and arrogance, anyway. Not that it was going to make a difference to the news she was about to deliver to him.

"Not even beating around the bush, huh?" Lucia asked, half joking.

Christian flashed her with a another charming smile, and even tossed in a wink for good measure. For another woman, that alone might have been more than enough to have her agreeing to whatever he wanted. Truth was, this man wasn't bad looking. He didn't give her a *bad* vibe, either. He clearly had wealth, status, and class.

Every woman's dream.

Just not hers.

"Listen," Lucia started to say, hoping to let him down easy, "it's not the right time for me to be ... dating."

Yeah, that sounded okay.

Mostly.

Christian's smile didn't falter at all. "Why not, *bella donna*?"

"For a lot of reasons."

And none that she wanted to share.

"Not even for dinner?" he asked. "A drink, maybe? Or … what if, as *friends*, or even … hmm, I happen to know a new gallery that's opening, and there's a painting I have interest in. Perhaps you could accompany me to it, and let me know what you think of it and if it's worth the price they're asking. Then, it's all business—nothing else to it, *sì*?"

Lucia *could* have agreed to that, if only to appease his request and get him off her back. The thing was, she seriously suspected that if she said yes to his offer, then he wasn't going to get the hint that she wasn't interested.

"Sorry," Lucia said, "I can't. I'm a little busy with family stuff while I'm here, that's all."

"Shame." Christian's smile softened. "Could I at least give you my number? In case you change your mind—not that I expect you to, of course."

"I—"

Quickly, he leaned over the table, and his hand came up to brush the loose waves of her hair over her shoulder. It was an easy touch—soft, and gentle. "You don't have to call, *mia cara*. It's a … *just in case*, kind of thing."

Fine.

"Sure," Lucia said, picking up her screen to unlock it.

Despite that, Christian didn't move. He didn't lean back to give her some space. No, he stayed incredibly close, and in fact, continued tucking her hair behind her ear. He had just taken the unlocked phone from her hands when a form over his shoulder caught her eye.

She blinked.

Breathed.

Her heart ached from the sight of the man walking toward them. Leather jacket on, dark eyes blazing with fire, and his gorgeous face searing into her memory. The reaction her body felt at seeing him was visceral, and *raw*.

Renzo's stride was not quite the same as Christian's as he approached Lucia's table. Instead of easy, smooth steps, his were firm and determined. He looked ready to tear something apart, but the only thing he was looking at happened to be *her*.

She sucked in a quick breath.

It ached.

It didn't feel like enough, honestly.

So many questions ran through her mind at the sight of Renzo. She had a bunch of shit right on the tip of her tongue—a breakdown was heavy in the back of her mind. He was too close, and yet, not nearly close enough.

This close, she was able to get a better look at him. He wasn't the same—the changes were small, but they were there. His hair was a little shorter. His gaze, a bit colder. Gone was some of the softer lines on his face that had given him his youthful appearance the last time they had been together, and in its place were the rough, hard lines of a *man*. The nose ring was new, too, but *fuck* … she liked it. A lot like the ink peeking out on his hand, and his throat.

New things for her to discover, maybe.

Jesus.

She went there quickly.

Finally, Christian seemed to notice Lucia's distraction as he went to hand the phone back over. It took one glance over his shoulder for him to see Renzo, but it was too late for him to say anything. Renzo's angry expression turned into something softer, and sweeter. He even smiled.

Showing off his white teeth, he winked at Lucia, and bent down to sling an arm over her shoulder, and kiss her right on the top of her head.

The action was familiar.

God.

He still smelled the same.

Leather, musk, and *man*.

"Hey, babe, sorry I'm late," he murmured against her hair. "We should head out of here, yeah? Don't want to be late."

Late for what?

What was he talking about?

Renzo didn't give Lucia the chance to ask those things before he helped her up from the table, and gave Christian a grin. "Sorry to cut this short—next time, maybe? I'm Ren, by the way."

Christian didn't miss a beat. "Christian."

Lucia was still wondering what just happened.

• • •

"What are you *doing*?" Lucia hissed as she tried to yank her arm from Renzo's firm grasp. He held tight even as he led her out of the hotel. She didn't actually want him to let her go—she liked the way his fingers felt curving around her arm, and keeping her close to him. But that was the problem … it left her confused and *sad*. "Let me—"

"Is that your guy?" he asked.

Lucia's brow dipped as she looked the way he pointed. At the car waiting just beyond the front doors of the hotel, and the man standing next to the back passenger door. "How did you know that was my driver? Are you following me?"

Renzo glanced down at her, and arched a brow. "He's driving a black car, is wearing a suit, and looked like he might come at me as soon as I dragged you out of the front doors. That all spells Marcello enforcer to me. *No*, I'm not fucking following you."

But he wanted to.

She could hear it in his voice.

Lucia didn't know what to think of that.

She glanced back at the man waiting by the car, and nodded. "Yeah, that's my car."

"Good, get in." He didn't exactly give her the chance to argue. Before she knew what happened, he was pushing her into the backseat, and leaning in the door. "Just smile, okay?"

"I don't understand why you just came up like that and—"

"I don't know what his angle is," Renzo uttered.

"Who, Christian?"

Renzo nodded. "Yeah, him."

"He's a businessman from Italy. I met him at the gallery where I work."

The laugh that came out of Renzo's mouth could only be described as *bitter*. Nothing else would fit the bill. It kind of shocked Lucia how harsh it sounded, and yet, the contrast of how good he looked doing it was bad for her insides.

So fucking bad.

His gaze leveled on her again, quieting her instantly. "Christian Savino is a hell of a lot more than *just* a businessman from Italy, and that's only a portion of my problem right now."

He didn't let her say anything else before he closed the car door. She watched, confused, as he said a couple of quick words to the enforcer outside of the car before rounding the back, and sliding in the other side.

The driver got in, too.

Soon, they were on the road.

All the while, Lucia glanced back and forth between the window, and Renzo beside her. Oh, sure, he kept a distance between them. A good two feet on the seat, but *still* … she could feel his warmth, and smell him. He was too close, and yet, not nearly close enough. All of those emotions she had been suppressing suddenly felt like rushing right back to the surface all over again.

Holy hell.

She really was a complete *mess*.

"Where have you been?" she asked him.

Renzo glanced over at her. "I don't know what you mean."

"Why haven't you answered me back? Why haven't you *called* me? Did you ever even fucking *look* for me, Ren? How long have you been out? Are you just … off living your life without even giving a second thought about me? Is that what you're doing now?"

Something darkened his gaze.

Pain, maybe?

Lucia didn't know.

"What—"

"I have thought about you *every single day*. Have you ever thought about me?"

Renzo blinked.

In a second—a *breath*—he was across the seat, and right in front of her. Those hands of his grabbed tight to her jaw, and he pulled her in. The kiss *burned*, but oh, it felt so fucking good, too. The way his lips melded against hers was hard enough to bruise. The dance was familiar, though. As was the taste of him, and the way every single part of him seemed to surround her, and the way the rest of the world disappeared. His tongue struck out against the seam of her lips, and she couldn't help but open up just to get a taste of him.

Yeah, all these years …

It still felt like yesterday.

It was *crazy*.

So good.

And bad, too.

All too soon, Renzo pulled away, and let out a shuddering exhale though he stayed close to her. Close enough that his lips grazed hers as he murmured, "I have waited five fucking years to do that again."

A tear escaped, then.

Lucia didn't wipe it away.

"I can't explain …" Renzo shook his head. "Ask your father, Lucia. Ask him about the *deal*."

She blinked. "Okay."

What else could she say?

"To the hospital, Miss?" the enforcer asked from the front of the car.

Lucia cleared her throat as Renzo gave her a bit of room, and she finally felt like she could breathe again. "Yeah, thanks."

She suspected the enforcer might have known about the fact her father was sick, as he was usually the one taking her to the hospital. So, she didn't feel like she had to watch her tongue around him.

Renzo gave her a look. "You're not sick, are you?"

It was second nature … just a slip of the tongue. "My dad—cancer."

"I'm sorry."

She frowned. "Yeah, me too."

But probably for entirely different reasons.

• • •

"Daddy?"

Lucian looked up from where the nurse was readying his port to take the line, and smiled at Lucia standing in the doorway of the hospital room. "Lucia, come sit with me, sweetheart."

She stayed where she was for now.

Her father didn't miss it.

"Something wrong?" he asked.

She gave the nurse a look, and her father seemed to understand. It was only when the nurse had finished her work, and the treatment had started that they were left alone to their peace and privacy. Once the door was closed, Lucia came to sit beside her father. She could feel him watching her, but she could only stare at her hands in her lap.

She felt too much.

She thought too much.

It was all way too much.

Renzo had walked her into the hospital, but then he said he had to go. He didn't explain anything else, or say when he might be back. He just left, and she was left more confused and hurt than ever.

She didn't want to feel like this.

"Did you know Renzo's back?" she asked, giving her father a look from the side. He said nothing, but maybe that was how she knew that yes, her father was aware. Lucian was quick to deny when he didn't know something—he wouldn't bother if he had to lie about it. "You know, I always wondered what happened to him because ... he just disappeared after he was transferred out of Rikers, and removed from the state's custody for his other set of charges. It was like he didn't exist—it was all gone."

Lucian still stayed quiet.

Lucia didn't mind.

"But he's back, and it seems like he's probably been somewhere for a while. He said ... I should ask you, Daddy. Something about a deal, I guess."

Her father cleared his throat. "Did he now?"

"Yes. You don't sound surprised."

"That he found his way back to you? No. That he couldn't stay away? No." Lucian smiled when Lucia's head snapped up, and her gaze slammed into his. "Things always find a way—life has taught me that."

She had so many questions.

None of them came out, though.

"Renzo is not the same as he used to be," her father said, "and that's partly my fault. That deal he mentioned ... it has to do with people in

Vegas and something that happened while you two were there five years ago. Someone died, Lucia, and he had to answer for it."

She blinked, realizing ...

"Do you mean Tucker?"

Her dad tipped his head to the side, saying nothing.

"Daddy, that wasn't Ren—"

"I know," Lucian murmured. "But that changed nothing between him and I ... not to mention, them. The young man who died was involved in something bigger than what it probably looked like, and someone had to pay for that death. A deal was made between me, Renzo, and the organization. A ... company called The League."

"What is *The League?*"

Lucian laughed weakly. "That's not as easy to answer, but I guess you could say they train people to do a great many things."

That told her nothing.

"Like what?"

"Bad things; good things," Lucian replied. "I'm not sure you would understand if I did attempt to—"

"Just say it."

Lucian sighed. "An easy description would be that they train assassins, but it's not as simple as that. Many of their members have a very specialized set of skills—they're contracted out to people in four- or five-year increments, if that's what they want to do."

Lucia stilled. "A *what?*"

"You heard what I said," her father returned quietly. "In his case—Renzo's—he couldn't *choose* to be contracted out for a term. He had to pay back a debt, so his contract was going to happen regardless. That was the deal. Five years of his life given to The League, and he had to follow their rules and demands during that time. I believe, from what I know, that one of those things was for him to stay away from here, and ... well, you, too."

Jesus Christ.

Was this real life?

"I have more questions," Lucia admitted.

Lucian nodded. "Later, maybe? I'm feeling nauseous."

Yeah, chemo was a bitch like that.

They didn't get a later to talk about it. Just as her father was finishing his chemo treatment, and the nurse had come in to remove the port, two men darkened the doorway of the hospital room. She saw them first, and felt the *pain* that radiated from both of her uncles.

Giovanni.

Dante.

"Lucian," Gio said quietly.

Yet, *firmly.*

79

Lucia saw her father's back stiffen as he was reaching for his phone on the table next to the chair he used to sit in when he was getting his treatments. He straightened a hell of a lot slower than she had ever seen him do before, and turned around even slower to face his brothers where they stood in the doorway.

For a long time, nobody spoke.

They just ... *stared.*

"Why?" Dante asked finally, breaking the silence. "*Why*, Lucian?"

Her father's secret was out.

"How did you learn?" Lucian asked his brother.

Dante's gaze darted to Lucia, and then went back to her father. "The driver for your daughter—he heard her say you were sick, and ... word came around."

"You mean, he ran right to you."

"Yeah, well," Dante countered, shrugging.

Gio laughed bleakly. "It should have been *you*. You should have been the one to tell us."

"I have cancer," her father snapped. "I don't owe anyone anything."

"Daddy," Lucia whispered, "be nice."

Chemo made him *pissed*, sometimes. Like that bad mood only got worse, but she understood. Her uncles might not, though.

Lucian looked her way, and then back to his brothers. "I was trying ... to handle it."

"Alone, though?" Gio asked. "We could have—"

"What?" Lucian asked, though Lucia heard it in his tone. The pain—the ache. He was tired, and he didn't want to do this today. "What, Gio, watch me get sick? Watch them pump poison into me so that it can kill another kind of poison? Watch me struggle to eat because it makes me want to puke? Watch me take twenty minutes to crawl into bed because I'm fucking exhausted? *What* do you want to help me with?"

"All of it," Dante said, softer than she had ever heard her uncle speak. "We would help for all of it, Lucian, whether you want us to see it or not."

Lucia saw the fight leave her father, then. Sure, she had more things to ask him, especially about Renzo, but it could and would wait for another day. They had other things—more important things—to handle right now.

She slipped out of the hospital room to let her father and uncles have some privacy, but not before glancing over her shoulder as she closed the door.

The three men inside were hugging. And *crying.*

She closed the door.

The world didn't get to see that. Not her father's breakdown, his brothers' fear, or their pain.

Ever.

NINE

Renzo kept his head down as he walked down the block leading toward his hotel room. The phone in his ear kept ringing with no goddamn answer, which only pissed him off more. He'd been trying to get ahold of Dare for the last two hours—since he left Lucia at the hospital with her driver.

No answer.

Or rather, Dare just wasn't picking up the phone because he was being a complete *asshole*. Maybe he was in a mood about someone else, or maybe he was in a mood about Renzo, specifically, but he bet that was the problem. Not that Dare couldn't answer his phone—the guy always had at least three on him—but that he simply didn't want to.

Renzo went another route.

Cree.

No matter what was going on, Cree would pick up his phone if it was someone from The League calling him. He might not be nice when he answered, but he would do it.

Renzo entered the lobby of the hotel just as Cree picked up the phone with a low, dark, "*What?*"

"Sleeping?" Renzo asked.

"Resting my eyes."

Right.

That's what Cree always said when someone caught him napping. It was like the guy didn't want to admit that he was just as human as everyone else around him. No, he wanted to be superhuman—or at the very least, make everyone else believe that was the case.

"What do you want?" Cree asked, his words mumbled a bit. "Don't you still have a job to do, New York? Lucky you that it's *in* New York now, huh?"

Renzo scowled. "Yeah, *lucky*."

That was one way to put it.

More like entirely fucked up.

Now was not the time.

Renzo went back to his problem. "Why isn't Dare picking up my calls?"

Cree grunted. "*That's* your problem? Because that sounds like Dare is sick of your shit for the moment."

"No, that is part of my problem. First this, then we'll talk about the second part of it."

"Ren, I don't know why he isn't picking up your calls, all right? And I'm not interested in hearing you whine about it, either."

Nice.

Really.

"I've been compromised," Renzo said, figuring it was better to just get that shit out there and over with quickly. Then, maybe Cree would see this wasn't just another regular call from Renzo where he rankled their chains. Sure, he pulled shit on them sometimes, but when there was a *real* problem, he wasn't the fucking idiot crying wolf. They knew that. "The Savino prick—he saw me, we shared words."

For a long while, Cree was silent. Sometimes, that could mean bad things, but other times, it just meant Cree was thinking. Problem was, it was often hard to tell the difference between the two things. Especially when one wasn't looking him right in the face.

"What words did you share with the Italian?" Cree finally asked.

Renzo sighed. "Nothing bad—I stepped in on a situation to divert what was happening."

He mentally patted himself on the back for not outing the fact that he stepped in on a conversation Christian had been having with Lucia because he was, in fact, an idiot. A jealous idiot who didn't like the fact that Christian was touching her, grinning at her, and getting closer by the second. Not to mention, giving her his *phone number* it seemed like. Why else would the prick be holding her phone and typing into it?

Sure, he didn't like the fact that the guy seemed interested in Lucia given his *business*, but it wasn't like Christian was any different than the other men in Lucia's life, or even *Renzo*, for that matter. They were all bad men. He couldn't say that was why he stepped in—he could blame it entirely on jealousy, though.

Because yeah, he was an idiot.

Cree made a noise under his breath before finally saying, "I know what Dare would tell you, so that's what I'm going to say."

"Shoot," Renzo muttered.

He'd not even left the lobby of the hotel because, depending on how this conversation went would determine what Renzo did after this. Whether he went upstairs, packed, and got the hell out of this city … or if he stayed. And if he did stay, well, there was a woman in this city who he figured that he owed an explanation to.

Lucia, that was.

After that car ride earlier … yeah, he owed her something.

A lot.

It scared him to death, and he wasn't one to feel fear. He shouldn't be scared of Lucia, but in a way, next to the love in his heart for her … the fear was ever-present, too. Because how might this end between the two of them—with her walking away?

God.

Renzo wouldn't be able to take that.

Nope.

He was not the same as he had once been. He was not the same person. And she didn't ask for *this*.

Neither had he.

"Are you listening to me?" Cree demanded.

Renzo blinked out of his thoughts. *Not really*, he thought, but instead, said, "Yeah, keep going."

He'd catch up to whatever Cree said, surely. There was no need to make the man think he wasn't listening, That would only piss Cree off, and the last thing Renzo needed was the man making a trip to New York to kick his ass because he felt like it. Knowing Cree, he absolutely would do it, too.

"Mmm, sure," Cree muttered. "I *said*, the job remains the same. Keep an eye on the Italian, and report back like you were told to do. Compromised or not, that doesn't change the fact that you know how to follow someone without being seen. As long as you're not constantly stepping in on Christian or his people, then I highly doubt he's going to notice you're even around, Renzo."

"But—"

"I'm not done." Cree sighed, and shifted on the other end of the phone. "Listen, there must be a reason why *M* wanted this man followed, and for you to do it. He's never sent you out on a job like this before—it's always something bigger, or he let The League contract you out for a job. So, this is … something. Maybe you don't need all the details, and that's why you didn't get them. I don't know. Point is, the job remains the same. Keep doing what you're doing."

Renzo frowned.

He shouldn't tell Cree what was on the tip of his tongue, but the words felt like they were about to come out without his permission, anyway. But if there was *anyone* he trusted from The League, it was Cree.

Besides, without explaining the full extent of the compromise he'd made of himself with the job, then Cree might not be giving him the right advice. If that came back on Renzo, then so fucking be it. He would handle it. But it wouldn't be *just him* who would answer for it—Cree would have to, as well.

That wasn't fair.

"The compromise had to do with Lucia Marcello," Renzo said quieter. "She was involved, and still is."

There.

He said it.

Renzo waited Cree's silence out again. The man knew the rules of Renzo's contract with The League, and M. He knew the rules that were expected of him, and that under no circumstances, was he to break them.

Would that change things?

Possibly.

When Cree didn't say anything after a minute, Renzo spoke again. "There is more at play here in this job than just the Italian. It's Lucia, too. I'm not good for this job, Cree, not when things like her also are in play."

Finally, Cree sighed. "He expected that, actually, and the job remains the same. Lucia or no Lucia, you stay and do your job."

"Who expected *what*?" Renzo demanded.

"All of them, Ren."

What?

Cree hung up the phone before Renzo could ask that question. *Shit.*

Frustrated, Renzo spun on his heel to head back out of the hotel's lobby. Hell, if he was going to have to stay in this city, then he had things to take care of while he was here. He damn near tripped over his own two feet at the sight waiting for him just beyond the exit doors.

Lucian Marcello, in a three-piece suit and looking ready for the day to be over, leaned against the back door of a black Mercedes. He'd folded his arms over his chest, and his gaze nailed into Renzo. There was no way for him to act like he hadn't seen the man when he was looking right at him.

Fuck.

He hated black cars now. They always reminded him of Capos on the streets, and the Marcellos coming for him in San Francisco. He'd bought three vehicles for himself since starting at The League, and not a single one of them were black for those reasons.

Lucian tipped his head to the side, and crooked a finger at Renzo as if to silently demand he *come closer*. Great, now he was regaled to the likes of a puppy. A simple gesture or a single word was going to send him running.

Renzo pushed his thoughts out of his mind, and headed out of the hotel. "Did you come here to tell me to stay the hell away from Lucia, then?"

Lucian arched a brow. "Is that what you want me to say?"

No.

Not at all.

Instead, Renzo muttered, "What do you want?"

Stepping away from the car, Lucian opened the back door, and then nodded at the inside of the car. "Get in?"

"So, I can never get back out?" Renzo asked.

Lucian gave him a look. "I see your smart mouth has become sharper over these last few years."

Renzo shrugged. "Yeah, well, gotta keep something for myself."

"Get in the fucking car, young man."

Hell, that was better than the *kid* he used to call Renzo.

Unfortunately, Lucian didn't seem like he was joking, or that he was giving Renzo a choice about getting in the car. Renzo stepped in, and the door shut behind him. Lucian slipped into the car on the other side, and the driver up front barely looked at the two of them in the rearview mirror as he pulled out of the hotel's lot. They drove for a good forty-five minutes, long enough to be all the way on the other side of the city, or damn near, before Lucian started speaking again.

"I want to make sure you know what you're doing here—with Lucia, I mean. She's ... strong, or that's how she seems," Lucian murmured, never looking away from the window. "So strong and stubborn, in fact, that I can count on two hands the amount of times she's had a real conversation with me before these last few weeks that she's been back home. She hated me for what happened, and perhaps, rightfully so. She's more like me than I gave her credit for, too. I always thought my boy was more like me than any of my daughters, but clearly, I was wrong."

"Why is that?"

"Only Lucia can hold a grudge like me."

Renzo chuckled.

Even Lucian grinned a bit.

"Nonetheless," Lucian added, still watching the buildings pass them by, "she seems strong, but there is still a very broken part of her that is barely holding it together. I suspect it falls back to what happened, and you, but she keeps it guarded. I want to make sure you understand that—you're back in her life, then you need to recognize her—"

"Wait, you came to talk to me about how I should treat *Lucia*?"

Because wow, that was a one-eighty from the Lucian he used to know. The Lucian he used to know would have threatened to cut off his arms for stepping anywhere near his daughter.

Lucian finally glanced away from the window, and gave Renzo a tired smile. "Things have changed, haven't they? I thought you knew that when I came to visit you in the prison with the offer about The League?"

Maybe so.

Renzo had still wondered if it really did change, though.

"I heard you're sick," Renzo said quietly.

Lucian's jaw hardened for a second, but just as quickly, he nodded. Using one hand, he grabbed the edge of his suit jacket and the silk shirt underneath. Moving the fabrics to the side, he flashed the port in his chest.

Renzo swallowed hard. "Sorry about that."

And he was.

Regardless of the shit between them, the bridges burned, and all the things that still needed to be said about what happened, Renzo wouldn't wish sickness on anyone. He just wouldn't—he wasn't the type.

"Don't pity me—I hate that."

"I feel a lot of things for you, Lucian, and pity isn't one of them. That doesn't mean I can't apologize for something horrible that's happening to you. It isn't the same thing. That's called sympathy and empathy. Despite whatever you might think The League did to me, they didn't take away the fact I am human. They just made me a stronger one."

"A better one, maybe," Lucian murmured.

Maybe.

Renzo wasn't going to think about it.

"The five-year deal isn't up yet with The League, correct?" Lucian asked him.

Goddamn.

"I know the five-year deal isn't up yet," Renzo returned, aching in his chest with every word that he spoke. "Trust me, I know exactly how much longer I have before it is. I know every single *day*."

That was an understatement. He probably knew it down to the minute if he wanted to be honest, but he didn't think Lucian needed to know those details. Some things were just better left unsaid in the grand scheme.

"I know in those five years," Lucian continued, "that she was something you were supposed to stay clear of, yes?"

Renzo blinked.

"Yes," he admitted.

"But you'll keep an eye on her while you're here in the city, won't you? Keep her out of danger, I assume."

"You don't even have to ask that."

Lucian nodded. "Good. Karver?"

The driver at the front of the car finally glanced in the rearview. "Yes, boss?"

"The Cordial, if you wouldn't mind, please. We'll drop our companion off there for the evening."

"A hotel across the bridge?" Renzo asked. "Because I would prefer to go back to my hotel in Brooklyn."

Lucian shrugged, but said nothing.

All too soon, the car came to a stop in front of the hotel in question. Lucian leaned over in the seat, and opened the door for Renzo to get out. He stared at the front of the hotel, and wondered what in the fuck was going on.

"Lucia changed hotels after leaving the hospital earlier," Lucian said. "I thought you might like to know where she was staying now."

Renzo's gaze widened as an understanding dawned on him. This was her hotel, and Lucian, the man he thought would *never* willingly take Renzo to her had just done exactly that. And he didn't look the slightest bit bothered by it.

Huh.

What was happening?

"Step out," Lucian said, "I'm tired and I know my wife is worried as I haven't gotten home yet, and today has been the worst of days."

Renzo didn't ask why, or question the man. He stepped out of the car, and then closed the door behind him. The very next second after he did that, the car pulled away from the side of the drop off, and disappeared out onto the street with the rest of the traffic.

He was stuck staring after it.

He thought two things, then.

One, he still owed Lucia that explanation.

Two, Lucian didn't ask about his job or why he was in this city. Renzo wondered if that was because the man didn't have to—did he already know?

TEN

Lucia knew it was Renzo behind the hotel door before she even opened it. How? Well, that she wasn't sure, but she knew nonetheless.

"Hey," Renzo murmured, never stepping beyond the threshold of her room. "You busy?"

There was a lot of things Lucia wished she could make sense of in those seconds—like the way her heart was screaming for this man, and yet, still hurt like hell, too. Or the fact that she finally felt a little less empty and alone because he was near, but she still seemed entirely too cold at the same time.

It had been so long since they were this close.

She *still* loved him.

Lucia shook her head. "No, I'm not busy."

Renzo smiled a little. A ghost of a smile. It teased the corners of his lips, but didn't lift up entirely. "Are you going to let me come in, then?"

"Not sure."

"Why is that?"

"I hurt all the time. I don't want to hurt more because I let you come in tonight."

There.

She said it.

Renzo could make of that what he wanted.

He leaned against the doorjamb, and hooked one combat boot over the other as he looked her over. He was bad for her senses, she decided. Bad for her heart, and the rest of her, too. He made her stomach do flipflops, and her blood rushed through her veins. There was nothing else like Renzo Zulla that could get her heartrate picking up as fast as he did.

It was crazy.

"How about I talk, then, and you can decide what you want to do," he said.

Lucia wet her lips, and glanced past him to the empty hallway. "Here like this?"

"You make the calls. It's all about you."

Yeah, she wished.

Unfortunately, very little was ever about her. He was also in the equation here. She didn't for one second think he had come *just* for her. He came because he wanted to, and so yeah, here he was.

"How did you know where I was staying?" Lucia asked.

"Your father, actually."

Lucia stiffened. "What?"

"Your dad let me know. Dropped me off, if I'm being honest."

What?

She was starting to feel like a fucking parrot that repeated everything because she couldn't make sense of it, and saying it out loud was the only thing she knew how to do instead. But *that* didn't make sense.

Her dad?

Since when did Lucian care about letting Renzo within breathing distance of Lucia? Never, that's when.

Renzo laughed like he could read her mind. "Yeah, that's probably how I looked when I figured it out, too."

"Huh?"

"Nothing," he said, waving a hand. "Anyway, can I talk and then you can decide where we go from there?"

Well, what choice did she have? Sure, she could say no, but that didn't mean she wanted to. In fact, that was the exact opposite from what she wanted. She had questions—Renzo was the only person with the right answers. If he wasn't the one to tell her, then how was she ever going to know? How was she ever going to get rid of this constant, heavy feeling in her heart that never seemed to leave her alone?

She wouldn't.

Not without him to help.

"Talk," Lucia said.

Renzo cleared his throat, and that gaze of his darted back up to meet hers. In a second, she was silenced. All it took was his eyes on her—pinning her in place and making her feel like the only thing in his world—for her to be thrust back five years to a better time when all of this shit hadn't happened, and she hadn't been alone without him for far too long.

Back when they had been different people.

A boy with a leather jacket.

A girl with a trust fund.

Two people who were young, dumb, and loved each other enough to do *anything* as long as they were doing it together. She didn't know if they were still those people, or if the time and distance between them had changed them into someone else.

He looked the same, sure.

And he didn't look the same, too.

"You know," Renzo said, breaking the silence between them, "the first thing I did when I started making money was put Diego in a private school for Rose."

"I bet she appreciated that."

Renzo nodded. "Do you want to know the second thing?"

"Sure."

"I tried to hire a private investigator to find you."

Lucia's heart clenched. "Oh."

"Yeah, but that didn't work because, at the time, I didn't realize how much control The League had over my life. Instead of getting any information from the investigator, I got a warning from The League. Five years—that was the deal. I owed them five years of my life, my time, and my skills, and during that time ... well, they decided how I got to spend it. And you were not one of the things they allowed me to have, you know? I mean, they told me some things here and there. Mostly to fuck with me, I think, and keep me in line."

Her brow dipped. "Things like what?"

"Do you remember a guy named Derek?"

It took her a second, and then another before she connected the name to a memory. "A friend in college was going to a concert with a new guy she was dating, but he had friend that wanted to come along, too."

"Derek," Renzo said.

Lucia shook her head, and gave him a look. "I went because my friend begged me—it was a blind date."

"They thought I might want to know."

Why was her throat so tight?

"That seems cruel," she whispered.

"Did you have fun with Derek?" he asked.

"I barely spoke to him. It was the first and last date I have been on in almost five years."

Not that men didn't *try*. They did—far too often. No one seemed to understand when Lucia said she wasn't interested that it meant exactly *that*. She didn't want to date, and she didn't want to try. It wasn't a matter of getting back on the horse and trying again—love couldn't be like that. Not when her love with Renzo had been ... so fucking amazing.

And entirely insane.

"But that bothered you, huh?" Lucia asked. "The thought of me with someone else."

Renzo's gaze flashed with something dark. "More than you will ever know."

"Yet, you never called. Never answered my letters back."

"What are you talking about?"

She ignored him, saying, "You never cared, clearly."

"*Lucia.*"

She refused to look at him. "That's all you had to do, you know? Make a fucking effort, Ren. Let me know *anything*."

"I couldn't."

"I don't think that's—"

"I *couldn't*," he said, harsher the second time.

Her gaze jumped back up to his. "You couldn't pick up the fucking phone and *try*?"

"You think that wasn't constantly on my mind? That you weren't still the first thing I thought about in the morning, and the last thing at night, Lucia? Because you were—still are. Every fucking day, and every single night."

She sucked in a sharp breath, but he didn't even give her the chance to respond before he continued on with, "But I made a *deal*—one they held me to regardless. One they *beat into me* constantly. It was bigger than me and you, and yeah, I know it fucking hurts, but some things are bigger than us, babe. They made me something when I was always gonna be nothing. I hate them for a lot of things, but fuck me, I respect them for what they gave me, too. I made a deal—my life for five years, and they didn't give me a choice but to follow it through."

Renzo shook his head, muttering, "My calls are monitored. I'm tracked—all the time. Anything that comes in and out from my place is already known before it even gets to me. I'm pretty sure they know the name of the guy that makes my coffee and bagel on Wednesdays. So yeah, the one time I tried to find you … they stepped in. You think Derek was the only thing they did to be *cruel*? Try seventy-two hours locked in a dark room with no windows, no food, and no contact with *anyone*. And that?" He barked out a laugh, harsh and fast. "That was an easy punishment, Lucia. That one was fucking *cake* compared to the others. At least that time, they didn't send someone in to beat me in the dark every hour on the hour."

God.

Her heart ached.

She wanted to believe he was just exaggerating, but she could hear it in his voice that he was speaking the truth. She didn't have to like it, but it was there. She had wanted to know. So there, she now knew.

What could she do with it, though?

She didn't know what to say to that. She didn't understand, really, because it hadn't been her in that position. She didn't know anything about this thing he and her father called The League, or what it meant for Renzo.

"Still hurts," Lucia whispered. "I can't make it *not* hurt, Ren."

"I know. I'm sorry for that."

She believed him.

That didn't help her heart, though.

Taking in a deep breath, Lucia made a choice, then. She stepped back from the door, and widened it a little. A silent invitation for him to come in, if he wanted to do so. She didn't say a thing one way or another, and let him decide for himself.

She already knew what he would do.

He came in.

Renzo drifted around her hotel room, never touching anything or lingering too long in one spot. Lucia didn't mind, as it gave her the chance to breathe, and think. Funny how that worked—after all this time, she still found it difficult to gather her thoughts and control her emotions when this man was around.

It was like time had just stopped.

Now, it was moving again.

"My dad said The League trains assassins," Lucia said.

Renzo's back stiffened where he was standing in front of the window. Silently, he began to unload the items in his jacket. He set each item onto the small table beside the window. Two guns, three knives, an extra clip of bullets, and a roll of wire. The final things he set to the table were a pair of leather riding gloves. Then, he shrugged off his jacket, and set it on the table, too.

She thought to ask him what in the hell he was doing—did he think he was staying, or something? Because she hadn't suggested that was going to happen. And yet, she stayed quiet because just like that, she realized, yes, that's exactly what she wanted.

For him to be here.

With her.

She needed him to stay.

Just ... *fucking stay with her.*

"You could say that, I guess. He's not entirely wrong."

"So, that's what ... you are, right?"

He let out a quiet chuckle. "I am whatever I need to be ... or whatever my boss needs me to be, Lucia."

"Do you just not like to put a title on your job, then?"

Renzo spun around fast, and cocked his head to the side. "No, I don't call myself anything because despite being *something* ... I don't know what I am. I know I'm alone, all the fucking time. I know I'm a prisoner who only *seems* like he's free. I know I am capable of amazing things, and horrible ones, too. I know I can be feared as much as I am respected. And I know I love a woman who I would die for, but I can't have her yet, either. These are all things that I know about myself, but because I don't have the one thing I want—you—I still feel like nothing. A nobody, Lucia."

He shrugged, adding, "So when you ask me what I am, I don't have a good answer. I don't have any answer at all."

Strange ...

That hurt her, too.

Not *for* her, but for him.

"And what about you, huh?" he asked.

Lucia found him staring at her in that way of his again—like she was the only thing in the world that mattered to him. "What about me?"

"Did you stop loving me?"

It seemed like such an obvious question.

He asked it *so* easily.

The answer was difficult.

Complex.

And yet, still obvious, too.

"Never," she admitted. "Not even when I wanted to. I couldn't."

Her heart wouldn't let him go.

Lucia blinked, and felt the tear escape from the corner of her eye. She quickly wiped it away, but not before Renzo saw it. He crossed the room quickly, already reaching for her though she wasn't sure if she wanted him touching her at all.

And then he was.

Suddenly, that was *all* she wanted.

Fuck it all.

His hand cupped the side of her face, and she swore it was instinct for her to just *turn* her head into his touch. To kiss the center of his rough palm because she needed to do it—needed that taste of his soft touch, and wanted the warmth of his skin against her lips. His thumb swiped away the tears that had streaked down her cheeks.

"Don't cry," he muttered. "Don't cry, baby."

"I just—"

"Loving someone shouldn't make you want to cry, Lucia."

"You're telling *me*?" She let out a sad, bitter laugh. "Love shouldn't hurt, either, but that's what it's always done to me when it comes to you. That's not what I want."

"Me, either. Never, you know?"

She didn't.

She didn't know anything.

Not until he kissed her, anyway. His lips found hers—a lot like the kiss in the car, this one was just as hungry and *vicious*. All teeth and tongue and lips working against hers. There was no questioning what he was feeling when he kissed her like this. Like it was the last thing he was ever going to do. She couldn't breathe, not properly. She couldn't drag in enough air to satisfy her lungs.

But it was lovely.

So good.

And like when he had touched her, she found this was all she wanted. The rest of her thoughts and sadness drifted away when she had him like this. It just made sense for her to reach for him—to peel that shirt he was wearing up over his body, and toss it to the side.

She froze, then.

Stunned.

Lucia blinked at the ink that colored up a good portion of one side of his body. She reached out with tentative fingers to trace the lines of the ink as he let out a husky chuckle. She didn't know what to say about the ink. The nose ring he wore was a new thing, too, but the ink … it told a completely different story than his new piercing.

Memories, she thought.

His tattoos were memories.

She recognized them easily.

A portrait of Diego on his bicep; one of Rose's favorite artworks down his inner forearm. Fireworks colored the space in between the larger pieces. A dreamcatcher drifted down his outer forearm. She was curious why he seemed to only tattoo the one side of his body, other than the ink she could see slightly on the back of his neck, but she didn't want to ask him about it. Mostly, her attention kept drifting back to the eyes staring out from the roses that seemed to be covering a face.

She knew those eyes.

She looked at them everyday in the mirror.

"He got them right, then," Renzo murmured.

She peered up at him. "The eyes?"

"Mmm."

Her fingers drifted over the tattoo again—over rose pedals and hazel eyes so expressive and lifelike, it was astonishing.

"Did you have a picture?" she asked.

"Memory," he replied. "I learned Rose isn't the only one who can draw, I guess."

Huh.

"They're just tattoos," he added when she stayed quiet.

No, she didn't think they were *just* tattoos. They were something else entirely to Renzo. Moments in his life that he didn't want to forget. Pieces of memories that he wanted to memorialize forever in a very permanent way.

It was kind of amazing.

And she was part of it.

"Is that really what you want to call them—*just* tattoos?" she asked, smiling up at him slyly.

Renzo swallowed thickly, and his tongue peeked out to wet his bottom lip as he grinned in such a way that flashed those white teeth at her. *Fuck.* He looked good like that—almost ready to eat her whole, she thought.

"I want to do a lot of things right now—mostly *to you*," he said, his grin deepening with each word. "But talking about these tattoos is not one of those things, Lucia."

She sucked in a sharp breath.

Her mind whispered *good.*

Her mouth, on the other hand, said, "Do those things, then."

"*All of them?*"

Lucia lifted a brow. "Anything you want, Ren."

Because she had a feeling that she was going to like doing what he wanted to do to her a hell of a lot more than feeling the way she had felt for the last few years. Alone, and empty. Entirely. It hurt, and yeah, this might hurt, too … but not right away.

He came for her mouth again.

Hungry, again.

The force of his kiss pushed her back to the bed, but he came with her. Never once did his lips break from hers as he worked her jeans down her legs, and then his pants followed soon after. His weight coming down on hers as he rested down on top of her was *perfect*. Just enough to make her feel pinned under him and it got her chest oh, so tight.

Her cotton-covered sex grinded against the length of his dick pushing against his boxer-briefs. She had no shame—she wanted the feeling of all the ridges of his cock rubbing against her slit and clit. All the while, his mouth followed a hot path down her chest. His hands pushed up under her shirt, and drove it higher around her throat.

Then, he found her breasts under her bralette. Those rough palms of his felt like sin tightening against her tits, and while his mouth traveled lower on her toned stomach, his thumbs tweaked her nipples into hard buds.

"*Fuck*," Lucia breathed, her back arching from the bed. "What are you doing?"

She meant it in a *what are you doing to me* kind of way, but Renzo took it quite literally when he replied, "I want a taste of this pussy, baby. Do you know how long it has been since I got my tongue on your cunt? Since I had your taste in my *mouth?* I want you on my tongue, Lucia. I want to fuck that pussy with my mouth, and then watch you lick it from my lips as I slide inside you."

The sound that escaped her throat was *weak.*

And primal, too.

Raw like she felt—the way he made her feel with his hands sliding down her stomach as his mouth hovered over her pussy. His fingers curved around the edge of her panties, and his gaze locked on hers as he dragged them down her thighs. There was something wicked in his smile; something *damning*, too.

She was going to be so fucked after this.

No doubt about it.

She lifted up her backside just enough to let him slip those panties down further. She felt the soft cotton graze her skin in the slowest way—an inch at a time. And then when he finally had them down her legs, and tossed to the floor?

He was back between her thighs in a *blink*.

That hot mouth of his worked her pussy like it had her mouth—rough and harsh. Like he was starved, her pussy was the meal, and he was never going to get enough. The textured pad of his tongue lashed against her clit over and over again until she could feel her heart *pulsing* through her sex against his mouth.

His fingers came down to work against her, too. Sliding through slick lips to find damp, hot flesh. His fingers slipped into her pussy to fuck her hard as his mouth drifted away from her clit just long enough for him to murmur, "Are you going to give me what I want, Lucia? Lick yourself from my lips as I fuck this pussy? Have you missed my cock?"

"Oh, my God."

Her back came off the bed again as sparks danced across her skin. She couldn't help but squeeze her eyes shut as the orgasm ravaged through her system. The noises that crawled out of her throat echoed through the room.

His name was the loudest thing, though.

She was still shaking when he drifted back up her body. He already had a condom in his hand. She was trying to figure out when in the hell he had grabbed that—probably from his pants—but figured it didn't matter. Not when she got to watch the way he slid latex down his cock as he came a little closer to her mouth.

Almost there.

Now, she kind of wanted to taste herself on him.

He'd teased her with the promise.

"Fucking missed you," he whispered.

Lucia swallowed hard. "Me, too."

She got to watch as he fitted himself between her thighs—the way he gripped the base of his cock as he slid it through the lips of her sex before coming to a stop right at the slit. He gave her just the tip, first. Pressing in, and then pulling back out. He did that over and over until he'd worked a good two inches in with each thrust, and the same lost when he pulled back out again. He kept that up until she was shaking all over, and *begging*.

"Fuck me ... just *fuck me*, please."

Renzo chuckled.

Dark.

And oh, so haunted.

She loved that sound.

It was the last thought to drift through her mind before he slammed inside her. It took one good thrust to fill her full, and shatter her mind. But those broken pieces were beautiful, too. Reflections of him and her like *this*.

He dragged himself away from her body again, and then slammed right back in. Harder than before—deeper, too, if it were possible.

"I wanna watch this, Lucia," he murmured. "I need to watch this."

She couldn't breathe again.

But he was fucking her now, so it didn't matter. It was the slapping of skin, and the sexy noises that slipped past Renzo's lips that dragged her back under into a greater state of bliss. There was nothing better than watching a man use your body the way he wanted just to get himself off.

He made it quite clear that he didn't intend to come until she did—*again*. His thumb found her clit and worked small circles into it with every beat of his hips against hers. The rhythm was enough to hit every nerve Lucia had.

"I'm going to come again," she gasped.

"*Good.*"

She came—faster and harder.

"Fuck, yeah," Renzo said thickly.

He fucked her harder.

She was all too happy to get on her knees when he was ready, pull that condom off, and swallow every drop he had to give her, too.

• • •

"You should go," Lucia whispered.

Renzo's head lifted the second he walked out of the bathroom, and his gaze instantly fell on her. There was no surprise in his eyes, and no disappointment. It was more like an understanding, she thought. Like he expected her to say that.

This whole thing …

Them … it'd been a lot.

Together, it had been too much.

Lucia needed to be alone again; she needed a second to breathe without him standing right there. She couldn't think when there wasn't any distance, and she had shit to work through, now.

Renzo nodded. "All right."

She wasn't even going to let him spend the night.

Fuck, she wanted to, though. There was a big part of her that was ready to beg for him to get back in the bed with her. To watch him enjoy the sight of her naked beneath the sheets with him, but she couldn't.

Lucia had realized something.

That shit she thought she was feeling for all this time—the stuff that held her back, and kept her lonely; the poison that filled her up like an old friend … she'd been holding it too tight, and keeping it too close. She blamed her father; put her pain on him, and let that contempt for him burn through her like a constant wild fire that was ready to devastate every time she fed into it.

The thing was, she wasn't just mad at her father.

Or even her brother.

97

She was mad at herself.

She was mad at Renzo.

She was pissed at life.

The world.

That was something she had to deal with alone—he couldn't help. She'd made friends with this way she felt. She'd found comfort in this contempt burning so deep in her heart that she was scared to know what it might feel like to live without it.

That wasn't on him to fix.

It was on her.

"I'm sorry," Lucia said softly, staring at her hands as they twisted into the sheet pooled around her naked waist. "I just … need some time to think, and figure some things out."

Renzo shrugged as he came around the edge of the bed, and silently, dropped a kiss to the top of her head. "Yeah, I get it, babe."

She sucked in a shaky breath.

"You asked what I meant," she murmured.

Glancing up, she found him looking back at her over his shoulder. "What?"

"I wrote letters. You didn't know what I was talking about."

Renzo's brow dipped. "I still don't."

Funny.

She couldn't forget.

Couldn't *let go.*

So much so, that she kept those fucking letters with her all the time. Bunched together with an elastic to keep them neat in her messenger bag that she carried with her *everywhere*, those letters were a constant reminder of pain and of something she didn't have. Of, what she had thought, was someone who didn't want her.

Lucia's gaze drifted to the bag sitting on a chair on the other side of the room. "There in that bag—all addressed to you, Ren. They were all sent back stamped with *Return to Sender.*"

"Do you want me to—"

"Take them," she interjected. "They were meant for you. You should have them."

He didn't ask how she had gotten an address for him, or how many letters had come back to her with that fucking stamp on them. No, he just crossed the room, and found the pack of letters in her bag.

Lucia thought maybe those letters had been a way she punished herself. For falling in love with him, and making the choice to run all those years ago … for not being able to help him that night in San Francisco, and for watching him sacrifice his freedom for the safety of hers as the charges piled up, and the courts gave him the sentences.

And then with each unanswered letter, the punishment changed. She kept them because she thought … he didn't want them.

He didn't want her.

Lucia thought she needed to be reminded of that, so she kept them.

Renzo turned to her as he packed up his jacket, and the weapons he'd discarded earlier. "About Christian Savino …"

Lucia gave him a look from the side. "What—we're not going to do a whole jealous thing, are we?"

"No, I was going to tell you to be careful. The man is … dangerous, Lucia. For reasons I know, and some that I am sure I don't know. He's involved in drug trafficking, but that's just scratching the surface. The problem is, he doesn't seem like the type, right? He seems to have some interest in you, so I just want you to be careful."

She laughed bleakly. "Are you like them now, too? They used to tell me that about you all the time—my family, I mean. You were *bad news*. A bad guy … I should stay away. Not that it matters, anyway. I'm not interested in Christian."

"It's not the same, baby."

There wasn't a *hint* of jealously in his voice. No heat, or anger. He wasn't trying to tell her to stay away from another man for his own pride.

She stilled on the bed, and met his gaze again. "I'll be careful, but he's probably not any different than my family, Ren. I'm not worried."

"I don't think he's like your family at all," Renzo murmured. "I think he's worse."

Well …

What did that mean?

ELEVEN

Renzo paced the length of his hotel room, and tried to ignore the giant fucking elephant that was taunting him from the bed. Not a literal elephant, no, but it felt like it. That stack of white envelopes felt like the weight of an elephant had come to sit on his chest from the moment he had them in his hands.

He'd flipped through them, briefly. Not in front of Lucia, of course, but after he'd left her hotel. Twenty-two, he'd counted. She'd written him *twenty-two* fucking times. Her last letter had been dated and stamped from a year ago—when she'd sent it out. The *Return to Sender* stamp on the front had been dated three months after that.

Every single letter was the same.

Dated to send.

Stamped to send back.

And yet, she'd kept sending them. Over and over again, she *kept trying*.

Renzo hadn't said anything to Lucia, but he recognized that address she had scrawled on the front of each envelope. It was a PO box The League used for different things—he'd never checked the box, sure, but he'd seen mail on Dare's desk more than once with that exact address on it. There was *no way* those letters didn't get in someone's hand at The League. There's no way someone—likely Dare—didn't *see them*.

Which only meant one thing to Renzo, now. Dare purposely kept them from him—another choice taken away from Renzo. Another way to control his life, and the contact he had with the outside.

Or … just Lucia, it seemed.

One by one, they'd allowed him to go back to people from his past in one way or another. Like the phone calls to his sister, for example. It was just Lucia who they kept away from him for all this fucking time.

And *God* …

It made him want to rage.

He still wondered who had given her an address to use to contact him—her father, maybe? Johnathan, possibly? Her brother had seemed to know something about his involvement with The League, so it was possible. Nonetheless, whoever it was that gave it to her, they'd *tried* to give her someway to contact him.

It was The League that had kept her away.

His fucking heart clenched as his gaze fell on that stack of letters again. Resting on the sheets of his bed, they looked innocent enough. Paper—that was all. Stacks of *papers*. Ink scrawled across the front in black and red.

Black, from her. Red, from the post office. Paper shouldn't be able to kill a person, but it felt like those might have done exactly that. Just looking at them, and before, when he'd shuffled through each of the twenty-two … they all felt like a slice across the muscles of his heart.

She sent letter after letter—they came back unanswered every single time. One after another. And yet, she kept trying. She kept sending.

She kept hoping.

What must that have felt like?

To hope, and then have it ruined.

To try again, and get another slap in the face.

Fuck.

It was no wonder she was stuck in her head about this—no fucking wonder she didn't know what to think, and why she was so hurt. For years, she'd believed Renzo purposely didn't answer her back. That *he* had made the choice to keep a distance between the two of them. That he was the one who refused to answer her back.

And now, she had to face the fact it hadn't been when she'd believed it for so long. No, he didn't blame Lucia for needing her space and time.

But *fuck.*

He hoped she figured it out soon. He needed her to get out of her head, work through her feelings, and come back better than ever. He was ready for that.

She needed to be ready, too.

This wasn't something he could fix for her, though. Whatever she was dealing with in her head and heart—he couldn't make it better.

His pacing had finally stopped, but that was just so he could glare at that fucking stack of envelopes, anyway. He had a complex about them. They came from her, meant for him, and for that, he loved them—adored that she took time to write him when that was a lost fucking art. And yet, at the same time, he hated those letters because they had so clearly been a source of pain for Lucia.

Yeah, a complex.

Before Renzo could think better of it, he reached over and snatched up the stack of letters. He was quick to flip through them again, noting the fact that Lucia had kept them all organized. From the very first letter she sent, to the final one a year ago.

Had she finally given up, then?

Was the last letter her *last* straw?

Renzo sighed, and went back to the first letter in the stack. A part of him didn't want to read these, at least, not without Lucia right there watching. Another part of him wanted to know what she had written to him—all those years ago, where had her mind gone without him? Had she been in a similar place to him?

Broken and alone?

Probably.

And that just bothered him more.

Not thinking it through, Renzo ripped off the side of the first letter. He tossed the rest of the stack down to the end of the bed, and sat down beside the pile. Tipping the envelope over in his hand, the single sheet of paper inside fell out to his palm. For longer than he cared to admit, he didn't unfold the three creases keeping the letter hidden.

He just ... stared at it.

What would be inside?

Pain, he knew.

Pain and loss.

He'd lived through that time once. He was still kind of living in it, if he was going to be completely honest with himself. Did he want to experience it from her side of things, too? Hadn't his experience been enough to tell him that he barely made it out sane the first time around?

It didn't matter.

She deserved to be heard.

Renzo unfolded the letter.

Renzo,
Do you feel like this, too? Alone all the time? Empty, too? That's me without you.
I don't know where you are, but I wish you were here.
And I'm sorry.
Love,
Lucia M.

It was short.

Maybe too short.

And then again, maybe those few sentences were all she could manage at the time. He didn't know, and since she wasn't here, he couldn't ask. He also wanted to know what she was apologizing for—none of what happened had been her fault.

Renzo tucked the first letter away, and picked up the second in the pile. It was dated one week *after* the first letter had been sent. That likely meant she sent out the second letter before the first had even come back with the *Return to Sender* stamp.

It, too, was short.

Ren,
I talked to Rose today, and Diego, too. I want to go back to New York just to see them,
but I can't go back because I hate it there, now. No, that's a lie.

I hate other people who are there, and that hate turns me into someone I don't want to be.
That's scary—I don't want to be this person. I don't know this person.
You know, I still feel alone without you.
I'm always alone now.
Miss you.
Love,
Lucia M.

He folded the second letter up, and stuffed it back into its home. The third letter had been sent *after* the first had finally come back with that *Return to Sender* stamp on it. It was short, too, but *angry*. The fourth was the same, and then the fifth, too. Yet, each time, in between her anger and confusion over her letters being sent back, she kept telling him the same things.

I miss you.

I love you.

I'm sorry.

I'm not me without you.

Renzo was about halfway through the stack of letters when his hotel phone started ringing—he already knew who it was going to be before he picked it up. Rose was the only person he had given it to, and since he was still in New York, he'd decided to let his sister know she could keep calling it, if she wanted.

With a letter in his hand, he leaned over and picked up the call. Balancing the phone between his ear and shoulder as he read through the letter, Renzo said the first thing that came to his mind because he *needed* to tell someone. Who better than his sister?

"She wrote me letters."

Sure enough, it was his sister.

"Who did?" Rose asked.

"Lucia," Renzo murmured, thumbing through the first letter that had been more than a single page. It wasn't as angry as the last couple, and she'd purposely written that in the first couple of lines. That she wanted to just … talk, and update him on her life with school, and everything else. "She wrote me letters that I never got—they all went back to her unopened. I never saw them, Rose."

"How many?"

"Twenty-two."

Rose made a noise under her breath. "Ouch."

"I don't know what to do. I mean, I didn't *get them*. And it's obviously something that hurt her a lot, so what—"

"You write her back," Rose said instantly, like it was the most obvious thing in the world.

Renzo let out a quiet laugh. "Rose, I don't think that's what she intended by giving them to me."

"Why not? That's obviously what she wanted when she first sent them. That's the *point* of writing someone a letter, Ren. They will then write you back. So, they might be a little late getting to her—who cares?"

How simple that seemed.

Renzo didn't know if it would be.

"Oh, and I am having dinner next week," Rose said, "that's why I called. I want you to come, and you *better* be here for it. As long as you are in this city, I expect you to show up."

Okay.

His sister wasn't fucking around.

"And what about Diego?" Renzo asked.

Because he still hadn't seen his brother since being back in New York. Rose was keeping that boy protected—as Renzo would want her to, but that wasn't the point. It was the fact that, in a way, she was keeping him protected from *him*.

That burned.

A little.

"Well, I'm not telling Diego anything," Rose said. "I don't want him to get his hopes up and then have them shattered again. So, don't fuck this up, Ren. I have to be the person who looks out for him now, you know? That means I stop things that hurt him—don't be something that hurts him again."

Then, Rose added, "And write her back."

His sister hung up the phone.

Renzo wasn't surprised.

• • •

The man who walked into the darkened restaurant didn't notice Renzo sitting in the corner. He'd perched himself in the back of a booth, and used the table to rest his foot a little higher than the rest of his body.

Lazy, sure, but fuck it.

In fact, the man walked halfway across the floor and was heading toward a back hallway where the sounds of keys clicking on a keyboard continued to tap away. Like it had for the last half of an hour since Renzo broke into the business, and found himself a place to sit while he waited for Johnathan Marcello to show up.

As he always did.

Seemed the man liked to end his wife's night where she worked by coming to get her, and taking her home.

Fucking *sweet*.

"John," Renzo said.

He took *great* satisfaction in the way John's back stiffened at the sound of Renzo's voice. Maybe the man had meant to spin slowly to face Renzo, but it was fast. He didn't miss the shock in John's eyes, either, even if he was quick to hide it.

"How did you get in here?" John demanded.

Renzo's gaze slid to the front door. "The same way you did."

"I have *keys*. The place is closed."

"John?"

The soft, feminine voice coming from the back hallway echoed out to their spot. John was quick to give Renzo a look before calling back to his wife, "It's fine, Siena. Keep working—I'll be back in a minute."

"If you're su—"

"I'm sure, Siena."

The woman in the background made an annoyed noise under her breath, and Renzo chuckled. "I bet she keeps you on your toes, huh?"

John looked back to Renzo. "Don't speak about my wife, yeah?"

Touchy.

"I meant it as a compliment—we all need someone who challenges us."

John seemed as though he was considering what Renzo said, and then nodded. "You still didn't explain how you got in here, or *why*, for that matter."

"I think the why is obvious, John. I like reminding people how close I can get to the things they love or care about, in some way. It's a good way to keep people in their place."

"Huh."

Renzo arched a brow. "What?"

"I was just thinking … you're a fragment, Renzo."

He blinked.

John chuckled. "Of who you used to be, I mean. Sometimes, it's shocking. I'm unsure if I should be pissed, or impressed."

"Or … I'm a better version of me."

"Yeah, maybe."

"I picked the lock—also, I didn't come here to remind you of your place, John." Renzo tipped his head toward the hallway. "I wouldn't touch her—I've watched you the last week, and her. I see how you feel, you know."

John cleared his throat. "So, what do you want, then?"

"Your business with Christian Savino. I'm curious about what the details are, and anything else you might be able to tell me. You weren't willing to talk the last time—I'm wondering if that's changed since then."

"He's a drug trafficker with a hand in some other shit I don't touch, Ren. There's nothing to talk about. I'm working a deal—or *trying*, he's a fucker on his good days—for some imports. We've got a deal already going on with Mexico for cocaine, but having more than one source doesn't hurt, you know? Why do you have such a hard nut for this guy?"

"I don't like that he seems to have taken an interest in Lucia, honestly."

There, better for him to just get it out.

John cocked his brow. "I—"

"You don't think it's a little … concerning that he just randomly had an art print to take to the same gallery where *your* sister works, John? It's what, just a coincidence that he had a fucking reason to get close to someone from your family while he was also doing business with you? And then he comes to New York, likely for business with you still, and approaches her *again* at the hotel she's staying at?"

"It could be just coincidence, yeah, but we don't have to worry about it, do we? Lucia is moved from that hotel—my father says she's not interested in the man, and apparently, you're keeping an eye on her along with the enforcer I posted to her. Should I be concerned? Maybe, but we're taking care of it."

John shrugged, quickly adding, "This business is fucking dirty, Ren. I would have been *more* shocked had Christian not tried to make some legroom for himself while he was here, you know? If I go somewhere for business where I don't control any territory, I try to make myself clear where I stand, too. Let them know how close I can get to them, so to speak—just like you did tonight."

Renzo's jaw clenched. "He's not going to do that with Lucia, though. I won't let it happen."

"Well, that's what I'm saying. It's taken care of."

"I don't trust Christian Savino, John."

"Me, either."

Yeah, but for the same reasons as Renzo?

That's what he didn't know.

There was something about that guy … something he didn't know and couldn't put his finger on, but it didn't feel *good*. Renzo wasn't the type to ignore a gut feeling.

"And there's nothing else about Christian that you know that could be useful to me?" Renzo asked.

John shook his head. "He's a possible business partner. Yeah, a dangerous one, but we all are, Renzo. So, look at it like that."

Nope.

He couldn't do that.

• • •

"Look at you, walking around in the middle of fucking daylight like an idiot."

Renzo's stride came to a sudden stop on the sidewalk, and he glared up at the sky with narrowed eyes, and a groan already on his lips at that familiar voice. Sure enough, when he turned his head slightly to see who was waiting, he found Corrado Guzzi grinning in a shadowed alleyway.

"What the fuck do you want, Corrado?"

The man flashed his teeth. "Checking up on you, New York."

He still wasn't sure if he hated or liked that nickname.

Probably both.

"Dare send you?" he asked.

"Cree," Corrado murmured.

Surprise, surprise.

For the most part, Renzo had been ignoring his phone for the last week. Or at least, he'd been ignoring Cree's calls who was the only person calling his goddamn phone. Maybe the guy would get the hint—apparently, not.

"What, did he get pissy because I don't want to listen to him bark at me?" Renzo asked.

"He thinks you're getting too … confident," Corrado returned. "His words, not mine. He thinks you might need a reminder of your place and whatnot, seeing as how you can't seem to pick up a call from him or whatever."

Renzo resisted the urge to roll his eyes. "I'm working a *job*."

"Mmm, in your old stomping grounds, too."

"Yeah, fucking *fun*, huh?"

Corrado gave him a look.

Renzo stared back, unbothered.

The differences between him and Corrado Guzzi were obvious on the surface, but it was the differences that one didn't know and weren't as obvious that made a bigger impact on Renzo.

Like the fact Corrado had *chosen* The League willingly, was a free agent for them, and could come and go at his will. They didn't control his life, or the choices he made. His life wasn't given to The League like a fucking present for them to unwrap.

Renzo was not the same.

Clearly.

"You can't get cocky," Corrado told him. "You know how Cree is, Ren. And you know how fucking *Dare* gets when he's in a mood, too. Just watch yourself, huh?"

"Just give me the message Cree wanted you to pass on, and go on your way. Let me get back to my fucking job, Corrado."

Corrado sighed. "You belong to The League until your contract is up in a couple months, Ren. Don't forget it, man."

Renzo, still unbothered, gave Corrado one last look before he continued his walk down the street.

Was that message supposed to be shocking?

A *revelation*?

It wasn't.

Renzo couldn't forget who owned him. They'd beaten it into him. Scars like those didn't leave—they only faded.

TWELVE

Lucia shoved the last of her things into her messenger bag as she waited for the phone ringing in her ear to finally be answered. Today was her father's second to last chemo treatment before he was finally finished—it was the hospital's tradition for those who finished their chemo to ring a bell at the nurses' station as a way to celebrate their achievement. Lucia wasn't sure if her father was going to ring the bell or not, it didn't seem like his style, but either way ... well, she was going to be there for his last treatment.

"Hello?"

Finally.

"Kelly," Lucia greeted, setting her bag on the bed so she could slip on her jacket. "How's California?"

Her boss laughed. "Hot at the moment. And dry. How's New York?"

"Polluted. Loud. Wet."

"So, feels like home, then?"

Lucia grinned even though the woman couldn't see it. "Yeah, it feels like home."

"Please don't tell me you've called to say you're not coming back because being home has made you want to stay. I don't think I could take the pain, Lucia."

She could tell Kelly was kidding, and at the same time, still serious.

"I'm not calling for *that*," Lucia murmured.

"But you are calling for something about that, I can tell."

Kelly was a smart woman.

"I know I am supposed to be coming back at the end of this week," Lucia said, "but I was thinking I might need to stay a couple weeks longer. I wanted to make sure that was okay—that you could work it out for me to get the time off, or let me know if it wasn't possible. I mean, I would understand if you couldn't."

Kelly was quiet for a short while, but then let out a dismissive sound. "Listen, it's all right, Lucia. I can figure it out. I'm sure you want to spend some more time with your dad, and all, so yeah. I can get it worked out."

Sure, her father.

That was certainly part of it.

Lucia was finally getting to a good place with her dad. No, they hadn't sat down and hashed out all of the shit that happened, but she didn't feel like that was necessary, either. At least, not yet.

It didn't matter.

They were in a better place.

Wasn't that what counted?

It was more about Renzo for the reason why Lucia wanted to stay for a little while longer. She had unfinished business with him, and she didn't think that running across the country would solve them. It certainly wasn't going to help her to put distance between them when what she wanted and needed to do was handle the emotional mess she constantly felt whenever he was around. They had things to deal with—she wanted the chance to do that.

She couldn't do it in California.

"So, you really don't mind?" Lucia asked.

She shouldn't have been surprised, but she still was, in a way. Kelly was a great boss, and always had been. She let her workers have a lot of legroom when other bosses would have had their employees on a very short leash.

Lucia appreciated it.

She didn't want to screw up the opportunity that Kelly gave her, either. This internship—the one Kelly offered her—wasn't that common. Not one with as many benefits as this one had, anyway.

"Yeah, I mean, I'm hoping you get back soon, but I under—"

Kelly's next words were interrupted by a knock echoing on Lucia's hotel door. She listened to Kelly rattle on in the background of the call as she headed for the other side of the room.

"Yeah, for sure," she replied to Kelly as she reached for the door.

Lucia didn't even think to check the peephole; she hadn't had any problems since switching hotels. The Cordial was just as nice and the employees kept things running smoothly. All good things.

She pulled open the door at the same time Kelly said, "Do you have a possible idea when you might come back, though? Just so I can work on a schedule and your hours."

"It won't be more than three weeks, for sure."

Lucia would make sure of it.

Or ... *try*.

On the other side of the door, a bellboy from the hotel stood with a smile on his face, and what looked to be a letter in his hands. "Miss Marcello, this was delivered for you this morning at the front desk."

Lucia took the letter the man offered, and looked it over. Other than her name scrawled on the front of it, there wasn't even a stamp or a proper address written on the front. Yet, it had been sealed shut, and felt light enough to probably be a standard letter.

But from who?

"This morning?" she asked the man.

Kelly still chattered on in the background, voicing her ideas for hours once Lucia was back, and some kind of project she wanted to put her on.

The man at the door nodded. "Yes, it was brought into The Cordial this morning and delivered right to the front desk—I was told he asked it be brought to you."

He?

"Okay, I'll let you go, then, Lucia," Kelly said on the call. "And let you get back to ... whatever you're handling."

"Sure, and hey, thanks again for the time off."

Her boss laughed. "No worries."

The call clicked off as Lucia thanked the man at the door once more, and then closed her door. Turning to face the empty hotel room, she tapped the envelope against her palm. She didn't think it was anything dangerous inside—wouldn't it be a little bigger, or heavier?

Lucia opened the side of the envelope, and peeked inside. A single sheet of folded up piece of paper came out onto her palm when she tipped it over. Chewing on the inside of her cheek, she opened the paper.

She was sure her heart stopped.

Oh, it certainly *ached.*

Renzo's handwriting—why she hadn't recognized it on the front, she didn't understand—stared back at her.

Lucia,

I was told to write you back. I'm sorry you're not going to get the response you wanted—from way back when, you know? I hope this is just as good.

I still feel that way. Alone and without. Unsure. Cold. I don't want to feel that way at all, but I don't know anything different.

It's uncomfortable.

The League taught me to enjoy discomfort.

Strange, huh?

It's funny, that. How I hate them, and respect them at the same time. I feel that way about your father, too. For the same reasons. He, and them, gave me the chance to be something, and to make something of myself ... I didn't realize the things I would have to sacrifice for it, and they never thought to tell me the cost.

The cost was high.

I love you.

I'm sorry if you ever thought I didn't.

—Ren

Lucia folded up the letter with more questions. None of them were questions Renzo could answer.

It was time to talk to her dad.

• • •

"You must feel like you can't get a second to breathe, huh?"

Lucian looked up from the book in his lap at the sound of Lucia's voice in the doorway to his room. His brother had just slipped past Lucia—Gio. Dante had been in first, and then switched with Lucia's mom, Jordyn. Gio went in before Lucia could see her dad.

It seemed like now that her father's secret was out, the entire family was determined to see him through these last couple of treatments. He wasn't given one single second alone. Someone else was always quick to step into the room.

Did he need a drink?

A snack?

Gio offered to sneak him in a joint—apparently, her dad had started smoking a bit of herb again after cutting that habit decades ago because now, it helped him to eat without getting sick. Her ma hadn't thought Gio's offer was very amusing, but Lucia did.

That was her uncle in a nutshell.

Lucian's gaze drifted past Lucia to the hallway behind her. "You know, I didn't think I would enjoy having everyone here constantly. I figured it would be too much ... they'd get on my nerves."

"And?"

Her dad smiled, and glanced down at the magazine in his lap. "I should have had them here from the start, that's all."

Yeah.

"Hindsight is twenty-twenty," Lucia murmured.

Lucian glanced back up then, and nodded. "It is."

Maybe it was the tone of her voice, or the way she stood in the doorway with her arms crossed. It could have been that posture, or the aura she gave off just from standing there thinking about all of the questions running through her mind.

Whatever did it, she swore her father just knew she was there to talk. That it was finally time for them to lay some of those cards they'd been holding tight to their chest down on the table. They needed to be honest, and speak the truth between one another.

Now was that time.

She kept saying this wasn't it—he was sick, and he didn't need this kind of shit while he was trying to fight the sickness in his body. She justified putting it off by saying it was better if he didn't have to deal with any emotional issues when clearly, he had enough on his plate. Right?

Lucia didn't give her father enough credit.

She should have known better.

After all, she'd come from this man.

She *was* his strength.

"Just ask what you want to ask me," her father said, still smiling a little. "Don't chew on it—your mother does that, too. You get that from her, not me."

Lucia laughed. "Probably."

Lucian shifted on the chair to get a little more comfortable. His gaze drifted to the IV pole, and the bag hanging from the top. The nurses always covered the bag of chemo with a sheath so that they couldn't see the medicine, and even the line that led to her father's chest was an opaque white color. She never understood that.

"Well, you're smiling," Lucian said, "so I'm going to say whatever it is, it's not going to upset me too much. Or you, maybe."

"All depends," she returned.

Lucian chuckled, and patted the seat next to his, offering it to her. Lucia didn't even think about it. She headed across the room, and took the chair next to her father's. It was funny because once she was sitting there, those words that she wanted to say—the questions she knew that she had to ask her father—suddenly stuck in the back of her throat like sticky tar.

They were not coming out.

Lucian waited her out.

Lucia couldn't speak.

Maybe that was all those years of keeping silent—of swallowing her words instead of letting them out. Maybe it was all that anger and contempt and pain that she'd kept tucked close to her chest like an old friend that felt more comfortable than *this*.

She wasn't sure.

"Renzo wrote me a letter," she finally whispered.

Without saying anything else, she pulled the letter out of her bag, and offered it to her father. Lucian took it from her fingertips, and she waited him out as he unfolded the paper, and read the letter silently. She knew when he was finished because his fingers tapped the edge of the letter, and he made a quiet noise in the back of his throat.

Contemplative, maybe.

Who knew?

"A reply to letters I sent him," she explained quietly.

"When did you send him letters?"

Lucia shrugged. "John gave me an address. Told me it wasn't about *you*, that it was between him and me, you know."

Her father said nothing.

Lucia wished it was easier to speak.

"Why, Daddy?"

Lucian sighed. "Why, what?"

"You helped him, didn't you? He says that, even if he doesn't like the way you did it. But you *did*—help him, I mean. I just want to know why you let me be angry for all this time. And why you let me *hate* you. Why not just tell me the truth—put it all in front of me, and let me see what you did. You helped him, got him free, and gave him an opportunity to become something, right? That's how he describes it. Had you just told me that, and let me see what you had done, then maybe this wouldn't have happened. All these years, they wouldn't have happened. Why let me keep blaming you and … hating you."

Lucian made another one of those noises. "You never hated me."

"I think I did."

"Hate and contempt are not the same, *dolcezza*. Hate is in your *heart*. The other, in your mind. Sometimes, they might feel like they are the same, but they aren't. You cannot hate the things you love. You learn that over time, or I have."

He wasn't wrong.

She still didn't know what to *feel*.

"I didn't tell you," her father murmured, "because I wasn't going to manipulate your feelings, or the reason why you offered forgiveness. And I felt that by giving you these things … telling you everything that happened that you didn't know about would do that. I would *hand you* a reason to forgive me, and that teaches you nothing. I didn't deserve that, either. You have to learn real forgiveness on your own, and in your own time. I can't hand you the roadmap for it, and expect you to come out of it better."

"You didn't deserve my anger and treatment, either."

Lucian hummed under his breath. "Didn't I? I only corrected my mistakes when it was already too late. I only realized the things I had done wrong—that I had hurt you and that young man—when it was already over. Your mother and I … well, we were never supposed to step in for our children. Not where love and life were concerned, and I did that with you. I made a mistake. I see it as life teaching me more lessons, and they're not easy ones. They're never easy when they come later in life."

Lucia blinked down at her hands.

Her father kept talking. "And part of that lesson was waiting for *you*, my girl. I had to wait for you to come back when you wanted to—when you were ready. It couldn't be about me when I'd already made it about me enough. I'm sorry for that."

She hadn't realized it until the first tear fell into her lap. She moved to wipe the wetness from her face, but her father was there to do it first. He used the pad of his thumb to swipe the tears away, and smiled at her all the while.

Funny.

He was getting chemo.

He was sick.

He needed love and care.

And there he was, comforting her.

Like he could read her mind, Lucian murmured, "It's what fathers do, Lucia."

"I love you, Daddy."

Lucian nodded. "I know, and I love you."

"What happens now?"

He shrugged. "Whatever you want. That's the beauty of it."

Was it?

So, why was she still scared?

Why did she still hurt?

• • •

I'm having dinner in a couple days. Do you want to come? Diego would love to see you again.

Lucia stared at the text from Rose as she left her father's hospital room. The nurse was just finishing up the treatment, and cleaning whatever she needed to clean. Lucian preferred to have privacy during that time, especially with there being so many people around now for his treatments. It was probably the one time he did get to be alone.

She hesitated to answer Rose back right away. It wasn't Rose's fault, honestly. More like Lucia's emotions swirling and threatening to drown her again.

Like usual.

She was getting tired of constantly feeling like she was two seconds away from drowning. Still, Lucia wasn't sure how many more opportunities she would have to see Rose and Diego before she headed back to Cali. And once she was back there, she had no clue when she was going to be back in New York.

Yeah, I'll be able to make it, she texted back, *just let me know the date and time.*

Rose's next text was exactly that.

Lucia left the hospital feeling like she might have finally fixed one thing in her life—the fractures between her and Lucian.

That just left one person, now.

Ren.

How was she supposed to deal with him?

She didn't have the first clue.

• • •

"Lucia!"

An almost nine-year-old Diego came her way with arms already opened. Lucia had hers ready to take him into her embrace the second she walked around the corner into the kitchen, and saw him reading a book at the island.

He was at that age, Rose liked to say. An age where it wasn't as cool to show affection, and he didn't want his hand held for every little thing. He wouldn't hold his sister's hand when he had to cross the street, and he liked to roll the bottoms of his pant legs for his school uniform up around the ankle of the Timberland boots he refused to *not* wear.

Apparently, the school called *a lot* about that. Rose had been called in for a lot of things regarding Diego, and the private school he attended. Fighting with other boys, school uniform code issues, and other rebellious things.

Diego didn't look four anymore.

Far from it.

He now reached Lucia's chest in height, and she swore he was growing taller with every passing day. He was a lanky kid, but Lucia knew that was only going to last a couple of more years before puberty hit. His dark blond hair had darkened into a light brown, and those russet eyes of his reminded her of his brother like nothing else.

So did his face.

Diego looked like a younger version of Renzo, in a lot of ways. His features were softer and more boyish, sure, but Renzo was *there*. In the way the kid smiled, and how one of his eyes would crinkle with a wink when he laughed. Some of his gestures were a mirror of Renzo, too, like the way his hands became more and more animated when he was excited.

Lucia didn't know if those similarities between Diego and his brother was a matter of nurture, or nature. Was it just in his DNA? Or was he, in a way, trying to hold onto the brother that he'd loved so very much for most of his life?

It was hard to say.

Lucia knew better than to ask.

Renzo was a touchy topic for Diego. She knew that he missed and loved his brother like nothing else, but the things he remembered about Renzo weren't always the *good* things. Because that was the thing about the mind, and trauma. It had a way of blocking out the good things so that it could keep hold of the bad details. Diego remembered running—he saw Renzo being taken away, and feeling alone.

Did he hate how he remembered his brother?

Lucia sometimes did.

Still, she knew it probably wasn't the same.

"Hey, buddy," she said, feeling his arms tighten around her waist.

"Hey, Lucia."

Lucia shot a look at Rose who was currently standing behind the kitchen island as she prepped some of the food for supper—it looked like a casserole. Rose smiled at the sight of the two of them, but quickly went back to her work.

Diego stepped back from Lucia, and grinned. "Rose got me a new book today. You wanna read it with me?"

Lucia smiled wider. "I would love to."

"*Cool.*"

Yeah, everything was *cool* to this kid.

Unless it wasn't.

Then, he could roll his eyes like nobody's business.

Lucia sat down at the island with Diego, and the kid flipped his book open. He went back to the page where he had put his bookmark, and said, "I'm not allowed to fold the pages—Rose said that's disrespectful."

She pressed her lips to keep from smiling as she shot Rose a look. The other woman in the kitchen *tried* to act like her name hadn't gotten said at all, but eventually, she just shrugged and laughed.

"What, it is," Rose said.

"Book-lovers," Lucia replied, like that would explain it all.

It kind of did.

She had a sister—Cella—who would gladly spend her entire life with her nose stuck in a book. Her sister had once used books to escape the pain in her life, but even after things got better for her, she knew Cella still found peace in a good book. And if someone was lucky enough to borrow one of Cella's beloved books, but it came back dog-eared?

God save your soul.

"What's the book about?" Lucia asked.

Diego beamed, and then quickly went into a whole discussion about the book—a discussion he mostly had with himself because all Lucia did was nod and agree. She was there to listen and spend time with him. Whatever he wanted to do, she was game for it.

"And there's dragons," Diego added.

"Really?"

Diego nodded. "They have to hatch them."

"How?"

"I don't know—that's the *point.*"

Lucia laughed at the look he gave her, but Diego didn't seem to mind. He went back to his book, and started reading out loud. He did well—only stumbled on one or two big words that he needed to slow down to get out properly.

It struck her then how much this kid had changed in the last few years. In small ways, sure, and in bigger ways, too. He just … wasn't the same. He'd had his own little personality back then, but now, it was bigger and more honed to him. She regretted having spent so much time away to punish someone else in her life because she'd missed out on a lot *here.*

But what could she do?

Hindsight was still twenty-twenty.

"And then Mar—"

A knock on the door interrupted Diego's reading. The kid pursed his lips, and annoyance flashed in his gaze at needing to stop his reading as he lifted his head from the book.

Lucia almost laughed.

Yep.

Just like every other book-lover in the world.

If only she would have focused on Diego, then, and not noticed the way Rose seemed to jump on the spot. She caught the way Rose's gaze darted to the hallway leading to the front door of the apartment, and how her hands instantly clenched into the dish cloth she had been using to wipe down the counter.

Were those *nerves?*

Why would Rose be—

"Sorry, let me grab that," Rose said quietly.

She didn't meet Lucia's gaze.

Or Diego's.

What was going on?

THIRTEEN

Renzo tried not to be nervous. He wasn't the fucking type to have nerves, anyway. He liked to bury that shit as deep as he could so it would never be used against him. Something else The League had taught him that he figured was good use in his daily life. Not that he was ever going to thank them for that.

He appreciated their lessons.

Respected them, even.

He didn't agree with the way they went about *teaching*.

That was the difference.

Knocking once more on the apartment door—he probably didn't need to, as he'd just knocked and it was likely the people inside heard him—he stepped back quickly and shoved his hands in his pockets. That way, he wasn't going to knock again, and hopefully when the door was opened, the person waiting on the other side wouldn't see how goddamn nervous he looked given that his hands were shaking.

Get it together, man.

This is crazy—stop acting foolish.

They love you.

All those thoughts ran like crazy in his mind, but it didn't make a difference to the way he was feeling. Maybe it was because in some ways, he'd had to work himself up to come here tonight. It wasn't that he thought he wouldn't be welcomed, but rather, the fact that he had been gone *for so long*.

Things wouldn't be the same, right?

They couldn't be.

That was the thing about time—it changed *everything*. And God knew he had been gone for a long fucking time, now.

"Hey, Ren."

The sound of his sister's greeting had Renzo lifting his head. She smiled at him on the other side of the apartment door, but even he could see the anxiety in her gaze. She did her best to hide it, sure—all of them were exactly the same. Maybe it was a Zulla thing to hide their emotions so that no one else could pick them out, even to one another.

"Hey," he replied.

Rose flipped the dish cloth she was holding over her shoulder, but didn't move to let him inside the apartment. "Ground rules for tonight?"

"Do there have to be ground rules?"

"Sure, if I feel like you might run again."

Renzo let out a hard sigh. "I'm not gonna—"

"Say *I'll see you later*. That's it. If you have to go … if it gets to be too much, or he asks you to leave, then that's what you say. Never goodbye, Ren. Goodbye scares him, even if he doesn't want to say it. So, we don't say that. We say something that means we'll be back again soon, simple as that. Got it?"

He could do that.

"Is that all?"

"No," Rose said, pursing her lips. "And make sure you play nice with my other guest tonight. I didn't get her here for you to chase her off. She's here because I figure the both of you could use a little help together."

Renzo blinked. "What are you talking—"

"*Ren?*"

He stiffened all over.

Like ice water had been tossed down his spine.

It wasn't the reaction he wanted to have when he heard an older, gruffer version of his little brother's voice, but there it was. Maybe it was because of the change in his brother's voice—older, and slightly deeper, although not so much so that it meant he was becoming a young man. Just enough to shock Renzo with the sound, and remind him of how many years he had missed with this kid.

Renzo found his brother quickly.

There he stood at the end of the hallway in black slacks rolled up at the ankles, a faded band T-shirt, and a face that reminded Renzo of years gone past. He stared at Diego, and the kid stared back. He took in the changes of his brother—the boyish features starting to form into the face of a young man, and the inches he'd grown since the last time Renzo saw him. He imagined Diego was taking in all the differences he could see in Renzo, too.

The tattoos.

The shorter hair.

The nose ring.

Just … all the different things.

Renzo felt like shifting on the spot. He just needed to *move*. Down the hallway, Diego looked to be in the same situation. The way the kid twisted his hands into balls at his side, and rocked from foot to foot as the silence stretched on.

It was funny, he thought.

They were the same.

And yet, they weren't.

"Talk," Rose muttered beside him. "Say something, Ren."

"Hey, buddy," Renzo finally said.

Fuck.

Buddy?

Really?

The kid wasn't four anymore, he was almost *nine*. Was buddy even a thing he liked to be called anymore? Did he have a fucking nickname? Was he hanging out with the right kids? Did he feel a need to refuse to conform to every single thing authority told him to like Renzo did?

Those were things he didn't know.

Things he *needed* to know.

Diego gave Renzo a small smile. "I missed you, Ren."

"Yeah?"

His little brother nodded.

All right, then.

"You're gonna stay for dinner, right?" Diego asked. "Like Lucia is, too?"

Renzo shot Rose a look.

Well, there was the other guest, he supposed.

Rose shrugged. "Don't be an asshole."

Really, that's what his sister thought he was going to do?

Whatever.

He put his attention back to Diego. "Could I get a hug?"

Renzo didn't miss the way that Diego hesitated, but he didn't blame the kid, either. He bet this was a little overwhelming, and all. Rose hadn't told their little brother that Renzo was coming tonight—rightfully so, considering—so he suspected Diego was having all kinds of feelings about this that he was keeping locked up tight.

He could have them, too.

Renzo would wait them out.

Finally, Diego nodded. "Yeah, a hug would be cool."

Renzo laughed.

Good enough for me.

He didn't waste time coming into the apartment, and closing the distance between him and his brother. Diego stood perfectly still until Renzo was close enough for him to reach out and grab him, then he did just that. Once he had his brother wrapped tightly in his embrace, another part of his life felt like it had slipped back into its proper slot. Like once again, his world was righting itself back to the correct axis.

Everything had been messed up for *so long*.

Nothing had been right.

Slowly, Renzo was getting it back.

One piece at a time.

"Missed you," Renzo murmured into his brother's hair.

Diego held him tighter. "You never came to see me, Ren."

He couldn't.

He didn't explain that—to Diego, it would be an excuse and not a real reason. It would be better for him to just not say anything at all.

"I'm sorry," Renzo said, pulling away to stare at his brother. "But I'm going to do better now, okay? I'll be around as much as you want me to be around, huh? I won't miss anything if you don't want me to."

Somehow.

He'd make sure of it.

Diego nodded as his gaze drifted to the colorful ink coloring up the side of Renzo's throat. "Did those hurt?"

Renzo laughed. "A little."

Some more than others.

"Want to see a cool one?" Renzo asked.

Diego nodded.

Without a word, Renzo shrugged off his leather jacket, and tossed it to the floor where it could stay for the rest of the night for all he gave a damn. Lifting the sleeve of his T-shirt, he turned a bit to let Diego see the portrait he'd gotten done on his upper, right bicep.

Diego stilled. "That's me."

Renzo smiled. "Yeah, Diego. Rose sent me a picture from your first day of school—I went in and had it done shortly after."

He was scared The League would take the photo away from him. They didn't let him keep very many things, and even that photo … they'd kept that from him for a good month after he'd finally been given an address to use to let Rose send some things to him. Another thing he was made to earn, unfortunately.

It was only then that Renzo noticed the figure hanging back by the kitchen island. Lucia stayed on her stool watching them, and saying nothing. She was smiling, though. A lot like his sister behind him.

Renzo wondered if Rose was trying to play matchmaker.

He'd deal with that later.

"Lucia told me you'd always come back for me," Diego whispered.

Renzo met his brother's gaze again. "When did she say that?"

"A long time ago."

Back then, he meant.

San Francisco.

The *bad time*.

He hugged his brother again. "She wasn't wrong, Diego."

"I know," his brother mumbled. "Missed you, Ren."

He had missed Diego more than this kid knew.

• • •

"Go wash your hands, all right?" Rose said from the head of the table.

Diego's smile faltered as his gaze drifted from Rose, to Renzo. "But—"

"I'll be here," Renzo said quickly. "We've got that game to play on the Xbox, right?"

"Right, okay."

Diego still peeked over his shoulder when he disappeared around the corner like he just needed to make sure Renzo wasn't going anywhere. To his credit, Renzo gave the kid a smile to reassure him without calling him out on it.

Once Diego had snuck from the kitchen to do his business, Renzo went back to the table. For the most part, Lucia had been quiet during the dinner. Sure, she joined in on the conversation when Diego or Rose pulled her into it, but otherwise, she didn't say much.

Renzo didn't think that was *because* of him. At least, not because of his presence. He suspected it was more likely because Lucia was trying to give him a chance to catch up with Diego as much as possible without inserting herself into it.

He appreciated that.

"Thanks," Renzo told Rose.

His sister arched a brow. "For what?"

"Everything, I suppose."

Lucia cleared her throat, but stayed quiet in her seat while the two siblings talked.

"You don't have to thank me for anything, Ren," Rose said.

Renzo disagreed. "Who else will? You stepped up, right. You shouldn't have needed to, I guess. He wasn't your responsibility, but I kind of threw him onto you when it was probably the last thing you needed at the time. And yet, you just kept on going—you did what you needed to do."

Rose nodded. "Maybe I had a good teacher, huh? Did you ever consider that?"

"No, why would I?"

"No, I guess you wouldn't," Rose replied in a sigh. "It was always second nature for you to take care of us. You never questioned it because it was all you ever knew, right? It was how it always was for you, so you did it."

"Of course."

And he didn't feel bad about it, either.

Rose shrugged. "I had an older brother who busted his ass day in and day out as I grew up to make sure I never went hungry, or cold. I learned what it meant to sacrifice because you taught me that it was okay to give up a piece of yourself for someone else if it meant they were going to be a little happier. As long as I loved someone else, then I would be loved in return. That's the lesson you taught me, Ren."

He shifted on his chair.

Huh.

He'd never thought of it that way.

"It shouldn't have been our jobs anyway," Rose said, "but we didn't have anyone else to take care of us, Ren. Not parents worth anything, you know. So, the only person I had to learn from was you, but I'm grateful for that."

"Yeah, I get it," Renzo murmured. Then, he had another thought. "Does she ever come around—or him, even?"

"Mom?"

Renzo nodded. "Or dad, I guess."

"Never."

He wished he could be surprised.

"Ever?" Lucia asked.

Her first time speaking, and this time, she inserted herself into the equation without someone else bringing her into it.

Rose turned her attention to Lucia, and smiled sadly. "Back when Renzo was first … uh, taken away, yeah, she came around. But that was only to try and take Diego away from me. She wanted the check that would come with him, basically. She put on a good show for the CPS workers, and everything, but she couldn't stay clean. I had a good lawyer. Hansen and Hansen Law were great—they didn't give her a fucking inch when it came to Diego."

Lucia stilled, and her gaze drifted to Renzo. "Hansen and Hansen?"

"Yeah, why?"

"That's a *really* expensive law firm," Lucia said quietly. "I know because my cousin's wife works for them—she's a partner."

Rose didn't even blink when she replied, "I know, at first I thought it was pro bono, but it turned out someone else was footing the bill for the law firm. I found that out later when some paperwork accidentally got mailed to me instead of the firm."

"I don't understand—"

"Your father, Lucia," Rose said. "He paid for my lawyers. He never asked for anything in return, and I never got the chance to thank him."

Lucia looked to Renzo again.

A silent question in her eyes …

Did you know?

He nodded, although it was never something that had passed his mind over the past years. Lucian had told him during his visit to Renzo in prison.

Lucian had done a lot for them—he did it all without asking for thanks, or seeking recognition. Renzo had come to realize that despite all the things the man had done to them back then was not an actual reflection of the person he was inside. He'd made mistakes. They all had. No one was ever going to be a perfect human being.

But he made amends.

He made them silently.

He didn't do it so that they would know.

He did it because it was *right*.

"Excuse me," Lucia whispered, standing from the table. "I need a second."

She was gone from the kitchen before Renzo knew what had happened. It was only the glare that his sister shot his way that made Renzo ask, "What?"

"Don't sit *there*. Go after her."

"I don't think she wants—"

"You're an idiot," Rose groaned, "stop doing that."

Well, fuck.

• • •

"Hey."

Lucia glanced up from the sink, and her gaze drifted to Renzo in the bathroom doorway. Maybe his sister had been right that Lucia meant for him to follow her—or maybe she just didn't care either way.

She hadn't been surprised to see him standing there, and if she hadn't wanted someone to see her washing the tears from her face, then she could have closed the door.

Instead, she didn't.

"I spent a lot of time being angry," Lucia whispered.

"I still am," Renzo replied.

"Me, too. A lot of the time."

Yeah, he knew that life.

"Do you want to talk about it—your dad, or whatever?"

He figured he should offer, despite the fact he wasn't even one-hundred percent sure on his own feelings regarding Lucian Marcello. It was kind of amusing, in a sick way. He still felt anger over the things that had happened years ago, yet he found himself respecting and liking Lucian more and more as time went on.

He was sure that wasn't supposed to happen.

It still was.

Renzo bet it was even more confusing for Lucia, in some ways. The man was her *father*. So, yeah, of course, she was always going to love him. She would *always* have that love in her heart for him no matter what. Through the bad times, and the good times. That was the thing about love—it never left. Not this kind of love, anyway.

Lucia shook her head, and let out a slow and steady stream of air as she watched herself in the mirror. "No, not right now."

"Okay, whenever you want, then."

She passed him a look. "Does that mean you're going to stick around more? What, do you plan to just walk right back into everybody's life like nothing ever happened?"

"Something happened, but yeah, I'm still walking back in, Lucia. Are you going to let me in, or keep pushing me away?"

He saw the way her throat jumped when she swallowed. He bet if he got his lips pressed against her neck where he could feel her pulse, that beat would be racing out of control right now. He loved this woman like *crazy*.

It didn't have to make sense.

"I don't want to push you away," she admitted.

Then, don't.

Renzo didn't say that out loud.

Lucia was allowed her feelings.

She could have them.

He'd still be waiting at the end.

"You okay?" he asked. "Do you want to go back out to the table, or …?"

Lucia used her damp hands to wipe the remaining tears from her cheeks, and took the hand towel he pulled off the rack when he offered it to her. She used it to dry her face, and then check her reflection one more time in the mirror.

"You look perfect," he murmured.

It wasn't a lie.

Crying, or with makeup done all up … natural, or a beautifully painted siren, she was always going to be perfect to him.

He didn't miss the way her lips quirked upward. "I didn't *ask*."

"You didn't have to. Besides, if I don't tell you, who is, baby?"

Her tongue snuck out to wet her bottom lip. "*Ren* …"

"I think about that all the time, you know? Drives me fucking crazy."

"No one is telling me when you're not," she said softly, her eyes lifting to meet his again. "You ruined me back then, and I'm still fucking ruined now. It's only ever been you."

Good.

He liked that too much.

"That makes two of us, then," he murmured, stepping closer to her.

Lucia laughed, and tipped her head down. He slid in beside her, and dropped a kiss to the corner of her mouth. He felt her smile grow all over again, and then she moved her head to the side just enough to catch his lips with her own in a slow, burning kiss. Her lips worked against his, and he felt that hunger growing.

Like a monster in a cage beating at the bars.

Fuck.

He loved this woman.

Loved her messy.

Loved her crazy.

Loved her *best*.

Renzo didn't care what anyone had to say about it—they couldn't possibly understand the way he felt for this woman.

All too soon, Lucia pulled away from the kiss, but her fingers came up, and the tips drifted across his jawline.

"What?" he asked.

"I just ..."

"Yeah, baby?"

"I just want to be close to you, maybe, but I don't like when it hurts in here," she admitted, clenching a fist over her heart.

"I'm sorry for that."

"Don't be. I still want to be close."

"Then, do that, Lucia." Renzo reached out to tuck a strand of her hair behind her ear. "Tonight, even. No expectations—once we leave, you come with me. We'll figure it out, and it's on you. Whatever you want, baby."

Lucia laughed. "I'm sure I know how it'll end."

Yeah, probably.

"I don't see the issue."

She shook her head. "Let's get back out there. Diego wants to spend time with you."

"You got it."

Like he said ...

Whatever she wanted.

• • •

They didn't even make it to the fucking hotel.

Renzo didn't know what it was—maybe she wanted to feel something other than the confusion that constantly followed her around, or maybe it was the fact that she wanted to feel *him*. He didn't know, but he also didn't care.

How could he when he pulled the car into the private, underground garage and Lucia was already crawling into his lap? How could he care when she was kissing him like she was going to lick the fucking color from his lips and suck the air right out of his lungs?

Renzo didn't even care about that.

He'd give her his *life*.

His hands skimmed under the skirt of her dress to drag it higher. He couldn't wait to get his hands under those black panties of hers, and feel the slick pussy he knew it was covering. There was something silky about her sex—like he was the roughness, and she was the *softness*. He was going to ruin her, and she would *always* like it.

God.

"I want you," she murmured against his mouth.

"You got me, baby."

More than she would ever know.

He didn't get the chance to feel her silky sex against his fingers because she grabbed for him, first. Her shaking hands worked the buttons and zipper on his jeans until she had them both opened. He lifted just high enough for her to get his jeans down. And when her hot palms found his length to wrap around tight?

Fuck.

"Yeah, shit, just like that," he grunted out through clenched teeth, watching her hands stroke him fast and hard. She knew exactly how he liked it—she *remembered.* That kind of made him hotter than ever. "Did you think about this, Lucia? Did you think about getting those hands wrapped around my dick when you touched yourself? Did you get off to me, baby?"

"Every night."

"Jesus Christ."

There wasn't any other response to that.

Lucia's kiss found his again as her hands kept working his dick. His balls were already tight—he couldn't fucking last with her. He just wanted to come so that he could bend her over, and fuck her *again.*

"Get me in your pussy," he muttered against her lips. "I need to be in you when I come, Lucia."

"Do you want me to get a condom—"

He had some in his pocket.

Always.

Just in case.

He just didn't *care.*

"You good?" he asked.

That's all he needed to know.

Because he was.

Just waiting on her …

"Yeah, I'm good," she mumbled.

"Then let me fuck you, Lucia."

He moved her panties to the side as she fitted the head of his swollen dick against her pussy. She hovered there for a brief second, dragging in heaving breath after heaving breath. Her lips were pinker than normal—her cheeks flushed.

"*Now,*" he uttered.

She came down on him, then. Fast, and rough. There was something about the way he stretched her open for that first pump—the way her pussy flexed around him, and her juices covered his dick.

"Love it," he muttered. "Ride me, then."

She did.

Wild.

Raw.

His hands curved tight around her ass as her mouth crashed down on his again. He could feel her shaking already—she was always so responsive to him. Always *right there* on the edge of an orgasm, and it only took the right words or the proper stroke from him to push her off into bliss.

He liked the way she looked like that.

A little desperate, and a touch needy.

"You wanna come?" he asked.

Lucia nodded fast—a jerky motion that accompanied her teeth biting down into her lip. That sight was enough to make him want to blow his fucking load as deep as he could get it inside her pussy, but he wasn't that selfish.

Her first.

Always her first.

He made her come hard when he stuffed a finger up her ass. She came even harder when he fitted a second one in there, and bit her throat right over her pulse point at the same time. It was the sound of his name coming out of her lips that took his control away, though.

Renzo came hard enough to take his words away.

His thoughts, too.

But that was okay.

He was with her.

FOURTEEN

Lucia knew the exact moment Renzo woke up because she could feel his eyes on her. She said nothing even as he shifted in the bed, inching onto her side of the mattress where she'd vacated a couple of hours ago. She didn't want to wake Renzo up just because she couldn't sleep—he looked like he needed the rest.

Did he ever relax?

She didn't know.

Tightening the Afghan blanket around her shoulders, Lucia sunk further into the chaise, and watched the clouds float by in the sky. Sitting in front of the large bay windows of her hotel room, she'd at least found some peace watching the sky instead of lost in her thoughts and emotions. She was still trying to make sense of that mess.

"What are you doing over there, huh?"

Lucia smiled and peered over her shoulder to look at Renzo on the bed. He was quite a sight resting amongst white sheets with his tanned, inked skin and sexy smile. He rolled onto his stomach and already had a hand reaching out to her.

Like he might pull her back to the bed.

She'd like that too much.

Instead of getting up to grab his hand and go back to the bed with him, Lucia reached out and grabbed hold of his hand with her own. She didn't move from her spot, and he didn't tug on her hand to encourage her to get up.

No, his thumb just stroked the side of her hand softly. It was enough to send shivers cascading through her body all over again. She loved his touch. She found that even after all this time, she still *craved* it.

He probably knew it, too.

Lucia peered back at him, and let her gaze drift over the ink on his skin. The portraits of people who he loved the most. The symbols and memories of her and them together that he'd made sure with one tattoo at a time to memorialize on his body.

That was kind of crazy to her.

And it wasn't at the same time.

She loved it.

She loved him.

"Ren?"

"Hmm, baby?"

"You know I love you, right?"

She felt his fingers tighten around her hand, but he didn't say anything in response to her question. Not that she blamed him. She hadn't *said* that. Not like she just did, anyway. She said it like a throwaway—like it didn't matter.

And that was the thing.

Her love for him was the *most* important thing. It was the one thing that continually held her back from moving forward all these years, and then at the same time, kept her going. That fucking love—as crazy as it was—kept her *alive*. She didn't want to put that knowledge on his shoulders. She didn't want him to know the struggle that had been so entirely dark for her all these years, but it was there.

She knew it.

"Hey," he murmured.

Finally, he tugged on her hand.

Lucia looked back at him again.

He was still grinning.

"You know, regardless of the rest, we're still just Lucia and Ren, babe."

She blinked.

"Are we?"

Renzo laughed. "A little messy, maybe. But yeah, why not?"

"Is it really *that* easy, though?"

"It can be, if you want it to be."

She did.

God, she *did*.

Lucia just didn't think it was that simple.

Nothing was ever simple or easy for her.

"I just ..." Lucia sighed, and shook her head. "How do you stop being angry, Ren? You know what I mean? I feel like it's been with me for so long—always *constant*—and I'm scared that I don't know how to live without it, now."

Renzo wet his lips, and chuckled. "You know, that used to be me, too. Grew up *angry*, babe. So fucking angry. And it feeds you, and you feed off it, if you get what I'm saying. It fuels you, and keeps you going when nothing else does."

He wasn't wrong.

That's what terrified Lucia.

Renzo shrugged one bare shoulder, saying, "I'm not saying it's gone now—I'm saying that it's not as constant for me, anymore. It's something I dig out and use when I need it, and when I need to be a different version of me. That's what anger taught me; it forced me to do better and be better. I was angry with the people in my life that didn't do anything for me, so I got mad enough that I did it for myself. I was so angry with life for fucking me over, and giving me the responsibility of shit that wasn't mine to begin with that I got mad and used it to keep pushing me through it. That's what you use it for."

"Never thought of it like that."

"It's not something we actively think about—we just *do it*."

Lucia nodded. "Yeah, maybe."

"No maybe about it, baby." Renzo tipped his head to the side, and winked. "But for *us* ... what do you want?"

Didn't he know?

"You."

Renzo smiled lazily. "Good because that's what I want, too. I don't know how to love anyone else but you. Not the way that I love you, anyway."

Yeah, she knew how that felt.

"What about when you have to go back to ... The League, and I go back to Cali?"

"We'll figure it out."

He said it like it was obvious.

Simple.

True.

She didn't have a choice but to believe him. God knew she wanted to believe him more than *anything*. They deserved to have the time to figure this out. Whatever this thing was between them, distance and time hadn't killed it—it wasn't dead yet. They needed to *fix* it.

Renzo tugged on her hand again, and Lucia did get up from the chaise that time. She fell into the bed with him, instantly locked into the bars of his arms as his mouth crashed down on hers. His kiss was hard—*demanding*. She didn't mind at all.

It was just her luck that neither of them had pulled on any clothes after getting up to the hotel, and shedding them the night before. It took him no time at all to pull Lucia up by wrapping his hands around her hips, and tugging her higher.

"Sit on my face, and let me *play*," he uttered thickly.

"*God*."

"Yeah, baby. You can call me God for a while."

Her thighs rested on either side of his head as he pulled her down on his face. His nose nuzzled in close to her clit as his tongue worked her pussy. He rotated between fucking her with his mouth, and his fingers. Getting her wet, and *ready*.

She was shaking before long.

Ready to come before she knew it.

"Right there," she mumbled, rocking her hips against his motions. "Fuck, right *there* ..."

One of his hands drifted behind her sex, and two wet fingers pushed into her ass as his tongue came up to lash against her clit while his other hand worked at her sex. She was getting him from all angles—driving her crazy three different ways.

She came harder than *ever.*

"Fuck, *Ren* ..."

"Yeah," he groaned, his approval thick as he pulled away from her pussy just enough to watch her down below. She shook her way through that orgasm, and his fingers only slowed in her pussy and ass when her trembling stopped. "Damn, that was something, huh?"

Lucia laughed.

"Yeah, *something.*"

He grabbed her hips hard, and pulled. In a breath, she was flipped over on the bed. Her knees pushed into the bed, and he yanked her ass high. Two smacks of his palms against her backside had her moaning into the bed.

He didn't say a thing until the thick length of his cock was pressing into her behind. Slow, at first, and then when he'd worked her pussy just enough to drive her crazy, he started pound into her harder. A steady, deep beat that she swore she could feel in her bones.

"Yeah, baby, let me fuck that pussy. Show me how you love it, Lucia."

She was *this close* to coming again when the ringing started. She wasn't the type to be able to ignore a sound like that, even during sex. If anything, it immediately dragged her out of the moment and into the present.

She cursed under her breath, a dark laugh following right after.

"No, no," he muttered when she grabbed onto his arm to slow him. "You know you don't wanna—"

"I have to."

He stopped fucking her instantly. "*Really,* right now?"

"Just let me answer it."

"Fuck," Renzo muttered, but it sounded a hell of a lot more like a whine than anything else. He pulled away from her like it was the last thing he wanted to do, and all she could do was laugh. "Keep laughing, and watch what happens when you get back in this bed."

"I look forward to it."

"*Goddamn.*"

She crawled off the bed, and headed after her ringing phone in the bag on the couch. She gave him a sexy wink over her shoulder as she pulled the phone out, and answered the call. She still had her eyes on Renzo the whole time.

"Hello?"

"Lucy, care to have dinner with me and a friend today?"

Lucia arched a brow, and turned her back to Renzo so she could talk to her brother. "John?"

"Who else calls you from this number?"

"I didn't check the ID."

"Ah, anyway … dinner today with me and a friend." John cleared his throat, adding, "Actually, you might want to see if you can get Renzo to come along, but stay in the background where he can't be seen."

Lucia didn't like the sound of that. "Who is the *friend?*"

"It's not important."

"It is to me."

John sighed. "Christian Savino. He's thrown out a threat that he promises to follow through on if I don't have a sit down with him over dinner, and—"

Lucia froze. "Bring me along, apparently."

"His request."

"Sounds like a demand."

Lucia turned at the sound of the bed shifting to find Renzo was already off the mattress, and getting dressed. Maybe he could tell something was wrong by the sound of her voice, but he didn't look pleased.

"Listen, John, I'm not involved in the family business, and I don't want to be."

"It can't be avoided," John said like he wasn't giving her a chance to argue, "but you'll be well protected the entire time. I need to get Christian the hell out of this city—my business with him is over."

"Apparently not if you're having dinner with him."

"Like I said, he made some threats. I don't like testing those. I don't want to get into details, Lucia, but if there was any way I could do this without involving you, I would do it. He's not giving me a choice."

Fuck.

"I could leave—"

"It's bigger than you; you're just part of the demand. And it *is* only dinner."

Right.

Only dinner.

"What time is the dinner?" she asked.

"Four."

"Text me the address."

"You got it, Lucy."

She ignored the nickname.

Again.

Hanging up the phone, Lucia dropped it to her bag. Renzo was already beside her, then, and frowning.

"What now?" he asked.

Yeah, right.

Because it was always *something.*

• • •

"Pull over here," Renzo murmured.

Lucia did as he asked, and pulled her rental to a stop about a block away from where she was supposed to have dinner with John and Christian. She didn't know who else was going to be at the dinner, but she would soon find out.

Hopefully, a whole army of Marcello people to keep the other side in line. But who was to say?

Once she had the car in park, Renzo leaned over in the seat, and pressed a kiss to her lips. Fast and fleeting, she wanted to pull him back for another kiss the second he was moving away. He just gave her a wink, and reached for the handle on the door.

"I'll walk the rest of the way, and then head in through the back," he explained. "Keep an eye on things, and stay out of sight at the same time. Just know I *will* be watching, all right? Fuck all is gonna happen if I'm watching in the background, babe."

Lucia nodded. "Got it."

"You good?"

Was she?

Lucia didn't know.

"I'm not sure," she admitted.

Renzo smiled a little. "It's just a dinner—you've had a few of them before."

"Cute."

"Just saying."

"Not a *sit down* kind of dinner, though."

"Look pretty; keep quiet." Renzo shrugged when she glared at him. "Isn't that what men like him want from a woman?"

"Well, probably."

"Then do that, babe. You can be loud and mouthy and messy to me later. I like you that way, anyhow."

Lucia smacked his shoulder with the back of her hand, then grabbed his jacket, and yanked him in for another burning kiss. She didn't say goodbye to him as he stepped out of her car—it was just better not to.

Goodbye felt final.

This wasn't the end.

Lucia pulled the car back onto the busy street as Renzo slipped into a shadowed alleyway. She wasn't sure how she would explain to John where Renzo was without giving his position away to Christian, but that was something she would handle when, or if, it came up.

Soon, she was pulling into the parking lot of the restaurant her brother liked to use to do business. One that his wife, Siena, also worked out of a lot of the time. She wondered if that had been another demand of Christian's for this dinner, or if it was something John had chosen to do.

After all, there was the upper hand in a person's own territory, right? Wasn't that how it worked?

A familiar Marcello enforcer was already waiting to open Lucia's door and take her keys before she'd even cut the engine on the rental. The man gave her a nod and smile as she stepped out of the vehicle.

"They're already inside waiting for you," the enforcer said. "They're the only ones in there, so you can't miss them."

Yeah, like she was going to miss her brother.

Or ... Christian.

Lucia knew there was a reason she hadn't felt anything for that guy from the start. Maybe she hadn't gotten the *bad* vibe from him, but she still hadn't wanted to get close to him, either. That spoke volumes.

Fixing the belt on her tweed jacket, Lucia headed for the entrance of the restaurant. From the front, it looked closed for the day. Even the sign hanging on the door said they were closed—despite the daily hours stating the place should have been opened.

The door was unlocked, but she didn't need to open it. A man she didn't recognize was waiting behind the door, and as soon as she stepped up to it, he opened it for her, and welcomed her in with a smile.

He didn't speak to her, so she didn't speak to him. Not that she needed him to say anything—he pointed toward the back of the restaurant where she knew a private section had been setup for John to do business or whatever else throughout the day. He'd always been like their father in that way, doing business somewhere he could eat all at the same time.

Maybe it was an Italian thing.

Sure enough, Lucia found her brother and Christian Savino waiting in the private area. Both men were already standing when she came to the entryway, like they had been expecting her or knew she was right around the corner.

"Lucia," her brother said stiffly.

His gaze drifted to Christian, but the man wasn't paying any attention to John. His gaze was locked on her. "Lucia, good to see you again, *mia cara.*"

She didn't like his sweet nothings, but she figured now was not the time to let the man know. How good would that be for this dinner?

"Now that you're here," Christian said, "we can finally get these negotiations started. Here, a chair." He pointed at the one *next to him*. "Sit, why don't you."

John cleared his throat. "She'll sit by me."

Her brother's tone offered no room for argument, and Christian didn't even bother to try. He shrugged, as if to silently say, *suit yourself.* Lucia came further into the private dining area, and took the available seat next to her brother.

She shrugged off her coat, and hung it on the back of the chair as her gaze drifted over the private dining area. There were men sitting at the other tables—some she recognized, and others, she didn't. For the most part, they were watching the meeting happening between John and Christian, but a couple of them kept their eyes on the table in front of them.

Strange.

"As far as these ... *negotiations*," John said, his tone twisting around the final word, "I already told you, I am doing this to entertain you, Savino. But that is it—we will *not* be doing any business together."

Christian laughed, and the sound made Lucia's gaze shoot to him. So cold, and unaffected, she thought. How quickly his masks could flip—she'd not noticed that before. One second, the man seemed happy and charming, and in the next, his eyes were icy and *dead*.

"See, you're mistaken there, Johnathan," Christian said, tipping a hand over to show his empty palm. "There was money on the table; we'd discussed business, and dollars. I don't leave money sitting on the table like that. Once you begin a business transaction with me, I intend for you to see it through."

John's jaw hardened. "No, *you're* mistaken. See, once you thought to seek my family out—my sister—as collateral for this business deal between us, it was over. I decided that, and let you know. There was nothing else to say after that. You go your way, and I go mine. That's what we're here for today. This ends it."

Christian smiled coldly. "She was back up, John. That's all. If things didn't go the way I wanted with the business deal through you, then I was going to use her to put you back in line. You can't blame me for that, can you?"

Lucia blinked.

"What?" she asked.

He glanced her way, still cold and unaffected. "Standard business practice, sweetheart. Don't be offended—you're pretty, sure, but not *my* kind of thing, if you get what I mean."

Jesus Christ.

She didn't even know what to say to *that*.

Christian didn't seem like he cared as he went right back to his conversation with John like he hadn't left it in the first place. "So, this is how we're going to go forward with this, John ... During my time in New York, while you were busy trying to ignore me thinking that I would get the hint and go away, I was *working*. And do you know what I do best for work, John?"

Her brother swallowed hard. "No, what is that?"

"I'm a finder." Christian grinned. "I find things. Things you care about—things you *love*. I find weaknesses, and then I find the ways to exploit them. I've had several weeks, and if we're honest, several months leading up to this meeting to find lots of things about you and yours, John, and I know exactly how to work them. Your wife—kids. Your father, and mother ... sisters, not including Lucia, here. I know details about their lives that *you* don't know. How about your son ... Lucky, is it?"

John stiffened in his chair, but he didn't look away from Christian. "My oldest, yes."

"Cute boy. Looks like his dad, huh?" Christian arched a brow, adding, "I heard he's severely allergic to ... what is it, shellfish? Shame, that."

Lucia's heart *hurt*.

Hurt for her brother, and her nephew.

Her brother said nothing, but she could see that muscle working in his cheek. Someone was threatening his son, and the rest of his family, but John was doing his best to keep himself in line. That in itself was a fucking feat. Lucia knew it.

"Imagine," Christian said, "if someone were to ... approach the fence that surrounds your son's daycare, John. They could get close to the chain link, and call to him. Does he go by his name, or *Lucky*? Anyway," the man said, flipping a hand as if to wave the question off, "imagine someone calling for him, and when he gets close enough, well, they'll grab him and put a bit of that shellfish in his little hands. He only needs to touch it, right? That's how allergic he is to it—I found that out. He'd be all the way at the other side of the playground, just far enough away that his teachers probably wouldn't notice he was struggling for what, a minute or two."

Christian flashed a smile. "Long enough, John."

Without emotion to his tone, although Lucia didn't know how her brother managed it, he asked, "What the fuck do you want?"

"Don't you want to hear how I'll go through the other people in your life? The plans I have for your wife. Or your sister—Lucia, I mean? She might not be my type, but damn, she's got a mighty fucking pretty mouth."

Bile rose in Lucia's throat.

She barely held it back.

"The money on the table," Christian said, "that's what I want, John. I start a business deal, and I finish it. That's how this works for me. There is no *backing out*. You don't get to jump into your feelings because you don't approve of how I do this business, you fucking got me?"

John tipped his chin back. "Yeah, I got you."

Christian nodded, and stood from his chair. "Good—remember that. Renegotiations for our deal will begin in three days. If you're not there with the money on the table to settle this out, I'll come for yours. I'll start with your sister, but your son will be a close second. And don't for one fucking second think that you can hide them from me."

"I'll kill you," John murmured.

The other man at the table laughed.

Lucia didn't think it was funny at all.

Marcellos didn't say those words easily. They didn't throw threats *just because*. When a Marcello man promised to take a person's life, it meant exactly what they said. They would do it, too. It might not be today, or tomorrow ... but *someday*.

That was a guarantee.

"I've heard that before, John." Christian snapped his fingers, and several men from the other tables in the room stood up, ready to leave. "We'll be on our way—keep in mind, the few that you see here ... triple that, and you might come close to the number of people I have watching your family. It only seems like I work alone, John, but the truth is ... I never fucking do."

"I'll be in contact," John said.

"Good."

Christian turned to leave the table, but not before asking, "I heard the Marcello leadership has changed a great deal—I look forward to seeing how that changes things for me."

Lucia didn't miss the way her brother's brow furrowed, but John stayed quiet. He didn't ask any questions, and he let Christian leave in peace with the rest of his men. Smart, probably. There was a good chance that if they attacked Christian here, then his men would counter attack. John wasn't the type to be irrational on his good days—he wouldn't put Lucia in that kind of danger, she knew.

"John, you okay?" she asked once it was just her, him, and the Marcello men left in the room.

John said nothing, but stood from his chair. Lucia felt the need to comfort him, even if she knew it wouldn't help. "It'll be okay, John. We'll figure it out."

Right, *she* would help him figure it out.

Sure.

"I want someone on her when she even *thinks* about leaving her hotel room," came a dark voice from the doorway.

Lucia found Renzo standing there. It seemed he did make it inside the business to watch from afar. Maybe that was why she hadn't felt *unsafe* during the meeting despite the threats that had been thrown around.

She just knew he was there.

John nodded, but didn't look up from his phone. "Yeah, that's the plan, Ren. Her, and everybody else."

Renzo didn't look away from Lucia as he said, "Make sure of it."

Then, to Lucia, John said, "When you go with Dad for his final chemo later this week, *do not* tell him what happened here, Lucia. He's sick—he doesn't need to be in a state about this, all right? I've kept him mostly in the dark, a lot like the rest of them. We're handling business; me and Andi, I mean. I don't want Dad worrying about it. Got it?"

Lucia shrugged. "Okay, I got it."

FIFTEEN

"Fuck," Renzo snarled, his hand coming down to smack the steering wheel with probably more force than was necessary. Frankly, he didn't care. He just needed to get some of this goddamn frustration out before he blew his top. Nothing ever ended well when he became angry, and reacted from it. At least, he'd learned that lesson before it was too late. "Where in the hell did he go?"

Pulling Lucia's rental to the side of the street, he cut the engine. Thankfully, the dark tinted windows all the way around the vehicle kept him out of view, but that did nothing to help him right now.

Christian was getting smarter.

Or ... more paranoid.

As soon as Renzo was sure that Lucia would be fine with her brother at the restaurant, he snatched her keys for the car, and headed after Christian. Maybe he hadn't been doing such a good job at this whole ... babysitter thing with the Savino prick. Renzo would knock it down to the fact that he didn't know *why* he was following Christian, and he didn't entirely trust whoever his boss was—M—for giving him this job without a clear reason.

Nonetheless, he hadn't been keeping as close of an eye on Christian as he should. Renzo figured that since Christian was in New York anyway, and apparently doing business with the Marcellos, that *they* would have their eyes on the fool.

But that wasn't the point of *Renzo's* job.

He was supposed to watch, and report back.

The Marcellos likely kept an eye on Christian for a different reason.

Fuck.

Hindsight was always twenty-twenty.

Stepping out of the car, although that probably wasn't the smartest thing, Renzo folded his hands behind his head, and turned one way, then the other. He glared at the empty street behind a bunch of warehouses down the left side, and then the right.

He'd turned in to follow Christian's car, because he figured he needed to know where the asshole was going after that whole meeting at the restaurant with John and Lucia, but the vehicle had vanished.

Apparently, into thin air.

In one of these warehouses, maybe?

But why?

Renzo eyed the row of warehouses, and let his mind run crazy. He'd been *maybe* twenty car lengths behind Christian's vehicle, and he'd been careful not to seem like he was following the idiot. Lucia's rental was a white Benz, and not the standard black car that most of the Marcellos and their associates seemed to prefer.

It was highly unlikely that the fucker driving Christian's car had believed someone was following him. So, if that wasn't what made them turn down this row of warehouses, then what was the fucking reason?

What was back here?

Renzo couldn't stay around here thinking about it, and fucking the dog for too long. For one, because he didn't want to be caught back here by one of Christian's men if they did end up coming out of one of these warehouses. And for two, because he needed to get Lucia's car back to her so that he could see her safely to the hotel where she would be protected.

Ugh.

What he wanted to do was scream.

Renzo had done a lot of jobs for The League—recon missions, a couple of jobs where explosives needed to be used; a robbery of a major bank in another country where someone's money had been held without authorization. Quite a few hits on big names in this country, and around the world. He'd done several rescue or recovery missions, and learned he preferred those.

Point was, he'd done *a lot*.

Why was *this* the one he found the most frustrating?

Oh, no … Renzo knew.

Because what was he even *doing*?

He didn't know.

He doubted *anyone* knew.

What a waste of fucking time.

Renzo had the greatest urge to shout out his frustrations, but he held it back. Yanking open the driver's door to the white Benz, he leaned in and grabbed the phone sitting on the passenger seat. Turning it on, he swiped to a GPS app he used to track the vehicle Christian preferred to use when his men drove him around. The one he'd been in today.

He'd put a tracker under the car when Christian's men hadn't been paying attention one day at the man's hotel. He had the chance, so he took it. Today, it was going to do him a bit of good.

Once he'd gotten the app up and running, Renzo waited for the damn dot to start blinking on the screen to tell him where in this maze of warehouses Christian went. It took ten seconds before the dot showed, and Renzo blinked at the screen.

He wasn't in any warehouse, now.

He was back on the fucking road!

Renzo clenched his teeth—apparently, by the looks of the moving dot on the screen, he was heading toward his hotel again.

Jesus Christ.

Maybe the man *had* known someone was following him.

What game was Christian playing?

Renzo figured he should probably get the car back to Lucia, grab his own rental, and then decide what he was going to do from there. Whether he should continue to follow Christian, or consider this day a total loss to his job.

The phone started ringing in his hand, and Renzo resisted the urge to throw it against the ground. The name on the screen prevented him from smashing the phone to bits, but also sent his irritation spiking a little higher.

Funny how that worked.

Cree.

Yeah.

Just his fucking luck.

Today couldn't get any worse.

Renzo was quick to jump into the Benz, and shut the door. He pulled back onto the road, and did a U-turn right there before heading back out onto the main drag as he answered his handler's call. It'd been a while since Cree had called him, so Renzo didn't think he would be able to get away with ignoring the man's call today. He'd backed off a little after sending Corrado with his warning, and Renzo respected that.

Appreciated it, too.

He wasn't about to test the man's line.

"Ren here," he said into the phone.

"I need a report, New York," Cree said.

"On what?"

Cree let out a dry laugh. "The only thing you're supposed to be doing, Ren. I don't know if you've been so busy elsewhere that you *forgot*, but your job right now is to be following a certain mark, and reporting back when I call about it."

"Actually, my reports are supposed to be once a week, thanks."

"So, this week, it's two."

Renzo's molars ached from how fiercely he was clenching his jaw. It wasn't even Cree, but just this whole fucking day. "There's nothing to report—nothing any different from the usual shit I've been reporting about Christian Savino. Pass the message along to my boss. I'm sure he'll appreciate it."

For whatever reason ...

Cree hummed under his breath. "Really, *nothing?*"

"No."

Christian was still doing the same shit he *had* been doing since he arrived in New York. He went to the same places, and met up with the same people. He was doing business with the Marcellos, or rather, now he was *forcing* them in to doing business with him. That was all the same shit Renzo had already been reporting to Cree to tell M over and over again.

It wasn't anything new.

"Same shit, different day," Renzo said.

"You're sure?"

"Cree, I said—"

"Your boss ... M, I mean, has it on very good authority that Christian had a meeting today. He has good reason to suspect you would have been in attendance at that meeting, or that you might have information to pass onto him about it. Are you telling me there was no meeting?"

Renzo stilled in the driver's seat, and his fingers tightened around the steering wheel. Maybe it was something John had said in the restaurant that finally made shit *click* in his head, or it could have been Cree basically helping him out here.

He'd assumed Lucian Marcello *knew* about Christian, and the shit happening in the city because of the man's presence. He thought that because he was sure things had been said in passing that suggested Lucian knew. Didn't Lucia talk to her dad about it when she was with him during his chemo?

Renzo couldn't be sure.

But John ...

John had said *not* to tell Lucian. That he didn't know—he didn't want him worried when he should be focusing on his health.

The thing was, Renzo's boss—the elusive M—had been watching this whole thing play out from afar through Renzo, in a way. He'd been getting regular updates; the kind of information that would be passed along to any member of the Marcello family when it came to Christian's involvement in their business and life.

M didn't have interest in hurting Christian. He didn't seem to care about the fact that the man had meetings with other people; he just wanted the basics of his work, and behavior. Where he was, what he was doing, and who he was doing it with. And then the Marcello thing ...

Fuck.

It was starting to fall together.

Renzo was beginning to feel like an idiot.

"Hey, are you listening to me?" Cree asked.

Renzo cleared his throat. "How much more time is on my contract, Cree?"

The man on the other end of the phone went quiet. "A few weeks, Ren."

Right.

A few weeks.

There was absolutely *no way* that The League, or M, didn't know Renzo had been around Lucia. It was their one line this whole time—the one thing they didn't allow him to even test with them. They made sure of that.

And yet, here he had been … for quite a while, in New York, with *her*. And her family. Publicly, on more than one occasion.

It was funny.

Renzo had forgot about it. He'd stopped worrying about being with her when he wasn't supposed to be because no one had stepped in to tell him to stop.

He had a fucking chip in his arm, tracking him. He had a phone that kept track of him, too. It probably recorded his conversations on a regular basis, for all he knew. That would make sense, considering other things that didn't matter right now.

The League knew where he was staying.

They probably knew where Lucia was staying.

And they didn't *know* he was with her?

That he had *been* with her?

Renzo called bullshit.

Or … someone, like his boss, no longer cared about seeing the contract out with all of those previous rules attached because Renzo needed to be close to Lucia now. He needed to keep an eye on her … and his boss didn't care, because his boss … M, was Lucia's father.

Lucian won the bid on Renzo.

Lucian was *M*.

It was Lucian.

"So, no update for—"

"No update," Renzo said.

Because he'd give it himself.

He hung up the phone before Cree could reply.

• • •

Renzo wasn't sure if it was just circumstance, but Lucian's final chemo treatment also fell on the same day that the Marcellos intended to meet with Christian to begin business negotiations. Or at least, Johnathan and Andino Marcello's side of things for the business—their people, and men.

"There's usually more people here with him," Lucia said as she dropped her stuff in the family room just down the hall from her father's room. "It's quiet today. I thought more people would—"

"Attention might be elsewhere," Renzo said.

Lucia's gaze lifted to meet his. "Oh … the Christian thing?"

"Yeah, like that."

"I hadn't thought about that."

Renzo didn't blame her.

He also didn't want her to worry.

"Let's go see your dad, huh?" he said, slinging an arm around her shoulder. Lucia grinned as he drew her close enough to his side that he could press a kiss to the top of her head. Her arm snuck around his waist, and squeezed, too. "Today's the last treatment, right?"

"Final round of chemo," she whispered. "Yep."

He could hear the fear in her voice.

But the relief, too.

"Everything is going to be great, Lucia," he told her.

Renzo didn't feel like it was a lie, either. Something told him that Lucian was going to be around for a long fucking time—probably riding his ass, and reminding him to stay the hell in line. He wasn't sure if he was going to mind that, or not.

He'd deal with it, though.

After he handled this little business of Lucian being the person who won the bid on him, and took over his life.

You know, that was a big thing.

It needed to be dealt with.

Renzo had zero intention of telling Lucia what he learned, though. He knew that her relationship with her father was just beginning to get back to a good place. He didn't think something like this would do any good for it.

And sure, he had his feelings about learning Lucian was *M*, but a part of him wondered if there was more to it than just the man wanting to control him. He wouldn't know if he didn't ask, right?

Lucia didn't need to be involved.

Simple as that.

"Hey, Daddy."

Lucian looked up to find Lucia standing in the doorway of the treatment room, and then his gaze quickly drifted to Renzo waiting behind her. He was already in the chair, with the IV pole beside him, and the line to his chest was connected—pumping in medicine. Or poison, depending on how someone looked at chemo.

It could go either way.

"And Renzo," Lucian murmured, arching a brow. "What are you doing here?"

Renzo tipped his head toward Lucia. "Thought I would give her some company. And it's close to lunch, so someone has to remind her to eat, right?"

Lucia gave him a look.

He stared back, daring her to deny it.

She just sighed.

Lucian chuckled, saying, "Food sounds good, actually. Something cold, I think. Ice cream."

Lucia's brow lifted high.

Renzo didn't miss it.

"You want something to eat? You never want to eat when you're—"

Lucian shrugged. "Gio found me a good strain of herb—it does wonderful things."

Renzo laughed under his breath.

Yeah, weed could make someone with food poisoning want to eat if it was the right strain of bud. He knew that from firsthand experience.

"I can go get you something," Lucia said. "I'm sure they have frozen yogurt downstairs in the cafeteria."

"That'd be great, sweetheart," Lucian said, tossing his magazine aside, and sneaking a quick look at Renzo, too. "Renzo can keep me company."

That was when Renzo knew.

Lucian was aware that he knew the man was *M*. He was sly as fuck, too, making sure to get Lucia out of the room so that the two of them could talk it out, or hash it out. Whichever way it went, he was up for it.

Renzo didn't think people gave Lucian enough credit. He was in his golden years, sure, and right now, he was just finishing up the battle of his life, all things considered. But the man was still dangerous—and *smart*, too. Maybe dangerously smart, if someone wanted to look at it that way.

His hands were still in the game.

He was still watching.

Retirement was a joke for men like Lucian.

Simple as that.

"I'll be back in a few minutes," Lucia said, heading back out the door.

Renzo dropped a quick kiss to her mouth as she passed him by. "Take your time. I'm sure he doesn't mind."

"It's fine," Lucian said. Once she was gone, the man in the chair getting his chemo waved at the door, saying, "Close it, hmm."

Renzo did.

Then, he turned back to Lucian.

"What do you want me to call you—Lucian, or *M*?"

Lucian grinned a bit. "You know, Renzo, I was so careful. I thought you'd never figure it out—I didn't want you to, either. Because I didn't want you getting a complex about it. I didn't want you to feel like ... those rules and the control that The League put on you came from me because they didn't. It was a by-product of your circumstances. How you came to them. They had to make sure they could scrub you from the world, and reinvent you. I didn't get a choice."

Renzo's jaw ticked. "You're saying you didn't bid and win my contract *just* to keep me away from your daughter, then?"

"Never."

He would have kept questioning Lucian on that. Called the man out on it, if he thought Lucian was lying to him. Something told Renzo that, in fact, Lucian was telling the truth. At this point, he didn't have a reason to lie, did he?

"Then why did you bid on me when the time came?" Renzo asked.

Lucian looked up from his lap with a sigh. "Someone was going to do it, if not me. All that work I did … all the effort I put into getting you free again, and giving you the chance to become something bigger than you were … what would it be for? All for someone else to come along, grab your contract, and get you *killed*? How was I going to tell her that, Renzo? How was I going to tell her I didn't do all that I could so that you could both have these moments again someday?"

He chewed on his inner cheek, unsure of what to say.

Again, Lucian didn't have a reason to lie.

Not now.

Not after everything.

He gained nothing.

The man already *had* everything.

"You should be following someone today, shouldn't you?" Lucian asked. "I still have a few weeks left to decide where you're supposed to be working. I believe, Christian is your current target."

"Yes, but *why*?"

Lucian laughed, and glanced away. "Years ago, my brothers and I decided to … step back from the family business, you could say. We allowed our sons to take control, and step up. We knew that if our presence was too *present*, that it would affect how they handled their business, and how the rest of the made men in our family perceived them."

"I get that," Renzo murmured.

"But that doesn't mean I am out of this game, Renzo. That doesn't mean I won't do everything I can to protect my family … my children. I promised my wife she would *never* bury a child, so whether they want me to keep an eye on their lives and business isn't my concern as long as they don't know I am doing it. And so, I do that from afar. You were simply one way I was doing that currently with John, but then Lucia got thrown into the mix, too."

He tipped his head to the side. "But why him—Christian, I mean? What is it with him?"

"He comes from a familiar place," Lucian replied.

"What does that mean?"

"It means what I said."

"But—"

The door opened, and Lucia poked her head in the room. "Hey, Daddy, I just remembered the gelato place down the street. Do you want that instead?"

Lucian's gaze drifted to Renzo, and then back to his daughter. "Yeah, sure. Take Renzo with you … he can carry it back for you."

Renzo shot Lucian a look.

The man just smiled back.

Yeah.

Dangerously smart.

More than anyone gave Lucian credit for.

Renzo wouldn't make the mistake of forgetting it.

SIXTEEN

"It's fine," her father murmured, kissing her forehead.

Lucia looked up at her dad, and frowned. "You're sure you don't want me to be here with you when you finish it out?"

Lucian patted her cheek with a tender palm. "I know why *you* want to be here ... but this is something I want to do alone, Lucia. You can understand that, can't you? This whole cancer thing has been more than sickness in my body—it's been in my mind, too."

Yeah, she bet.

Her father ... always strong and never fallible had finally met his match. Sure, he was going to beat it, and yeah, they'd have to wait another six months before they would officially get the *all clear*, but she understood what he was trying to tell her.

"I love you, Daddy," Lucia whispered.

Lucian smiled. "That's all that matters to me, *dolcezza*."

"We'll take a walk around the hospital," Renzo said from the doorway, "and then circle back around, Lucian."

Her father nodded. "I appreciate it. Also, check in on ... well, you know what I want you to check in on, Renzo. Make sure they don't need you, or whatever. That should be happening soon, yes?"

Lucia cocked a brow, and glanced between her father and Renzo. It seemed like the two of them were having a silent conversation that she wasn't included in on, and one that she didn't understand. She figured it would be better for her *not* to question it. If the two of them were getting along, then she wasn't about to go and ruin it with her curiosity.

"You got it," Renzo replied. "Come on, Lucia."

He held his hand out to her, and despite the fact that she still wanted to sit with her father to be with him while he finished his last bit of chemo, she stepped back. Taking Renzo's hand in hers, he directed her out of the room as his fingers weaved with hers, and held tight. Like he was going to keep her right there with him, lest she try to dart back to her father.

"He's going to be fine," Renzo said, chuckling before he dropped a kiss to the top of her head. "Let him do this alone, Lucia. We all need those moments sometimes."

Fine.

"He didn't even want Ma here today," she said.

"He's got a lot going on, I think."

"Yeah, about that."

The two of them slipped down a stairwell, and Lucia turned fast with a sly grin on her face. She poked him right in the chest, and all Renzo did was arch a brow as if to challenge her. "What was all that about back in the room, anyway?"

"I don't know what you're—"

"Don't even try it." She put a hand to her hip, and squared him with a look that she hoped said she wasn't fucking playing around, now. It was hard to say whether or not Renzo would take it as a challenge, but she welcomed it either way. "I saw that whole … silent conversation shit you and my dad had going on. Don't even try to lie to me."

Renzo tugged on her hand as they came to the first landing in the stairwell, and he took the door leading out to a floor that looked … empty. Wordlessly, he tugged her hand, peeking into door after door until he found one that he seemed to like. Renzo pulled her into the room behind him, and then kicked the door closed.

It took Lucia two seconds to realize they were inside a damn storage room. Rows of metal shelves had been filled with medical supplies. But hey, it gave them a bit of privacy for this talk, which she appreciated.

It was something.

"What are you doing?" she asked him when Renzo gave her a grin, and a wink.

"Come here," he demanded roughly.

He pulled her closer to him, and his hands slipped up under her jaw. Tipping her head back, all she could see was him clouding her vision.

And God …

She loved it.

Loved *him*.

He dropped a quick kiss to her mouth, saying, "Don't worry about it, Lucia. Me and your dad, I mean … it's not about you."

"But—"

Renzo kissed her harder.

He was trying to distract her, and it was working. Lucia wasn't even sure if she minded, or not. She did like his hands on her. Loved the way he kissed her like he was hungry, and couldn't get enough. It was enough to make her wet between her thighs even if *here* was the last place that she should be feeling that kind of way.

He probably knew it, too.

He knew exactly what he was doing to her. He had to, considering the way he drifted closer to her, shoving her body against the wall, and pressing his hard form against her softer lines. She was suddenly glad that she had decided on a flimsy dress for the day when it made easy work for one of his hands to slide up under her skirt and grip her inner thigh while his other one kept a firm hold on her jaw.

She couldn't move.

She didn't want to, either.

"God, you're awful," she breathed when he finally pulled away from their kiss.

Renzo chuckled. "Am I?"

"Just … it's okay, right?" she asked, peering up at him. "You and my dad, I mean. You're both okay, right?"

He nodded. "I promise."

Okay.

That was all that mattered to her.

Lucia didn't need details.

"But *you*," he said, cocking a brow.

Lucia wet her lips. "What about me?"

"You get in a state here, I think. Watching him and worrying. I don't like that."

He moved a little closer.

His hand on her thigh moved higher.

Christ.

"This is not the right place for—"

"Tell me to stop, then," he dared.

She couldn't, not when his fingers were grazing her sex overtop her panties.

"I hate you," she lied.

Renzo laughed. "Why?"

"I don't have any control with you."

"Just let me make you feel good, baby."

How was she supposed to say no to that?

"Make it fast," she muttered. "We do *not* need to be caught in here."

"You got it. Scout's honor."

"You are so far from a fucking scout that—"

"I know," he said, grinning.

His words were punctuated by his hand slipping up under her dress. Those deft fingers of his stroked her pussy overtop her panties. He knew *just* how to touch her—to curve his thumb against her clit as the tips of his fingers dragged across her cotton-covered sex.

"You're already wet enough for me to feel it through these panties," he murmured.

"Is that a surprise?"

Renzo winked. "I love it. I *want* it like that."

Yeah, she knew.

His fingers drifted under the gusset of her panties to glide along her sex beneath the fabric. She felt him drag her wetness from her slit to her clit, and then he pressed hard, fast circles against the throbbing bud. Her thighs trembled and his mouth descended on hers. That tongue of his lashed against hers violently as his fingers went back to her slit. Two pushed in deep, and curved against the wall of her pussy. He hit her G-spot *perfectly*.

"Oh, my God," she mumbled against his mouth.

Renzo chuckled again.

That same dark, husky chuckle.

She could come from that sound alone, surely.

"Come, and then get me ready with your mouth so I can fuck you," he demanded.

Yep.

Damn.

That did it. Just his rough voice filled with the promise of sex, like his words, and the smell of him in *leather*. It was all the same to Lucia. It all spoke of man, sex, and love to her. Could someone bottle that scent for her?

She needed it.

Lucia came hard, but Renzo was quick to cover her mouth with his other hand to keep her noises muffled *just enough*. His laugh came off entirely too sexy. The way his gaze locked on hers made her feel *crazy*.

"You gonna get a taste of me on your mouth, baby?" he asked.

Lucia nodded, and he uncovered her mouth. She was fast to drop to her knees, then. He was already working his pants open, and shoving them down a little. His cock—already hard, and pulsing in her palms—came free from the confines of his boxer-briefs easily enough, and all she could think about was getting him in her mouth. The silkiness of his cock against the roughness of her tongue; the taste of his precum as he watched her swallow him whole ... she wanted all of it.

"Lucia ..."

She peeked up at him.

Renzo arched a brow. "Love you, huh?"

She smiled. "More than you know."

There was nothing quite like the sound Renzo made when she first took him into her mouth. It was guttural, and raw. Like he was aching from the inside out just from the feeling of her lips wrapping around his dick. She could get lost in the way he sounded out his pleasure as she sucked him off. It was beautiful.

"I thought you wanted *fast*," he said through clenched teeth.

Christ.

She loved the way he looked like this. With her on her knees, his cock in her mouth ... he looked like he was losing control in the best way. He was always steady—she made him unsteady. Nothing turned her on more.

"Because this is going to end *way* differently if you keep that up," he warned.

He didn't let her keep it up, either. He was quick to pull her off his cock, and make her stand. Those strong arms of his wrapped around her waist, his hands palmed her ass, and she found herself backed against the wall. Her hands worked between their bodies to get her panties pushed aside, and his cock where she wanted it to be.

Her back hit the wall hard at the same time he thrust in. Those fingers dug into her ass as his cock stretched her open in the best way. She barely got her legs hooked around his waist, and found support by holding onto his shoulders, before he was pulling out and then slamming right back inside of her again.

She swore his cock hit every nerve she had.

And her fucking G-spot, too.

"Oh, God, yeah," she breathed.

Renzo leaned in close, his lips grazing hers as he spoke. "You want that cock, baby?"

"Yeah, give it to me, *fuck.*"

He did.

Hard.

And fast.

So deep.

Every snap of his hips against hers drove her a little higher. Closer to the peak of bliss, and the promise of an orgasm. His mouth slammed down on hers, swallowing every single noise that dared to slip past her lips. His tongue worked against hers—a war. And a gift, too. With a kiss, she swore he could hand over his entire soul to her.

There was so much about this man that was perfect.

Too much, really.

"Fuck, come with me?" he uttered against her lips.

Lucia nodded—it was the best she could do.

She was close.

So was he.

She could feel it in the tightness of his back, and the way his fingers trembled against her ass. Maybe that's what did it for her, then—the idea that he was barely hanging on. That his control was about to slip, and he couldn't hold it back.

"Yeah?" he asked her. "Yeah, you there?"

"Fuck yeah."

She fell off the edge at the first feeling of his cock jerking inside her. He muffled her cry of his name with another bruising kiss, and he didn't release her from that kiss until they'd both stopped shaking.

Only then did he let her down from the wall … with a mess between her thighs. She couldn't even find it in herself to care, not when her legs felt like jelly and her mind was still humming with the orgasm she'd just experienced.

Damn.

"And you know what else?" Renzo asked as he found a paper towel to help her clean up. "Because don't think I forgot."

"What is that?"

"You didn't eat lunch." He tossed the used paper towel to a nearby trash can, and helped her to fix her panties and dress before he bothered to worry about tucking himself away and zipping up his jeans. "Just like I said you wouldn't."

Lucia sighed, and refused to meet his gaze even as his hands came up to cup her cheeks and his thumbs stroked her skin. "I just worry about my dad when I'm here, okay? Don't judge me."

"No judging, but you're going to get food down at the cafeteria right now. I have to make some phone calls, anyway."

Yeah … for her dad, probably.

Lucia settled herself on not asking questions.

"You have time to grab something," he told her. "He's not going to be finished for another half hour, or so."

She nodded.

He wasn't wrong.

"Fine, I'll go get something to eat."

Renzo dropped another kiss to her lips, and looked her over one more time to make sure she looked okay before they left the room. "That's my girl."

• • •

Lucia knew something was wrong the very second after she stepped out of the cafeteria's doors. The sandwich and apple in her hand suddenly held very little appeal as she stared at the knot forming in Renzo's brow as he talked faster into the phone.

"What the fuck do you mean he's not answering calls, man?" Renzo shook his head, and he still hadn't noticed Lucia standing right there. "I checked the fucking trackers—I put two others on the cars his men used. They haven't left the hotel."

Renzo was silent as the person on the other end of the call replied to whatever he was talking about, but it only seemed to piss him off more.

"I know the meeting should have started ten minutes ago, but that doesn't mean—" Renzo cursed under his breath, adding, "Maybe he picked up another car, John. One I didn't get a tracker on, right. It's possible. I have to sleep; I can't have my eyes on him twenty-four-seven."

"Ren?" Lucia asked.

Finally, he looked her way. He didn't seem all that surprised to find her standing there. He gave her a halfhearted smile, and a nod. It didn't seem true. It felt more like he was trying to placate her, but something was certainly *wrong*.

She felt it in her bones.

"All right, don't move," Renzo said. "Don't let anybody leave in case he's got an ambush planned for when you all leave. I *knew* we couldn't trust him. I knew this fucking meeting was a ruse for something else. *Fuck*."

He hung up the phone, but didn't give Lucia the chance to ask him anything before he was grabbing her hand, and tugging her toward the bank of waiting elevators. It would take them up to the floor where her father would probably be just finally finishing up his treatments. Renzo stayed quiet as he hit the button for the elevator at the far end, and five seconds later, it opened up for them to step inside.

It was only after the doors closed, and they were moving upward that he finally spoke.

"You're going to have to stay here with your dad," he said. "I have to head out. Your brother needs me for something."

"For *what?*"

Renzo didn't look away from the elevator doors that had yet to open for their floor when he replied, "That meeting for Christian, Lucia. It was today. But the fucker hasn't shown up, and all the beads I have on him are dead right now. I figured he was planning something, but John was thinking with his emotions, you know."

"Because of the threats, you mean."

He nodded. "Yeah. And I get it—he was worried about his kids, and you. His fucking wife. I *get it*. But you can't trust someone like Christian. He's not the type to have *one* plan, not when several works far better."

Something cold dripped down Lucia's spine. It felt like it seeped into her bones and blood, then wrapped around her lungs, and finally, her heart, too.

It froze her to the spot.

Silenced her.

"Where are they?" she asked.

"At the meeting location," Renzo replied.

"I don't understand—"

"Approximately twenty Marcello men, including several of your direct family members, are in a warehouse in Brooklyn right now, ready to do this meeting with Christian as he demanded. Problem is, he hasn't shown up, he isn't picking up calls, and I don't know where he is, either. That spells bad news."

Lucia wet her lips, but damn, her mouth felt dry. She found Renzo's hand with her own at her side, and wove their fingers together. She just needed to feel him a little closer to her—maybe his warmth would help her.

It did.

And it didn't at the same time.

"Do you think he has something planned for them?" she asked quietly.

Lucia didn't miss the way Renzo's jaw ticked. "I would bet on it, actually."

God, no.

Not her brother.

Her *family*.

"Do you think they're waiting for them to leave the warehouse?"

"Possibly," Renzo said. "That's why I need to get out of here, and get *there*. Scout the place, or see what in the hell is going on around them. I can feed John information from the outside, and then we can decide what to do from there."

That made sense.

And terrified her.

It meant Renzo was about to go right into the line of possible fire, too. Wasn't it bad enough that her brother and cousin was there along with God only knew how many other people she loved and cared about?

It was almost like he could feel her fear.

Like he could read her mind.

Renzo looked down at her, and his fingers tightened around hers. Lucia looked back at him, and didn't hide the tears welling in her eyes.

"Why is he doing this?" she whispered.

"Christian?"

She nodded. "Is it because of me … or the business with John? I don't understand why he would do something like this for that, Ren."

The doors to the elevator opened to her father's floor, but she didn't look away from Renzo. She needed an answer to her question.

"Is it personal or business?" she asked. "Is something like that enough for a man like him to come after us like this?"

"It's not about you, or business … or even John," came a voice from just outside the elevator.

Lucia found her father standing there, dressed in his suit, and ready to go, it seemed.

"Business is the only thing John has with Christian, right?" Lucia asked her father.

Maybe that's what her dad and Renzo had been talking about earlier. *This mess.* Christian, John, and the meeting. It all made sense. It's exactly why he knew what they were talking about when the elevator doors opened without having to ask what they were discussing.

Lucian looked up from where he was finishing buttoning the bottom button on his suit jacket as he said, "This isn't business, Lucia. It's a vendetta."

SEVENTEEN

Renzo shared a look with Lucian, and the man seemed to hear his unspoken words as he nodded, asking, "Is there a problem I should know about, Renzo?"

He almost wanted to laugh.

A problem?

That didn't seem like the right word for what could possibly be happening on the other side of Brooklyn. It didn't feel like a *big* enough word.

Sighing, Renzo replied, "Yeah, a problem is one way to put it."

Lucian pressed his lips into a thin line, and fiddled with the cuff on his suit jacket. Renzo recognized those actions for what they were—a man trying to keep his cool, and maintain his calm composure. Lucian didn't seem like the type to overreact because of emotions or fear. He understood that.

"Lucia," Lucian murmured, "would you mind giving us a quick minute to talk?"

"Sure, Daddy."

Renzo could have spoken up then and let Lucian know that Lucia already had a pretty good idea about what was going on, and having her step away was pointless. But if it made Lucian feel better to think Lucia wasn't worrying about the current drama, then what would it hurt for Renzo to stay silent?

Stepping out of the elevator, Renzo waited until Lucia was around the corner before he turned to Lucian with a grim expression. "You want the details I know first?"

Lucian shrugged. "I would appreciate it."

Renzo went through a quick rundown of the shit he knew—the fact that John had went to the meeting as he was supposed to, and the approximate number of men he and Andino had brought along for the arrangement. He sped through the details of Christian not showing up, not answering calls, and currently, being entirely off Renzo's radar as his vehicles were still showing parked at the hotel he'd been using for his stay.

Lucian only started to become visibly agitated when Renzo moved onto the fact that John—his son—and the others were currently in a warehouse, and had reason to suspect that leaving would be a bad thing. Be it because of an ambush, or something else.

They were stuck.

"Your turn," Renzo said when he was finished. "Why is it a vendetta and not an asshole with a big ego and an even bigger Caesar complex?"

Lucian chuckled dryly, and shook his head. "I didn't have a reason to suspect that's what it was, Renzo, but it *could* have been. And that alone was enough for me to make sure there was someone watching Christian Savino from the time he walked onto my son's radar."

Interesting.

Except ...

"That tells me nothing," Renzo said.

Lucian sighed. "I told you earlier, I might not be *in* the game anymore, but I am always watching from the background. I will step in should I need to in order to keep my children safe, regardless of what they want or think."

"Yeah, I get it."

"Well over three decades ago," Lucian said, his voice lowering, "there was a man in Italy named Bruno Savino. He would have been Christian's father, but as far as I know, he didn't even know his father. He was kept in seclusion until he was five, and when his father died ... well, I don't know what happened after that, but he came back into the public eye."

Renzo cocked a brow. "You've *tracked* a dead man's family? Why?"

Lucian gave Renzo a look. "Bruno Savino kidnapped my son, John, when he was a baby. He was going after one of my brother's wives, and my son was the way he thought to do that. Obviously, it didn't work—John is alive, and fine. I can't say the same for Bruno, or the small handful of men he brought along to help him."

Shit.

Yeah, that explained *a lot.*

"Italians love their vendettas, huh?" Renzo asked.

Lucian scrubbed a hand down his jaw. "Usually, we make it known when we've got a vendetta with somebody else. We tend to ... like for people to see us coming, if you get what I'm trying to say."

He did.

So why was Christian different?

"I suppose he couldn't get as close to your family as he did if he was going to make it known what he was coming to America for, huh?"

Lucian nodded. "And consider ... the event where we killed his father happened *years* ago. Decades, Renzo. Our family has moved on, and we never spoke to our children about it. It was something we wanted to leave in our past. And when our sons began to step into our roles and take over our families, we promised to step back and let them have full control of the family, business, and how they wanted it all handled. It's not a surprise that John wouldn't recognize his name, or know what happened decades ago."

"You know," Renzo muttered, "this fucking information would have been great to know *months* ago. I could have taken care of this issue before that asshole ever got to New York, Lucian."

"I didn't want to step in unless I had to. Give me some credit—I couldn't *know* it was a vendetta without him acting against us in some way, or making it known. And he did none of those things until it was too late."

Renzo didn't think so.

The second the asshole approached Lucia would have been a big red flag waving high. It was. At least, for him. He wanted to kill Christian right then, but he'd held back because he believed it was his jealousy getting worked up, and he tried not to give into his weaknesses like that.

Be a better man, and all that shit.

Fuck.

"Well, enough of what could have been done," Lucian muttered under his breath, "because what we need to figure out right now is what we're going to do about *today*. And my son in a fucking warehouse on the other side of Brooklyn. He's got a wife and kids to get back to tonight, Renzo. And Andino, my nephew? He's got a wife and a handful of kids, too. Why haven't my brothers—"

"I suspect they know," Renzo said. "But maybe they also know what you're trying to handle here, Lucian, and they factored that in on whether or not to call you."

Lucian scowled. "Fucking stupid."

"Yeah, well—"

A chime echoed in the hallway, and Renzo figured out what was making the noise quickly enough when Lucian pulled a cell phone out of his pocket. The man said nothing as he unlocked the screen, and his brow dipped at whatever he saw waiting for him.

"What in the *hell?*"

"What is it?" Renzo asked.

"A video," Lucian murmured.

Wordlessly, the man turned the phone around to give Renzo a peek at what was on the screen. The video text had come through from an unknown number, but it didn't take him too long to figure out who had probably sent it considering the video was of Johnathan and a hell of a lot of others walking into a warehouse.

"He was watching them?" Renzo asked more to himself than Lucian.

God.

That was cold.

It made *him* cold, and he wasn't even the one in the fucking warehouse. Because that was just creepy as hell. Like Christian was watching his work go down with no problems, and maybe enjoying it.

Yeah, *creepy.*

Renzo finished watching the video through, and before it had even finished, a second text came through. A *link*. No words accompanied the text to explain what the link was or what it might lead them to, but he didn't think for a second that it was … a mistake.

Christian *wanted* them to check that link.

He wanted them to click on it.

Lucian went to click on the link, but Renzo was quick to bat his hand away, almost knocking the phone to the ground in the process.

"What the fuck?" Lucian growled at him.

"I don't know what that link does—is it a *trigger*, Lucian? You click it and something activates? I don't know."

That was the explosives specialist in Renzo talking. Sure, it'd been a hot minute since he had to fuck with a bomb, set one, or disengage one, but still … the second The League put him in front of a dismantled bomb and gave him access to explosives, that shit was always in the back of Renzo's mind.

Something just *clicked*.

Bombs felt like his anger.

Dangerous.

Explosive.

Deadly.

It gave him control, and made his mind *run*. It engaged him like nothing else ever did when The League was training him. Some people could name every gun ever made in the world, but Renzo?

He could do *bombs*.

"Yeah, shit," Lucian muttered.

Then, his phone started ringing.

The same number that had sent the texts.

Lucian passed Renzo a look.

That was a risk—it too could be a trigger. Pick up the call, and it activated something. A person could do anything with the right code to get it done. It was that simple.

"I should pick it up," Lucian said.

"That's a risk," Renzo returned.

"It's *him*, clearly."

The phone kept ringing; Christian wasn't giving up.

He wanted to talk.

Renzo didn't think it was a trigger. "Pick it up, then."

Lucian connected the call, but put it on speaker phone. He was quick to turn down the volume in case anyone was listening nearby as he said, "Lucian Marcello speaking."

"Ah, Lucian. It's nice to finally speak to the man I've been watching for … well, most of my life, now."

Renzo glanced at Lucian, but the man's face was a mask of *nothing*.

"Funny," Lucian replied calmly, "I've been watching you, too, Christian. It seems we have the same idea about one another, no?"

"Well, you're a little late to the game. I've already made my moves, Lucian. I'm waiting for you to try and catch up, now."

"Came to finish the business your father never got the chance to?"

Christian made a noise on the other end of the phone—anger and pain, Renzo thought. That's what it sounded like. He was quick to hide it with his next sentence, but it didn't matter because he'd still heard it.

"The only vendetta I was willing to follow through was the one I held onto for your family, Lucian," Christian said, "so let me get down to the details, okay? You might even appreciate this, if you think it through."

"Doubt it," Lucian murmured.

"You will."

"Get on with it, Christian."

Christian clicked his tongue. "Listen, this is *my* day. It's all on my time."

"Well, I'm about a minute away from vomiting—chemo is a bitch, you know. Make it fast, or you're going to be talking to the sound of a toilet flushing."

Renzo pressed his lips together to keep from smiling because *damn*, Lucian didn't have time for this shit today. Who wouldn't appreciate that?

"The warehouse where your son, nephew, and ... well, a good portion of their men are currently situated, it's live wired to a bomb that will level half the block," Christian said. "They were fine to enter, but the second they leave ..." The man trailed off with an amused laugh, adding, "Well, it's going to go *boom*, in a beautiful way. Mind you, I have a kill switch, Lucian, so if something goes wrong, I only have to press a single code into my phone as a text, and that'll be it for them."

"What do you want, then?"

Christian was quiet for a second, and then said, "Nothing, Lucian."

"Nothing?"

"I want to watch them die like you watched my father die years ago. It's what you deserve. You'll hurt like I did when I lost a man I never got the chance to know. I think it's a fair trade, isn't it? Oh, and the link I sent you, well, that's just a live feed to watch them inside. You can call them and talk ... their wives and children can chat as well, if you want to punish them that way. Say goodbye."

Renzo met Lucian's frantic gaze and mouthed, *Ask about a timer*.

Lucian nodded.

"Is there a timer backup, Christian?" Lucian asked.

"No timer unless someone messed with the bomb. Then, yes, it'll begin ticking down. But otherwise, I just wanted to watch them panic like rats before they finally figured out there was no real way out. And don't for one second think someone from the *outside* could hold the doors open for them, either. They all have sensors to tell the difference. They're in there now, and there's no way out. Appropriate, don't you think, Lucian?"

"How so?"

"My father tried to blow you all up once, didn't he? All three of you brothers at the same time ... he failed, unfortunately. I won't. Have a good day—this will end the vendetta between us."

Christian hung up the call before Lucian could do it. Renzo had to physically *take* the phone out of the man's hand so that he didn't break it into pieces. Renzo could see it in Lucian's eyes that's exactly what he wanted to do with the phone.

"Don't watch the live feed," Renzo told him. "Don't do that."

Lucian glanced his way, but quickly looked away. Not before Renzo saw the line of water streaking through his eyes, though. And his jaw—stretched tight, and taut. His muscles worked with every clench of his teeth, and swallow of his throat.

"I can disengage it," Renzo murmured. "Let me try."

Lucian shook his head. "Impossible. You heard what he said—he's got three backups on the bomb, Renzo. It'll blow if a door opens to let someone *out*. It'll automatically begin to count down if you start fucking with it. And he's got a kill switch in *his hand* as he watches a live feed."

None of that mattered to Renzo.

"I can disengage it. I *can*."

Lucian's hands shook, but he hid it by shoving them into the pockets of his slacks. "It's a death wish."

"I could get them out. Somehow, there has to be a way out, right? I just ... let me *try*. I can't know if I don't go in there and try, Lucian."

"Renzo—"

"You have to let me try, Lucian. Look at everything you did, and gave to me. This is what I do. *Let me try*."

EIGHTEEN

"Hey, *dolcezza*."

Lucia looked up from her lap to find her father standing in the doorway of the hospital room wearing a smile that felt a little forced. She wasn't going to tell him the truth—that she'd stayed just beyond the corner where he couldn't see her so that she could listen to the *whole* conversation he had with Renzo, and the phone call that followed.

Oh, yeah.

She knew *everything*.

Lucia knew, without a doubt, that her father had enough to worry about. His son being trapped in a warehouse that, at literally any moment, could blow up. And, what could her father do about it?

Nothing.

Hospital policy meant he was going to have to sit in this room for at least another hour so that they could monitor him after his treatment. Sure, he could probably force his leave, if he wanted, but that still wasn't going to change the situation her brother and other members of her family were currently in.

It would only put her father closer to danger.

Wasn't it bad enough that her brother was there? And now ... *now*, Renzo was on his way there, too. Because yeah, she heard that. He hadn't even said goodbye, but she understood why. She didn't blame him.

That would have been the fight of his life against her—she never would have let him go willingly, and he was smart enough to know that he was going to have to just *go*. She was pissed, sure, but she would deal with it later.

Right now ... she had to figure out a way to help. To help her father, her brother ... the rest of her family.

Renzo.

They needed all the help they could get, even if they wouldn't ask for it. So, she would do it. Somehow. She just needed to figure out *how*.

"Everything okay?" Lucia asked.

Her father nodded. "Fine, but I'm not feeling great. Nauseous, you know."

Yeah, she bet.

And not just from the chemo, either.

"Come sit down," she told him. "One last day for this, right? And then you're done with all this, Daddy."

Lucian smiled, and for a moment, it did look genuine. That fear and panic in his eyes that he wasn't very good at hiding disappeared for her, although it was quick to come back, too. He crossed the room, and dropped into his chair with a groan. Scrubbing a hand down his face, he swore under his breath.

"*Cazzo*. What a day, Lucia."

"But it's almost over, Daddy."

Lucian nodded. "It is."

He wasn't looking at her, though. He was looking at the ceiling. She didn't need him to say it—he didn't need to tell her what he was doing, then.

God wasn't a *big thing* to Lucia. He was there on the back of her mind, and she went to church. God and religion was as much a part of being a Marcello was as anything else in their life. It was engrained into their *culture*, honestly.

He was praying.

Silently, sure.

Privately.

Her father did that a lot.

She didn't mind.

Lucian's silence let Lucia run through the shit in her mind. The things she knew about Christian Savino, and this plan he had made. It seemed like the man planned for everything, didn't it?

Backup after backup.

A timer.

A kill switch.

Just in case.

Lucia wondered ... what if she was able to take away one of those backups? If she could possibly give Renzo a little extra time, or if she could take away one of the backups altogether, would that give him the chance to do what he did best?

He'd never explained his specialty with bombs to her in detail, although to be fair, she had also never asked. So much about his time at The League and the person it made him were not topics that he wanted to discuss with her, and she didn't push.

She didn't have to push.

Renzo was just *Renzo* to her.

But could he do it?

And if she was able to help ... would it give them a better chance? Should she even *try*?

It wasn't even a question for her. *Yes*, she should try, if she could. For her family because she loved them more than anything. Her father hadn't just spent months of his life fighting to be healthy just to end it by watching his son and nephew *die*.

For Renzo, though?

God.

Hadn't she spent enough time without him? Hadn't all this time been enough? They'd just started again—just came together again. There was no way in hell she was going to give up.

That was *weak*.

The easy way out.

Without him, there was no point to her.

She was not her without *him*.

Lucia would rather be dead.

But how could she help?

How could she take away one of the backups?

Lucia's gaze drifted to the item sitting at the top of her bag—her cell phone. She eyed it for a second before it clicked in her head like a lightbulb going off. It should have been obvious, but nothing seemed to be coming easy to her lately.

Why would this be any different?

Christian *had* given her the number to his phone.

Hadn't he?

He'd plugged it into her phone at the hotel.

Would a man like that pass up the chance to rub salt in the wound if she was practically offering herself to him?

She didn't think so.

Lucia passed her father another look. He was still staring upward, but now, his lips moved silently. Probably mirroring the words he was speaking inside his head where no one but him and God could hear.

She just needed to get away from her father.

Luck would take care of the rest.

Hopefully.

• • •

"Daddy?"

"Lucia, just … don't."

The retching sound behind the door came again, and she cringed. Stepping back from the door because there was no way her father was going to let her inside the bathroom to help him, she glanced at the doorway of the hospital room.

This was her *only* chance.

She felt like shit for doing it. Her father was at his weakest point right now—sick, and in need of her help, or someone's help. He didn't need to come out of the private room's bathroom just to find she had snuck out on him.

But how else could she do it?

When would she get the chance?

Lucia would apologize later.

That's what this whole thing with her father had taught her. That's what *he* taught her, and Renzo, too. There was nothing that couldn't be fixed later. It didn't matter when the apology came, just that it did, and it was genuine.

So yeah, she could apologize later.

Her father would understand.

She hoped …

Lucia headed out of the room after grabbing her things. Slipping her coat on, and slinging her bag around her shoulder, she fished the cell phone out as she came up to the nurses' station. The woman who had been checking up on her father every ten minutes looked up at Lucia with a wide smile.

"Everything okay?" she asked.

Lucia shrugged. "He's getting sick again. It's not passing. Maybe some meds this time?"

The nurse frowned, but nodded. "Sometimes that happens. I'll bring something in right away."

"Thanks, and uh … could you tell him I just had to run down to grab something to eat from the cafeteria? I'll be right back."

All lies.

The nurse didn't know.

Neither would her father.

But it might give her at least twenty or so minutes to get ahead of her father, and anyone he might think to send after her if he caught onto her plans. That was all she needed—a head start to help Renzo.

Lucian wouldn't understand.

Not now.

The nurse smiled. "Will do. I'm sure he appreciates you being here, Lucia."

"Yeah, I'm sure." Inside her head, though, she was thinking *lay that guilt on a little thicker, please.* "Thanks again."

Before she could talk herself out of it, Lucia headed down the corridor. She just stepped out of the double doors for the section when she finally found Christian's contact in her phone. The asshole had even put in a winking emoji next to his name and number like that was supposed to be cute, or something.

It wasn't.

Fucking annoying, really.

Lucia hit the call button before she could think better of it, and then put the phone to her ear. She kept walking toward the bank of elevators waiting at the end of the hallway as the call rang two, and then three times. She was sure it was going to go to the voicemail, but halfway through the fourth ring, he picked up.

Because just like she thought … yeah, Christian was that kind of man. He'd rub the salt in the wound. He'd be the asshole to spit on the grave. He'd kick a man while he was down.

Today, that man was her father.

And the love of her life.

So yeah, fuck him.

"Lucia?" Christian asked carefully.

She heard it in his voice—the hesitance. Like maybe it wasn't going to be her on the other end of that call, but it was.

"Hey," she said, desperately trying to keep her tone calm. She didn't think it would help her cause for him to know she was panicking, and her heart felt like it was about to come right out of her chest. She never had been able to deal with anxiety well. But who could? "This is Christian, right?"

"It is. Why are you calling me, *bella?*"

Oh, he was still on the sweet nothings, huh?

Good.

"I'm heading for the airport today," she lied. "Heading back to Cali, but I didn't know if I would get the chance to see you again. I haven't even seen my family today, but I think I've seen enough of them to do me a while, anyway."

"Why's that, *donna?*"

"Bad history. I'm ready to leave."

"Ah, I understand. So, why the call today?"

Lucia wet her lips, and prayed her lie came out as easily and smoothly as she heard it in her mind. "I was hoping we might be able to meet up. I didn't get the chance to speak to you again, and I might not get to see you when I'm in Cali?"

"I was done with the art print business," he admitted. "Surely, your family has called you today, haven't they? Don't they want to spend some time with you?"

Yeah, there he went.

Testing the waters.

"I ignored their calls earlier," she said. "I mean, if you're busy, then maybe we can figure something else—"

"No, no. Not busy," Christian said. "I'll text you the new hotel's address. Expect a man to be there to check you when you arrive. I hope you understand. I have … some things going on today, so we're being careful."

Lucia smiled.

Stupid man.

"You got it. See you soon."

She let Christian hang up the call first. His text for the address where she had to go came less than two seconds later.

The man wasn't fucking around.

Good.

Neither was she.

• • •

Lucia stepped out of the cab after paying the man, and pulled her phone from her pocket. She didn't even think about it—she had her head start, now. Her father could do with it what he wanted, if he needed to. She just needed that extra time.

She sent a single text to her father.

The address of the hotel.

And then, *I love you, Daddy. I'm sorry.* She dropped her phone in a trashcan as she passed it by, just because. There was supposed to be a man who would check her, right? She didn't think it would be good for him to find that message in her phone.

Lucia didn't even have to open the front door of the hotel. The man in question was waiting there to do it for her. He said nothing, but took her bag after she said, "I'm here to see Christian Savino."

Silence.

That's all she got from him.

Ass.

He checked her bag, and then her coat when he waved for her to hand that over, too. *Jesus.* Once he was satisfied that she wasn't trying to pull anything on them—apparently, he hadn't seen her toss the phone into the garbage can outside—he handed over a single key card.

305.

That was the room number.

Lucia didn't even bother to thank the man. He hadn't said a single word to her. Heading for the bank of elevators at the other end of the hotel's main entrance, her nerves finally started to pick up once she pressed the button. It got worse when the elevator opened.

Lucia sucked in a breath to force herself to be calm, and stepped inside. Once the doors were closed, she felt like there was no turning back now. She didn't know what was going to be waiting for her upstairs, but she couldn't stop.

Now or never ...

She suspected the man downstairs had let Christian know she was coming up because by the time she arrived at his hotel room, the man was waiting for her at the door. He looked slightly disheveled, more so than she had ever seen him before. His usually put together appearance was mussed with a wrinkled shirt, and his wild hair.

Still, he smiled.

That *charming* smile.

Lucia smiled back.

All lies.

"Are you sure you're not busy?" she asked.

Just over his shoulder, she could see the spread of monitors that the man had set up on a table. Four monitors, to be exact. On one, showcasing the outside of what looked to be a large building—the warehouse, likely—a dark car pulled up.

She recognized that car.

It was Renzo's rental.

Time for a distraction, then.

Lucia smiled a little wider at Christian, wanting to keep his eyes on her. "I can come back, if—"

"No," he said, tipping his head to the side, "the show is just getting started. I think it'll be even better to watch it with you."

Fine, if that's what he wanted.

She needed to get his phone, though. That's what he'd told her father, right? He needed his phone for the kill switch.

NINETEEN

Stepping out of the vehicle, Renzo felt the cool rush of air sweep under his jacket. He eyed the exit door of the warehouse where he knew the Marcello men were currently stuck inside, waiting for the bomb to blow.

Figuratively.

And *literally*.

Shooting a look to the side at the sounds of murmurings, Renzo found another small army of cars and men. A few, he recognized just from having grown up on the goddamn streets. Anybody hustling on the streets knew the important faces of the crime families controlling New York. It wasn't smart to play stupid on that sort of thing.

Renzo hadn't seen these men in years, though.

Not even on the news.

Giovanni Marcello shoved his older brother away when Dante came closer, and then jabbed a pointed finger back at the warehouse. His mouth opened to shout at the other man, but he quickly snapped it shut when the two realized Renzo was standing there watching their little spat without any shame.

If people were going to have public moments, then they should expect the public to consume it. That's what humans did.

Giovanni was quick to straighten up, and fix his suit jacket. Dante was already turning to greet Renzo as he came closer to the two men. A couple of cars away, a group of gathered men were huddled in a semi-circle. Probably discussing a plan to get the others out of the warehouse, although Renzo couldn't be sure.

He knew if that *was* what they were discussing, well … he had bad news for them. There was no way out from the outside. Someone was going to have to *go in*, and work it out from inside. He doubted any of these people wanted to go inside that fucking warehouse. It was human nature to not want to be the sacrifice.

Renzo didn't blame them.

And he was the only person in this city who might be equipped to deal with a bomb of this standard. Especially if everything Christian said about the bomb was true—that it was big enough to level a good portion of this block; that it had several backups to blow if the first and second didn't work; that he had a kill switch.

Problem was … Renzo wouldn't be able to know if those things about the bomb were true unless he *went inside*. He had to get his eyes on the bomb. He had to get his fucking hands on it, and see how it was wired.

Look at all the bits and parts—the electronics attached, and the method used to make it tick.

Then, and *only* then, would Renzo be able to determine if what Christian said was entirely true, or only partly true. And if it was all true, then he had to figure something out for these people, and *fast*.

Because they were all fucked.

Every last one of them.

"You're gonna have to get out of here," Renzo told the only Marcello looking his way—Dante. "As I know it, that bomb is big enough to blow this place out, and the block, too. Anyone standing within a block of this place could be in serious danger."

Dante nodded, and opened his mouth to start to say, "Yeah, I got—"

"We're not fucking going *anywhere*."

Renzo's gaze drifted to the angrier of the two. Or shit, maybe Giovanni—Andino's father, as far as he knew—was just terrified. His son was inside. He couldn't go in. "You want your wife to bury a son, nephew, *and* a husband when they finally dig your bodies out of the rubble?"

Giovanni's jaw hardened in his frustration. "I can't *go*. He's right there," the man snapped, pointing at the fucking wall like Renzo couldn't see it. "He's right *there*, okay. He's just beyond that fucking wall, and you want me to *go?*"

"Emotions are a bit high here," Dante murmured. "We got the same messages as Lucian, and the live feeds. We're all informed on what's inside, and how it's going to go down if someone can't get them out, or disengage the bomb."

The other man let out a hard laugh, and threw his arms up in the air. He stared at the sky, and let out a shout that echoed over the alleyway between two warehouses. The other men who were standing in their semi-circle immediately quieted, and shot Giovanni a curious look. Or maybe it was one of worry.

The man looked ready to *go off*.

Renzo didn't blame him.

"You have to relax," Dante told his brother. "This isn't good for anyone, Gio."

"That's my *only* kid, Dante," Giovanni barked at his brother.

"I know that!"

Gio shook his head wildly. "No, you don't. You can't possibly know because he's not yours. He's *mine*. He's the only fucking one I got, okay? And he's got kids at home that he needs to get back to—and a *wife*. And I've got a fucking wife I have to go home to and explain what happened here today. If I go home, and I have to tell her we're going to *bury* him ... oh, you just ... you can fuck right off with that shit."

"Gio—"

The other man started to walk away from his brother with a hand tossed high over his shoulder. "*Fuck off.*"

Renzo sighed, and gave Dante a look. "Listen, let him be angry. This is a high stress situation, and you don't have a kid in there, right?"

Dante shook his head. "One is on call right now for us—he's a trauma surgeon. Another is flying to California today. So, no."

"Get the surgeon closer; within a couple blocks."

The older man cleared his throat, and glanced away. "You think—"

"Nothing. I think *nothing*. I know it's better to prepare for the worst and hope for the best, though."

"Yeah, all right."

"But for the record …" Renzo cleared his throat, and shifted on his feet as he shoved his hands into the pockets of the leather jacket. "You need the surgeon closer for anyone *around*. Because if that blows, he won't save anyone inside. You all do need to get as far away from here as you can while I'm inside."

Dante let out a quiet noise. "I don't know if I can get Gio—"

"Then you fucking drag him out of here. It's not negotiable."

"Can you minimize the impact of the blast in any way?"

Renzo shrugged. "I can't tell you anything about that bomb until I'm inside there, eye-level with it, looking at all the parts of it that make it tick. But typically, from what I know about bombs like this … no, I won't be able to minimize the blast should it go off."

"*Fuck.*"

Yeah.

Fuck was right.

Dante calmed his outburst, and turned to Renzo with a final nod. "Okay, I'll make sure the area is clear. Anything you need before you go in?"

Renzo had to think about that one—there was one thing he really wanted, but he couldn't have it right now. He wanted to speak to Lucia.

He wanted to tell her that he loved her, and if today didn't end the way he was praying for it to, that he was sorry they didn't get the chance to see this thing between them through like they should have been able to.

He wanted to apologize for leaving the hospital without telling her goodbye, but he was just like his little brother, honestly. He was like Diego because *goodbye* scared him, too. Goodbye, to him, felt way too final, and he wasn't trying to go away forever. He was trying to get back to her. He didn't think she would understand.

He wanted to tell her that she was worth the fucking world and *more* to him. Always would be.

That's why he was here today.

For her.

But she messed up his head—it wasn't even her fault because he loved it, usually. But today, he couldn't afford for her to put him off his game.

So, Renzo shook his head and replied, "No, I got everything I need in my pockets, thanks."

Dante pulled out the phone in his hand, and asked, "What's your phone number—I want a direct line while you're in there."

Renzo rattled it off as he headed for the side exit door that he suspected had been left unlocked for everyone to go inside the warehouse without issues. Yeah, he bet Christian had been planning this for a while, and now it suddenly made sense why the asshole had been playing down in this district of Brooklyn when Renzo followed him.

Not that it mattered now.

He had other things to do.

• • •

Renzo had just stepped inside the warehouse, and let the door close behind him with an audible *click* as the phone in his hand buzzed. He didn't want to look down at it and see whatever message was waiting for him when in that moment, he had to drag in a breath and calm himself. He had to feel the full weight of the realization that now, there *was no going back*.

He was inside.

Leaving meant death.

This was it.

Once he took that breath, he lifted the phone in his hand to check the message scrolling across the home screen. A text from Dante, it looked like. Renzo might have been fine with that if not for the words the man had sent him.

That sent his anxiety spiking.

Lucia went after Christian, the text read.

There was a part of him—the stupid part that still wasn't very good at thinking things through, for the most part—that suddenly wanted to turn the hell around, and head for the door. It was dumb because as soon as he opened it, everything was going to hell. This whole place would be bombed sky-high, and every person inside—including him—would be dead.

That was reality.

And yet, that part of him still wanted to leave. He still wanted to go after her because *what the fuck, Lucia?* What was she thinking?

He wondered if their conversation at the hospital between him and her father hadn't been as quiet as they thought it had been. Or maybe ... the woman was just smarter than the rest of them gave her credit for, and she stayed close enough to listen.

Either way ... *what the fuck?*

It was the only thing that felt appropriate.

Get her away from him, Renzo texted back.

What else could he do?

Fuck her for doing this.

Now his head was *screwed*.

"So, they send you in, huh?"

Renzo glanced up from his phone, and met the gaze of Johnathan Marcello. Lucia's brother looked like he was dead inside staring back at Renzo. Like he couldn't fucking feel *anything*, and this was just another day for him.

He knew that couldn't be true.

But hell ... a situation like this could do a lot of things to people. No one was going to react to it the same way. He wouldn't expect them to, either.

Behind John, another man stood close with his arms folded over his chest. Andino. Lucia and John's cousin. The main boss of the Marcello organization, as far as Renzo knew, while John was the boss of another New York faction for the Marcellos.

"Yeah, they sent me," Renzo said. "Anyone find the bomb?"

John looked like he was chewing on his inner cheek before he muttered, "Toward the middle of the place. There are some ... uh, car lifts and things. It was setup right between two of them. You know those lifts with the fucking cement holes beneath them for someone to go under and work on the cars?"

Renzo nodded. "Yeah."

"Those."

"Are there cars on the lifts?"

John shrugged. "On both, yeah."

"So, he was trying to hide them, then. Or ... make them blend in a bit."

The man behind John let out a hard sigh, and passed the two of them a look. "How the fuck are we getting out of here, huh?"

"I don't know yet," Renzo replied.

"Well, don't you think you better fucking figure it out?" Andino snapped. "Because I've got fifteen men inside this warehouse, not including *us*, and they send in you. You're supposed to be the goddamn bomb specialist, right? That's what John said. So, why don't you stop talking about bullshit, and get on with telling me how you're going to get me out of here and back to my wife and kids."

Renzo arched a brow. "No."

Andino turned to face Renzo head-on. "I beg your fucking pardon?"

"I don't have to tell you or anyone else anything. This is *my* show. What I want, and how I work, and the way it's done ... that's all on me. I can work while you watch, or I can work alone. I *will* work silently, unless I choose to do differently. My work? It's fucking *intense*. I'm controlling, and focused.

You don't like it? *Fuck off.* Get used to it, man. Step up and let me do what I'm here to do, or step the fuck off."

John cleared his throat as the silence between Renzo and Andino stretched on. "Listen, he's wound a little tight right now. He doesn't mean to be an asshole, he just doesn't deal with this kind of shit well, that's all."

Well, that was all nice and great.

Except for one thing ...

"I'm in here, too," Renzo replied. "I'm going to die, too. So, fuck off, and let me work."

• • •

This is not good.

Oh, this was so not good.

Renzo used the tip of an icepick-like tool from his small kit to peel up a cluster of wires so that he could get a better look at where it was connected to. The problem was that the setup used for this particular bomb was not the norm—it didn't mean that Renzo didn't understand what he was looking at, but rather ... he understood what it meant to be looking at this fucking mess.

Actually, calling it a mess was ... offensive.

This bomb was amazing.

Brilliant.

Deadly.

Typically a large cluster of wires on a bomb would go to the same fucking place—the cluster would connect into the same general area, but not on this bomb. No, on this one, the cluster then broke off into several snakes of wires that went to all different places on the bomb.

To several batteries to keep the electronics running. The problem with that? It removed Renzo's ability to cut the power source when there were several, and he was sure, just by the electronic setup, that if he cut *one* power source, it would set the timer currently sitting still at ten seconds to start counting down.

Ten seconds.

That's what he fucking *had.*

All of ten seconds after he cut a wire to *move.*

He couldn't get to the other side of this fucking warehouse in ten seconds. That was a *joke.* This bomb was a guaranteed death trap, and he wished he knew who had built it for Christian. It could be any number of bomb experts. There were only a handful in the world who could create a masterpiece like this. If only Renzo could nail it down to *which* man had made this bomb, then he might know where to look for the failsafe.

Every bomb expert made a failsafe. The one wire to cut on a bomb, or the one piece to remove that would disengage the whole thing. They made sure to put a failsafe on because it was always possible during transport or creation that something could go wrong that would start the bomb's timer before it should begin counting down.

Renzo couldn't find the failsafe.

He didn't know *which* wire to cut because there were too many—too many leads to be cut *all at once*. He didn't have enough hands to cut every single power source at the same time. He didn't have enough tools to use the hands of the other men in the warehouse to cut the wires, either.

"Anything?" John asked.

For the most part, Renzo had to give John credit. And all the other men in the warehouse. They stayed away from him—they stayed quiet. They let him work, and didn't step in. They didn't make demands, or bark at him to hurry the fuck up.

That's what he needed.

It still wasn't going to make a difference, it seemed.

Renzo swallowed hard—an idea trickling up his spine. "They're all at the back, right?"

John nodded. "Yeah, that's what I said."

"And there's no camera back there?"

"That's why they huddled back there, yeah."

"Is there a door?"

John cleared his throat. "There is … but—"

"It's wired, I know."

Renzo pulled his icepick-like tool away from the bomb with a careful hand, and rested his arms over his bent knees. Staring at the bomb, he ran through the only options he had. His chest felt tight because there was only *one* thing he could do—and even that wasn't a total failsafe.

Christian still had a kill switch he could pull, but if he couldn't see the men on the cameras escaping the warehouse, then would he pull it? If he didn't have a reason to pull the kill switch, would he set it off?

Renzo didn't think so …

But it was still a risk.

"What are you thinking?" John asked.

"I can get you all out. You'll have—*at most,* John—two minutes. That's it, all right. Two minutes, and you gotta run as far and as fast as you can. Get these guys in alleyways between buildings. Huddle down to the ground, and cover your heads. Even better if you can get *inside* something."

"I don't understand—"

Renzo pointed the tool at the wires on the bomb leading to just *one* battery source—it connected the Wi-Fi for the bomb, but was also a failsafe power source. "These wires that are twisted … unless I cut through the latex tubing around them, I can't see which is which inside. One is leading to the Wi-Fi, and the other … to the power source for one of the batteries for the timer." He gestured at the timer in question sitting at ten seconds. "There is a split second at which a wire is cut where power is *still* running through the wires. As long as I can see the exposed wires, I can hold together the wires leading to the timer to stop it from counting down."

Tipping his head to the side, he sighed. "I can let the other wires hang— the ones that'll override the tripped doors. It'll allow you all to get the fuck out of here, but I gotta keep my hands on the other wires beneath the latex tubing to keep the timer from starting."

"Ten seconds won't be enough to get us all out of here," John pointed out.

"I can hold the wires after I cut them to keep them connected, so the brain on the bomb won't know the difference until I let them go."

"You couldn't twist them—"

"Not these types of wires. I have never been able to twist them in such a way that the brain couldn't tell the difference. It isn't a risk I am willing to take. So, while I hold it, you all can get out."

John quieted above Renzo before he quietly said, "But you won't get out. You have to hold the wires. That's what you're saying."

Ah, so the fucker was finally getting it.

Renzo's jaw ached from clenching his teeth. It ached like his heart, and his chest. His lungs beneath his ribs felt like they were expanding beyond the point that they should. It *hurt*. Like his mind, and his soul.

Because this meant one thing.

One person would die here today.

Him.

"Ren," John whispered.

He didn't look away from the bomb. "I don't want to get inside my head about it, okay? Get them all at the door, and waiting."

"But you have to—"

"This is the only way, John."

God, he *knew it*.

He'd spent the last twenty minutes going over every inch of this bomb, and the wiring. All the electronics. He looked at every possible angle he could to find that failsafe, but he couldn't see it. He didn't know where it was.

Because it didn't exist.

There was no way to disengage the bomb.

It was Christian's *last* backup, Renzo realized. Making sure that there was no way to disengage the bomb just in case because the man planned for everything here.

Renzo dragged in a hard breath as he pulled that one latex tube out with the two twisted wires, and held it there with his icepick-like tool. "You'll tell her I love her, won't you?"

Because he couldn't call Lucia right now to tell her himself. Who knew where she was? Still with Christian, probably. Nobody had updated them like they promised they would when they got Lucia away from the asshole.

Renzo glanced up at John. "You'll tell her that for me, won't you?"

John stared back, and the deadness in his eyes from earlier was gone. Instead, it'd been replaced with thick emotion, and a line of water. "Every single day, Ren. I'll remind her every day."

Yeah, okay.

That seemed like a fair trade.

"Get to the door, John. I'll call it out."

"*Fuck.*" John gave Renzo one last look, and muttered, "At least *try*, okay?"

"I don't know how I could."

"Me either, but *try.*"

As John passed the cars on the lifts, he struck out with a fist and it connected with the metal control box. It caused the control box to go off, which made the cars on the lifts lower until they were almost level with the cement holes beneath them.

Like a cover.

Metal on top of a cement box.

He stared at it for longer than he should have … because was it possible?

"At the door," he heard called out.

That broke his daze.

Renzo turned back to the bomb, and pulled out the tool that he would need to cut the latex tubing, and the wires. A skilled, fast hand was the only thing that would make this work. Maybe, in those moments, he shouldn't have been thinking about The League and their training … but he kind of wanted to thank Cree for cracking his knuckles with a flexible metal switch every time he didn't move fast enough when he worked on wires.

He didn't *know* how to be slow.

They made sure of that.

Renzo held the wire cutters against the latex, sucked in a breath, and *cut* as his fingers instantly pulled back the latex to expose the wires, so he could slip the ones he needed back together again before the circuit would realize it had been cut. It took all of a half of a second to do, and someone would have missed it had they been standing right there watching him do it.

At the same time, he yelled out, "*Run.*"

The timer stayed steady at ten seconds.

His heart, though?

It was dead.

TWENTY

Cars were pulling away.

Next to the sight of Renzo kneeled down in front of a bomb on one of the screens, that was the other thing that Lucia noticed. She had the hardest time trying to tear her eyes away from Renzo as he looked over the bomb on the cement floor of an unknown warehouse. Every single time he touched the bomb, she noticed his hands were fast but *steady*.

He made deliberate choices.

He thought before he touched.

He didn't just *tinker*.

He was careful.

But fast, too.

Not that any of it made a difference to the way Lucia was currently feeling. Like her heart had suddenly jumped inside her throat, and was beating harder than it had ever beat before. Racing. Like a thousand hooves of horses.

If it kept up, she might puke.

But the other screen … the one watching the outside of the warehouse was the one that caught Lucia's attention for a split second. The cars filled up fast, and backed out of the alleyway where they had all gathered. She recognized the faces of her uncles before they too disappeared into a car, and backed out of the alleyway.

Where were they going?

What was *happening*?

Lucia's attention flipped back to the screen with Renzo. Well, he wasn't entirely alone anymore. John had been watching over his shoulder for the last little while, but her brother didn't look like he was speaking, and Renzo didn't seem like he was talking, either.

Just working.

But would it make a difference?

"A good vendetta can last years," Christian murmured beside her. "And the feeling when you finally watch it come together?"

The man made a rough, deep noise.

"Beautiful, really," he said, smiling coldly.

Lucia had the greatest desire to strike out at him, but she didn't think that would work out well for her. He'd already put his hands on her once— she refused to sit where he wanted her to, so he grabbed her by the hair of her head, and dragged her to the bed himself.

She was going to sit where he wanted her to sit whether she wanted to or not. Or, that was his fucking idea.

"Do they think this is going to work?" Christian asked, more to himself than her as he looked at the motions happening on the many screens. "There is no way out of here. Every backup ruins another failsafe for them. It's impossible."

"Did you expect them not to try?"

He looked over at her, and then nodded. "I did—I wanted to watch them try to figure it out only to finally breakdown when they realized there was only one way out of this."

Lucia swallowed the thickness in her throat. "Death, you mean."

Christian chuckled. "Yes, exactly that."

She didn't know how she was holding it together watching the scene play out on the screens. At some point, she had become a little too numb. Like if she let herself *feel* the emotions that were trying to ravage her insides … well, then she would be entirely useless.

She wouldn't be able to feel anything *but* that.

Lucia couldn't take that risk.

"Isn't that the young man who interrupted us at breakfast?" Christian asked as he watched Renzo look over the bomb.

She opted not to lie. "Yes."

"Do you love him?"

"With everything that I am," Lucia whispered.

Christian smiled again. "Oh, well, this is going to be difficult for you."

Fuck you.

The words were right on the tip of her tongue, but somehow, Lucia managed to keep them inside her head. After all, her scalp and cheek were still burning from the last time she tried to do anything against Christian.

Christian got up from the foot of the bed, and inched closer to the screen while being slightly bent over at the knees. He tipped his head one way as he peered at the one screen, and then the other way when he looked at the others.

She didn't know what he was looking for.

"The rest of them—they've all left the line of the cameras, haven't they?"

"You should have put some in the back," she muttered.

That's where she had watched them all go. Whoever else was inside the warehouse with Renzo, John, and her cousin, Andino. They'd all headed toward the back of the place, for whatever reason. Maybe because they knew where the cameras were, and didn't want to be watched like rats about to die in a large metal box.

But who was to say?

"I didn't *put* the cameras anywhere," Christian muttered. "They came with the damn place—an associate sold it to me before I came to America.

I thought it would work well for my plans. I'm regretting not having someone go in and add more to the security system."

"Fascinating."

It wasn't.

She didn't even try to hide how dry her tone came out.

It wasn't lost on Christian because he glanced back at her over his shoulder with an arched brow that *dared* her to continue without even saying a word. Her gaze darted to the screen behind him—the one showcasing Renzo nodding as John walked away from him. He pulled a tool out of his pocket.

It looked like a *cutter*.

A wire cutter.

Lucia swallowed again—that lump was bigger, now. She needed to keep Christian's attention on her. Renzo would only have cutters if he was going to *cut* something, right? Like the wires … had he figured out a way to disengage the bomb?

Would it still work if Christian pulled the kill switch?

She didn't know.

Still, she could *try* to keep his hand off that kill switch on his phone for as long as possible. She needed a head start, right? Maybe Renzo needed one, too.

"You know," Christian said, "you are beginning to become boring to me, Lucia."

She smiled back at him, unafraid. "That's funny."

"Why?"

"Because you were boring to me from the first second I met you."

That did it.

That pissed him off.

Christian spun around with a hand already raised to hit Lucia. Instinct made her turn her head, and raise an arm to cover her face, but not before she shot one last look at the screen where Renzo was working. She watched him cut the wire, and sucked in a sharp breath at the same time before she closed her eyes to prepare for that oncoming slap.

Christian didn't miss it.

That slap never came.

"What was he doing?" Christian demanded. Lucia opened her eyes to see Christian right up against the screens again. "What did he cut? Why isn't it counting down? *What did he fucking do?*"

His voice become progressively louder until he was just *roaring*. Lucia covered her ears because it hurt to hear it.

She didn't have time to think on it for long. He was already reaching for the cell phone he'd set beside the screens.

"Kill switch it is," he hissed.

No.

The word screamed inside her mind. She didn't even hesitate to jump up from the bed, and smack the phone out of his hand. She heard the phone skid across the floor at the same time Christian swung around with a closed fist that connected with the side of her face.

Pain bloomed.

It exploded in her mind.

Her vision blurred and stars burst in her eyes.

Lucia was sure she hit the floor from the force of the hit, but she couldn't be sure, either.

Holy shit.

"Fucking *bitch*," he snarled at her, "stay down there like the dog you are."

She blinked in just enough time to see Christian turning his back to her. He bent down like he was trying to find the phone as Lucia got up to shaky legs. Her vision still wasn't all that great, and her ears were ringing like crazy.

It didn't matter.

He couldn't touch that fucking phone.

She grabbed the first thing she could to throw—one of the monitors on the desk—and threw it at his back. The screen crashed over the back of Christian's head, and sent him sprawling to the floor. It wasn't enough to keep him down, though.

When he got back up, he came for her. She didn't even have the chance to turn and try to run before he was taking her to the floor. His punches rained down on her one after the other, and the only thing she could do was try to deflect them, or protect her face. Sure, she got in a couple of her own hits—she scratched her nails down his face, too, but it didn't do *anything*.

He wasn't the least bit fazed.

God.

But he didn't have that phone in his hands.

He didn't have the kill switch.

That was all that mattered to—

Pop.

The quiet noise was all Lucia heard before the heavy weight pinning her to the floor, and the constant pain echoing through to her bones was suddenly gone all at once. Christian fell to the side in a heap—a single bullet hole bleeding out of his forehead.

She gasped in air.

Tears streaked down her face.

Her whole body trembled.

"You got it, Lucian?"

Lucia looked up to see her father rushing into the room before he called over his shoulder, "Make sure they're taken care of out there, yeah."

"You got it."

Lucia just kept blinking. "Daddy?"

"*You crazy girl*," he muttered thickly, pulling her up from the floor with shaking hands. "You crazy fucking girl—*why?*"

Lucia sobbed as her father wiped the tears from her face. "I had to *try*. Didn't I?"

"Lucia—"

She glanced over her shoulder to look at the screen where Renzo was still in front of the bomb. She looked in just enough time to watch him let go of whatever he was holding, and dart backwards toward the car lowered on the lift right next to him.

He disappeared.

She didn't know where he went. *Where did he go?* She dragged in a heavy, painful breath. And the bomb blew.

The cameras went black and so did her vision right before she hit the floor.

TWENTY-ONE

Let go.

Let go.

Let the wires go, Ren.

It was a fucked up thing to know you were about to kill yourself when that wasn't something you wanted to do. A bad analogy for it might be the Band-Aid—suck in a breath, and rip the Band-Aid off as fast as possible to minimize the duration of the pain. It was still going to hurt *a lot*, but at least by doing it quickly, it wouldn't last as long.

That's how it went, right?

Well, this was *kind* of the same.

Just a thousand times worse.

Renzo's fingertips slipped on the wires ever so slightly. Certainly not enough to break the circuit and make the timer start counting down, but it was enough to get his fucking heart leaping into his throat. Which just reminded him all over again that this was not what he wanted. He was not fucking ready for *this*.

He hadn't been given the chance to *grow up* into somebody. Never got married, or had kids. He didn't know what the world looked like when he wasn't pissed off at it. He couldn't remember what the sky looked like when he woke up that morning, and now he was wishing he had one more morning to see it.

He hadn't said goodbye, even if he didn't like goodbyes. He hadn't told his brother and sister that he was sorry for being a fuck up, and that he loved them. He never got the chance to show them the better man he wanted to be, only the man they had always known. Was that a good enough man for them?

He never got the chance to tell his parents that he forgave them because he knew they just didn't know how to *be* parents that loved their kids, and he didn't think it was all their fault. They were sick in their minds—addiction and life made them that way. He wanted them to know he forgave them for himself, but he couldn't ever forget.

He was never able to thank Cree for being such a prick because the man knew that's exactly what Renzo needed to push him to make him break. Cree made him into a better *human*. He taught him the tools to slaughter and bury the parts of him that he didn't want to be anymore, and he owed the man *something* for that.

He never got to tell Lucia he loved her again.

Every single morning.

All the nights of their lives.

Life owed him that—they wouldn't get it.

Yeah, he wasn't ready for this shit. He was never more aware of that fact than right now, and it fucked him straight up.

Instead of letting go of the wires like he should, because if he didn't, there was a good chance the idiot watching the cameras would just pull the kill switch anyway, he was stuck in his head going over every single moment of his life that he could.

People liked to say when death came quickly, a person's life would flash behind their eyes. This death for Renzo wasn't fast—it was painfully slow.

His memories came in the same way.

Like a trickle.

One drop at a time.

It hurt more this way, he figured.

Way more.

Renzo let the wires go—he didn't want to hurt anymore. He'd planned a *just in case* for when he let go of those wires, but he didn't think it was going to work, but fuck him if he wasn't going to at least *try*.

Spinning around fast after he let go of the wires, he ran right into the car that had lowered on the lift after John punched the metal control box earlier. Pain bloomed in his shoulder from the impact, but he didn't even feel it.

The adrenaline was rushing through his veins, and all he could think was *move, run, go*. He could hear the timer on the bomb beeping behind him. He was hyperaware of that sound, and it also seemed like it was chasing him.

Beep, beep, beep.

It felt like it was echoing in the quiet warehouse. The same way it reverberated in his mind, and heart. His body became the echo chamber for those beeps and the seconds that they represented with each new *beep*.

Beep, beep, beep.

Six seconds.

Four to go.

Renzo dropped to his knees, and squeezed in beneath the car where it was covering the cement hole beneath the lift. He fell in *hard*. Once he got through that space, he dropped ten feet down, and his back hit the bottom with a *crack*.

If he broke something, he didn't know.

It felt like it.

Probably his fucking skull.

Renzo stared up at the bottom of the car covering the hole for an entire second. The fall had taken his breath away, and he needed just a moment to catch it and realize how far he had fallen before he hit the ground.

It was long enough to hear the bomb *beep* one more time before he rolled over, tucked his body as close to the cement wall as he could, and covered his head with his arms. He still didn't think this was going to work, but he also still needed to try. It wouldn't be him if he didn't go out of this world giving it all he fucking had, right?

Beep.

He'd done what he could.

Beep.

It was all on God now.

Beep.

Please, I don't want to die, Renzo prayed. *I'm not ready to die yet.*

His thoughts were the last thing he heard.

• • •

What hell was *this*?

Or was it heaven?

Renzo didn't think it was heaven—a person couldn't physically *hurt* in heaven, right? Their bones didn't feel like they were separating from one another when they were in heaven, surely. He was sure heaven didn't make someone's head feel like it was going to explode, either.

Heaven wasn't supposed to be *pain*.

Why couldn't he open his eyes?

"… the coma is …"

"… the team in, I'll pay. Get them here …"

"… going to change your …"

It was strange, in a way. Renzo's body was weightless—indefinitely floating on … something. Or nothing at all. He couldn't *feel* his skin, or his hands, or anything else. But he could feel the pain.

The pain was ever-present.

Constant.

Behind the black space of where he was sure should be his eyes, all he saw was darkness. Not even streaks of colors, or the fuzzy shape of something. No, he just saw streaks of different shades of darkness.

And there was color.

Not a lot, sure.

Just a little.

A pin hole of color—bright, and yellow. It was warm, he thought. Warmer than his unfeeling body floating in a sea of nothingness. That light welcomed him closer, and called to him without making a single noise.

He just *felt* it.

Like everything else.

And nothing at all.

"… code blue …"

"… give me twenty more …"

"… call it after five …"

"… *Ren* …"

The light got smaller all of the sudden, and he was *angry* at it. He was angry that it promised something beautiful and wonderful and warm, and then it went away. He was pissed it became smaller, like a pin prick in the back of his mind that he couldn't reach no matter how hard he tried to get to it.

He ignored the light, then.

Ignored the warmth.

Ignored it when it got bigger.

Pretended it didn't come closer.

The pain was back again.

Fucking pain.

So was the floating feeling.

This is not what I asked for, he told God.

He was pretty sure he heard God laugh back.

"… Ren?"

"… Hey, Ren …."

"… Renzo …"

"… I don't want to hate you for doing this. Don't make me hate you for this, *please* …"

• • •

"Can you … *stop?*" Renzo snapped.

The nurse took a wide step back from his bed, and he immediately felt like shit for barking at her like an asshole. He was just sick and fucking *tired* of being touched. Every time they touched him, it felt like his skin was crawling. Not to mention, the goddamn *pain*. With every IV change … the broken bones that were just beginning to heal … the hairline scar from where they'd cut open his head to remove *three* clots inside his brain from the trauma.

It all hurt.

It never stopped.

He was done with being touched.

Done.

"I'm sorry," Renzo muttered, his throat thick and his tongue dry. "I just … been awake for two days, and you all won't leave me alone."

Not that those two days had done a lot for him. His vision cleared after the first day, and he could finally move today. Or … as much as was expected considering his injuries and the trauma to his brain. It was going to take a while for him to get out of this bed and even walk to the bathroom by himself, as much as he hated the very idea.

But it wasn't this woman's fault.

He bet this nurse took shit a lot from patients, and families. People didn't understand the hell nurses went through on a daily basis. They were the people still at the hospital long after a patient fell into a restless sleep, and the family had gone home. They were here cleaning the patients, feeding them, and making sure they stayed alive.

Nobody understood.

Nobody appreciated them for what they did.

"I'm sorry," he said again.

The nurse gave him a smile, saying quietly, "I guess your IV does look okay—just a little bit of blood in the tube. I suppose I can leave it until just before my shift change. How about that?"

God.

That sounded perfect.

Renzo nodded as best he could against the pillow. "Thanks."

Sometimes, his words still came out slurred or confused. Sometimes, he thought he was saying one thing, but he was saying another. It was annoying and frustrating, to say the least, but it was expected.

Or at least, that's what the neurosurgeon explained.

His brain had to heal.

It would take a while.

He was grateful that the hospital managed to keep the detectives out of his room since he woke up. Although, he heard them loud and clear out in the hallway promising to be back as soon as the doctor approved it for them to have a conversation with Renzo. He didn't know what to tell them—the last thing he remembered was going down an elevator.

He didn't even know why he'd been in the elevator. He didn't know who had been there with him, or why he left it.

He knew nothing.

The brain is a funny thing, his doctor said.

"Ah, your first approved visitor," the nurse said, drawing him from his thoughts. She smiled at the person standing in the doorway, and it felt like it took minutes for Renzo to turn in that direction, too. He didn't know who he thought would be standing there, but he knew very well who he *wanted* it to be.

It wasn't who he wanted.

It wasn't Lucia.

Lucian smiled in the doorway, and rested his hands at his front while holding a manila folder. "They decided—and by *they*, I mean your team of neurosurgeons that were called in from overseas—that I would be the best person to meet with you first. One person a day, and they will progressively allow in those who may cause you more upset or emotional reactions as the days passes."

The nurse gave Renzo a small smile. "Do you understand what he's saying?"

He did.

He also didn't like it.

Something beeped hard in the room.

"That sent his blood pressure up," the nurse muttered.

Lucian chuckled. "Yeah, I bet. Do you need to be in here, or …?"

The nurse shook her head. "No, but there is the call button should you need us. Do not hesitate to use it."

"Will do."

It felt like hours before the nurse was gone, and Lucian was sitting beside Renzo's bed on a hard, plastic chair he'd pulled closer. He knew it wasn't hours … but his brain just wasn't connecting seconds, minutes, and hours to the reality of his situation.

It confused him more.

"A team?" Renzo asked.

Lucian seemed to understand what he was asking even though he hadn't given him a lot of details about his question. In his head, he gave all the details … his mouth didn't work to say them, though.

"A friend of my brother's … he worked with a team of neurosurgeons overseas for an old head injury. Any medical professional worth their weight in head trauma say they are the best of the best, and we all knew that was what you needed, but you were never going to survive the trip, Renzo. They could barely get you into the OR without you coding for that first couple of days. But the clots became worse … they didn't have a choice."

"A team?" he asked again.

In his head, he asked, *and they came here for me?*

Lucian arched a brow. "They were worth every penny, clearly."

Were they?

Renzo didn't know.

"I know right now it seems like nothing is right," Lucian said, "but that's your brain, Renzo, and it's just trying to heal. You've got to give it time to heal. Every day, something will get better or easier. The more frustrated you are with your recovery time, and the more you fight it, the longer it will take."

Yeah, okay.

Had he said that out loud?

Renzo didn't know.

"Lucia?" he asked.

Lucian sighed. "She'll come in on the last day with your sister and brother. The team has a way they like to introduce people or things that they know are going to … cause you emotional upset. That's all."

He still didn't like it.

"The doctors say you don't remember a lot about what happened," Lucian said after a moment.

Renzo passed the man a look, but said nothing. What could he say?

Lucian nodded. "Once the police have been around, they do their thing, and we believe they are satisfied in what they've gotten—or not gotten, in your case—from you, then everything will be explained. I'm not purposely keeping it from you because I think you'll tell something that you shouldn't, but rather, you might not be able to control it, Ren. Okay?"

"Okay."

Lucian lifted the folder he'd been holding for Renzo to see. He waved it a bit, and smiled. "Now this … you should understand very well what it means once I tell you what it is. Your contract with me and The League. You were in a coma for a little over a month, and that means during that time, your contract ran out."

The man put the folder on Renzo's lap in the bed. He couldn't pick it up—his arms were tired from the exercises from earlier, and he still didn't trust his brain to tell his limbs to do the right thing. He just looked down at the folder instead of reaching for it.

"You are a free agent," Lucian said. "You can go or do whatever you want, Ren. You've paid your debt. Is that congratulations worthy, do you think?"

Huh.

"Yeah," Renzo mumbled.

"Congrats, then. You earned it."

TWENTY-TWO

"You okay?"

Lucia looked up from her jittery hands to find her mother standing in front of her with a to-go coffee in each hand. "Uh, yeah, I think."

Jordyn nodded, and then gave a little laugh. "You know, with the way you're shaking … I'm not sure that I should give you this cup of coffee."

She had to give her mom credit. There was something to be said about a person who could call you out on your shit without saying it directly. That was Jordyn Marcello in a nutshell. She was too polite to say something that someone might feel was rude, but she wouldn't hesitate to still call you out in her own way.

Lucia had been acting like everything was fine leading up to this day. Every time someone asked her if she was okay with how everything was shaking out, she would nod and agree because she didn't want them to know how nervous she was.

This wasn't about *her*.

This was all about Ren.

His recovery.

His health.

Just *him*.

Today was the first day she was going to be allowed in to visit with him since he woke up almost an entire week ago. She'd spent day after day next to his bed wearing his sweater he'd left at her hotel room, and *begging* him to wake up. Because then, they didn't know if he would. And if he did wake up, they didn't know if he was going to be the same.

He'd looked like *hell*.

Like death in a bed.

Battered, bruised, and fragmented.

Broken bones.

Blackened eyes.

Swollen skin.

The injuries faded as they kept him in that induced coma, sure. The swelling went down, and in some cases, the casts came off for some of the broken bones that weren't as bad as others. His face lost that blackened color from the worst of the bruises, and it was only then that they could confirm that the hairline fracture on his orbital sockets wouldn't need surgery. The swelling had been so bad that they thought the X-rays were not showing them the full extent of the injuries.

It had been bad.

So bad.

Thing was … Lucia just sat there talking to him. She didn't care if he woke up and wasn't the same as he had once been. She didn't care how long recovery would take, or the fact that he might never be one-hundred percent the same again.

She just needed him to *wake up*.

And then she got mad … she got mad because look at what he did to himself. He almost fucking killed himself, and she had to sit there day in and day out just to watch him fight for a life that she didn't even know if he wanted.

If he did want his life, would he have done what he did?

Then, the guilt would come.

Because if not him … then it would have been her brother, her cousin, and so many others being buried. He was willing to sacrifice himself for them. For people who had never given him a second glance because that's just who he was.

Lucia couldn't settle it.

She couldn't settle her feelings, or confusion.

She went from anger to guilt to hope … to a million other things she didn't understand. But wasn't that selfish of her to feel that way? It wasn't her lying in that bed. It wasn't her who made the choice to let the bomb blow.

It wasn't *her*.

It was him.

"I was angry at him," Lucia whispered. "For doing what he did. I told him that I was angry at him—that I would hate him if he died."

Jordyn let out a quiet sigh, and dropped down to crouch in front of her daughter. She set the cups of coffee to the side, and rested her arms over her jean-covered knees. God knew she appreciated her parents more than ever lately. They were always there doing whatever she needed them to do. Whether it was words or actions, they were at the ready for her.

Like now.

Lucia refused to look up at her mom. It was just easier this way to stare at her trembling hands and pretend like she wasn't cutting herself up inside because of shit she had let slip out of her mouth when she was reacting from emotions and a bad situation.

"Lucia," her mom murmured.

She still wouldn't look at her.

Jordyn didn't push, thankfully.

"For one thing—he was in a coma for over a month," Jordyn explained, "so whether or not he even heard you is a toss-up. Second—you're allowed to *feel*, Lucia. You are allowed to have feelings about this, and you don't have to understand them. Absolutely no one, and him included, will expect you to have all of this processed just because he's alive and awake, okay? That's not how this works."

"But he's—"

"Not the only one who is dealing with trauma," her mother interjected firmly.

Lucia blinked.

She hadn't thought of it that way.

Jordyn smiled when Lucia finally glanced up to meet her gaze. "We're all human, Lucia. We all say things when we're angry or hurt that we should never say—things we wish we could take back the second they come out of our mouth. And words hurt, no doubt, but words are also *just* words. Words can be corrected. They can be fixed with actions, and new words. But it's what you feel in here," her mother said, touching the spot over Lucia's heart with her fingertips, "that makes all the difference. It's in there that you know what matters. I promise, he's going to know it, too."

"Lucia?"

She looked up to find the nurse standing in the doorway of the waiting room with a clipboard in her hands.

"Yeah, that's me," Lucia said.

"He's ready whenever you are."

Now or never.

Jordyn smiled, and leaned in to kiss Lucia on her forehead. "Say hello for me and your dad. I heard his sister and brother are coming in today, too, so try not to get him too worked up while you're in there, okay?"

Lucia laughed.

Right.

She was the one who would work Ren up.

It was always the other way around, right?

• • •

"You know, I worked twice as hard all week so that I would be able to sit up on the side of this bed to greet you, Lucia. Don't make me regret that because you just want to stand in the doorway."

Lucia smiled, and let out a laugh. Her gaze fell on the man sitting up in the bed, and her heart clenched in the best way. Oh, it hurt, sure, but it felt damn good, too. Like dragging in a deep breath that burned your lungs after holding your air for too long.

It burned.

And it relieved.

Yeah, that's exactly how it felt.

Renzo grinned at her from the bed, and she just stared. Maybe it was stupid, but she just wanted to look at him. From the moment he woke up, she had been kept away. She didn't want to, but the team of doctors were *adamant* this was what would be best for his brain. One step at a time, they kept repeating. His brain needed to process one thing at a time—including people.

The remaining bruises were pretty much gone—all the swelling was nonexistent. He still had a cast on his left arm, and one on his right foot up to his knee. She knew the one on his arm would be coming off within the next couple of weeks, and they would use a sling. The one on his leg ... that was going to be another couple of months.

Maybe three.

Who was to say?

"You coming in, or ...?" Renzo teased.

She wanted to cry.

His voice was *normal*.

His words were clear.

His smartass was back.

Those were all things that people had reported to her that he was struggling with over the last week. His words would get jumbled, he'd get confused when people couldn't understand what he was saying to them, and then he'd react from that. Sometimes angrily, and other times, he'd be emotional.

It was a toss-up.

His brain heard one thing.

His mouth said another.

This meant good things, though.

Right?

"Lucia," Renzo murmured.

"I was so scared," she whispered.

Renzo swallowed hard, and nodded. "I know—I'm sorry."

"Don't ... God, don't apologize for doing an amazing thing, Ren."

He tipped his head to the side, and chuckled. "You know, the police finally stopped hounding me yesterday, and your father explained the bits I was missing. Some of it came back, and some of it was still a black hole. I still can't remember *why* I decided to let the wires go. I remember that I didn't want to die."

Oh, God.

Those tears she had been holding back finally made their appearance known when she blinked. They tracked lines down her cheeks, but she didn't even bother to wipe them away or try to hide her emotions.

"I wasn't ready," he said after a moment.

"But you still did it."

Renzo let out a loud exhale. "I don't know why, though."

Lucia nodded. "But would you do it again?"

That took him a little longer to answer. She didn't know what he would say, and she didn't have any expectations about it, either. It was his right to answer her question the way he wanted to—honestly, if he wanted. Or a lie, if he needed.

"Knowing what I know about the situation and the bomb ... and the fact seventeen men were able to go home and tell someone they loved them again, yeah." Renzo glanced up and met her gaze. "Even if that meant I didn't get to do that same thing again—you already knew, right? Did you need me to tell you again?"

Lucia dragged in a ragged breath. "I need you to tell me that every single day of my life, Renzo."

"Okay, baby. Okay."

It seemed like with that out of the way, an invisible rope had come to tie itself around Lucia's middle. Something yanked on it, and her feet started moving. She couldn't stop, either. Not until she was all the way across the hospital room, and got her hands on this man she loved entirely too much.

She loved him *crazy*.

Lucia wrapped her arms around him, but not too tightly. Not that it mattered, he tried to wrap his other arm around her back—his only one that wasn't in a cast. She felt the tremor working its way through his arm as she pulled back, and he tried to touch the side of her face with his palm. His arm just wouldn't *lift*.

Renzo let out an angry noise, and shook his head. "Sorry, I just—"

"No, it's okay," she whispered quickly, dropping a kiss to his scowling lips to make him smile again. "Promise."

When she felt his lips curve against her own, she kissed him again. And then again until her lungs were burning with the need for air, but she didn't care. She needed his kiss as hungry and desperate as it was. She needed his lips working against hers to bring her back to reality because it felt like she had been in hell for far too long.

In the background, something *beeped*.

Entirely too loud.

Renzo pulled away with a chuckle, but tossed a glare over his shoulder at the machine that had made the offending noise. It looked like it was monitoring his blood pressure and heartrate. "Fucking thing—it gives me warnings."

She grinned, and stroked his face.

Someone had shaved him.

It should have been her.

"Does it?"

Renzo nodded. "Yesterday, when they let Cree come in ... it kept beeping, and they made him leave. I couldn't get them to understand that's what I needed. He was pushing me, and I needed it."

She gave him a look, and Renzo only tried to shrug, but it didn't come off right. She didn't acknowledge it, and neither did he.

"Cree gets it," Renzo muttered.

"He's the guy that handled you at The League, right?"

"Yeah."

She didn't press for more.

He didn't offer.

Lucia went back to hugging him where she stood between his legs, and used her fingertips to trace over the line of his features. He was happy to sit there, close his eyes, and let her do whatever she wanted. He couldn't know, but she was imprinting his features to her memory.

She had been terrified she would forget them.

"Wait, wait, wait ... we don't want it to be a surprise for him!"

"Ren! *Ren!*"

Footsteps followed the shouting.

Diego's shouts.

"Ren!"

"Young man, you wait just a sec—"

The machines started beeping.

Diego came into the room *crying*. "Ren?"

Lucia thought to step back from Renzo, and let his little brother come to greet him, but he didn't let her. Instead, he used *her* to help him get off the bed. On shaky legs, sure, and an unsteady body, but he did it. She was sure he would need help to get back into the bed. She knew it probably took every bit of energy he had, like sitting up wasn't already a taxing event for him.

And he waited for his brother to come to him. Because that was Ren. He'd always think about them before he ever thought about himself.

He didn't know anything different.

• • •

Five months later ...

Lucia tossed the keys to her apartment into the glass bowl at the same time she kicked off her heels. There was nothing like coming home after a long day, and just ... breathing. Something about that was comforting to her. She needed it to keep her sane.

Although, lately, Lucia had to admit that California didn't feel like home. She'd been back for almost three months—the second the doctor gave Renzo his walking papers, so to speak, from the hospital, she had to come back here to finish out her internship with Kelly and the gallery.

More than anything, she wanted to be in New York. That's where Renzo was doing the majority of his recovery, although he did travel quite often to Vegas, and more recently, directly to her, too.

She also missed her family.

All the time.

And Renzo.

She missed him, too, even if he'd just walked out of her place after visiting for a span of days. It never got easier, and that's how she knew.

Lucia wouldn't be staying in California for very much longer. She'd let Kelly know before she left the gallery that day, too. The woman seemed to understand, and even admitted that Lucia just didn't seem like her attention was where it needed to be after coming back from New York.

She'd almost laughed at that.

Understatement of the century.

How could her attention be where it needed to be here when her heart and soul was somewhere else entirely?

She had another month here before her internship would be finished. Kelly was kind enough to offer Lucia a full-time job at the gallery, if she wanted to take it. The pay was incredible, as were the benefits and the experience she would get from it.

It was her dream.

She could live that dream elsewhere, too.

Heading through the apartment, the first thing Lucia did was pull her phone out of her pocket. She was already calling Renzo's cell before she even entered her kitchen. She froze all over at the sound of that ringing in her ear also echoing from somewhere in her apartment. Pulling the phone away, she listened.

Sure enough …

The ringing was coming from the back of her place.

Lucia shook her head, knowing exactly where he was in her place. Sometimes he did this. He just showed up, and she came home to find him sleeping in her bed, or sitting in front of the television with his favorite bowl of cereal.

She never asked Renzo what sent him running back and forth. She didn't know if he just wanted to be around her, or if he wanted to escape something else.

He didn't talk about it.

She didn't ask.

Soon, she found him.

Lucia leaned in the bathroom doorway and eyed Renzo where he rested in a dry bathtub. Him, and those fucking bathtubs. All these years, and he still did it. It was sad in a way, but also amusing.

Whatever he needed.

"When did you get here?" she asked.

Renzo glanced up, and flashed her a sexy smile. "About an hour ago."

"Did you come from Vegas?"

He shrugged. "Cree was driving me crazy."

Lucia didn't respond, but she didn't need to.

Renzo was *far* better—he was even back at work for The League, although now, as far as she knew it, he decided what jobs he wanted to take, and which teams he wanted to work on, if that was the case. He was mostly healed, and back to normal. All his injuries were gone, and he looked perfectly fine.

But she knew ...

Sometimes, his hands still shook.

Sometimes, his mind took a second to catch up.

Sometimes, he just didn't feel like him.

That's where Cree came in, or so he said. Cree was the therapy and the recovery that he needed. Cree was the person pushing him mentally *and* physically. He was the one person Renzo could go to, and know if he needed to break without being judged for it, then Cree would be there to do it.

She didn't think it was easy.

She knew Renzo left those sessions exhausted, but not ready to give up. He came out of them stronger, even if he was weaker for a time.

Lucia peered up at the ceiling. "I thought you weren't seeing Cree until next week?"

Renzo grunted under his breath as he worked his herb grinder back and forth, and the briefest whiff of freshly cut bud drifted through the bathroom. "Needed to get my mind off some shit, I guess."

"Like what? Because you know I'm here, too, right?"

He did look up at that statement, and his hands froze on his grinder. "I know that, Lucia."

"Just making sure."

Renzo smiled.

She winked.

He needed what he needed.

She didn't judge or push.

"I found my mom," he muttered, going back to his work as soon as he let those words escape his lips. "I thought ... it'd been years, you know? Maybe she would be willing to try now. Maybe she was sick and tired of being sick and fucking tired, Lucia. I thought a lot of things, and so I went looking for her."

"You didn't tell me you wanted to find your mom."

"I was going through some shit about her."

"Oh," she whispered.

"She can't get better for me and Rose, you know," he said, sighing. "It's too late for us—we're adults, and doing our own thing. But Diego, he's still a kid. She could get better for him. Make a fucking effort, and fix the shit that's wrong before it's too late like it is for the rest of us."

"Ren …"

"She just asked me for money and then when I wouldn't give her any, she called me a bastard and said she was gonna call the cops on me."

Lucia wished she could be angry.

Or surprised.

Really, she just felt numb.

A lot like the way he sounded.

"Diego's got what he needs, Ren," she said.

He nodded. "Yeah, but he also needs a mom. He doesn't need someone who acts like his mom, or whatever, he needs *her*. The real fucking thing. I know, Lucia, because I needed her. I needed her and all she ever wanted to do was give everything she had to the drugs she pumped into her body. Our father, well, he's a lost cause. Dead, I guess."

"What?"

"He had a heart attack a couple months back," Renzo said, dropping cut up bud into a folded up paper to roll. "I know where he's buried. Haven't been there yet, but it's on my mind lately, too. So, yeah … I went looking."

She could tell he was just talking to *talk*. He was giving her details because he felt like she needed to know them. She wanted to know, sure, but it was always up to him on whether or not he was willing to share.

She didn't push.

"You want a minute?" she asked.

Renzo licked the line of the paper, and passed her a look. "Depends on if you want to share this smoke with me, baby."

Lucia laughed. "Not while you're in the tub."

"You're no fun."

"Listen, *some* of us use the bathtub for its intended purpose, Ren, which is to take a bath."

"I use it for that, too."

"I know. I'll be in the kitchen."

"*Fine*. Christ, smoking is supposed to relax me, not make me give it more effort, Lucia."

She rolled her eyes, and left him behind in the bathroom as she headed for the kitchen. He was quick to follow behind her, and she had already pulled out a bottle of water from the fridge to have while he shared his smoke with her.

Renzo already had the joint lit and burning when he took a stool at the kitchen island. Unlike him, who could smoke and smoke and smoke before he was satisfied that his mind was as high as he wanted it, she only needed just a few pulls to be good. He worked the joint down to a good point for her, and handed it over to let her have whatever she wanted off it. He leaned in as she took her last drag.

"Gun it, baby," he murmured.

Lucia grinned, and pulled him closer by fisting her hand into his leather jacket. He hovered over her mouth, lips parted as she let the smoke come out. There was something sexy about the way his eyes locked on hers as the smoke drifted from her lips to his, and she loved it.

He inhaled her smoke, held it, and kissed her hard.

Renzo's lips curled at the edges, and he inhaled every drop of the smoke she passed to him. His pupils blew wide while his gaze drifted down her face, and lingered on her throat. He closed the distance, then, his tongue lashing out against the hollow of her throat, and his teeth grazing her skin with the *promise* of more.

Her mind was *light*.

Her body, hot.

This was the part she liked the most about finding Renzo at her place when he decided to randomly make a trip. Time apart always seemed to bring them back together in the *most* brilliant of ways.

Sex was just one of those.

Lucia crawled over the top of the island at Renzo's urging hands. Her legs hung off the edge as one by one, he stripped her of the clothes she had on. Then, she got to take her time to admire his body and the two new tattoos he'd had done on his stomach during his recovery—one read *Ten Seconds* and the other, a Madonna. She figured, in a way, they were self-explanatory. Renzo loved art as much as she did, just in his own way.

Once he was undressed, she eyed the red, puckered scar on the inner section of his left bicep. She used the tips of her fingertips to trace the scar—he'd gotten The League's chip removed a couple of months back so they couldn't track him anymore if he didn't want them to. She understood why he did it, and frankly, was surprised he hadn't gotten it taken out as soon as he got out of the hospital.

The cool air in the apartment whispered over her skin as he widened her legs, and kneeled down until he was eye-level with her pussy. She swore he licked his fucking lips too before he grinned up at her.

"Look at that—all pink and wet already, baby."

Lucia couldn't even find it in herself to be ashamed. "You should have a taste—it's been a while."

"You're fucking telling me."

Something wicked and dark flashed in Renzo's eyes as he closed the distance between his mouth and her pussy. His tongue found her slit as she tipped her head back to just *feel*. There was nothing like his mouth working against her sex to put her in the best place. And he knew just what to do to get her higher than she already was. His tongue slipped between beating a fast pace against her clit, and then back down to her slit to work her there, too.

"You're such a fucking *tease*," she breathed.

Renzo's chuckles rocked against her sex.

A deep bass.

God.

"You want to come, then?"

"So bad," she admitted.

"Don't hold back."

Lucia laughed breathlessly. "Never."

Yeah, sometimes his hand would still shake. And sometimes he got frustrated over little things that would have been nothing to him before. But when he wanted something to work … when he was focusing in on the things he loved to *do*—her—then everything was just fine for him, and her.

She swore Renzo took it as a challenge to see just how fast he could make her come. And being the kind of man he was, who loved a good competition, he liked to see if he could beat his fucking time. This was no different.

All it took was his tongue lashing against her clit, and then just as she started to climb that oncoming peak of bliss, he sucked the nub in between his teeth. The pain was sharp, and the orgasm was intense.

"*Ren.*"

She was still trembling when he pulled away from her sex, flipped her over on the island, and pulled her down so that her knees were on the two stools. He fitted in behind her, his pants shuffled down, and her pussy was *still* clenching when he filled her full. That first thrust sent her body sprawling against the countertop.

He pushed one hand against her back, keeping her pinned to the countertop. His other hand wrapped in her hair, and pulled tight. He fucked her hard from behind as her sounds echoed through the quiet apartment. She was sure her neighbors were going to be happy people when she finally moved out, and they didn't have to hear this every few days.

She couldn't even meet their eyes anymore.

Fuck it.

"Fuck yeah," Renzo muttered behind her, "back into that cock, baby."

Was she?

Christ.

His pace picked up as her sounds got louder. He pulled her hair harder, and pushed her firmer into the countertop, too. There was something about giving her control to him that did it for her—it made her wetter, if that was possible, and got her body even hotter.

Insane, really.

"Fuck, *there*," she breathed.

She came again.

Shaking.

Breathless.

So high.

He followed soon after, painting her back with streaks of come that warmed her skin up all over again. She felt his fingertips drag through the fluids before coming to rest at her backside. Trembling fingers. He leaned against her, and his breath pulsed against the back of her neck.

"Fucking love you," he mumbled.

Lucia grinned. "Love you, Ren."

"Sit up, huh?"

"What?"

He didn't explain, simply helped her to turn around on one of the stools until she was facing him. She didn't even care that she was naked, and he was already tucking himself away. She was going to have to clean the mess they made, but that was a background though, too.

Especially because he looked … *nervous*.

"Ren?" she asked, smiling.

He cleared his throat, and laughed. "So maybe now isn't the right time."

"For what?"

"Just, I'll get you dressed first, okay?"

She just shook her head, but if that was what he wanted. It took a couple of minutes for them to clean up, and pull on clothes again until both of them dressed. He set her right back up on the stool, and both of his hands came to rest on her thighs as he came close enough to press a soft, lingering kiss to her lips. He kissed her until she smiled, and then he dropped another kiss to the tip of her nose, and her forehead.

Sweet kisses.

She just wanted more.

"Okay, now's good," he murmured.

"I still don't know for what, Ren."

One of his hands snuck into the pocket of his jeans, and when he pulled it back out, he held a letter. Renzo smiled a little bit—just a tiny grin that had her heart fluttering.

"One last letter," he murmured.

"Oh?"

"I've replied to every single one you sent me, right?"

"Every single one except the last one."

Sometimes, she would just wake up and a letter would be on her nightstand. Sometimes, he sent it in the mail. Other times, he gave them to her himself.

Renzo nodded. "This is the last one, baby."

She took the letter when he handed it over, and unfolded it to read the words written inside. Water blurred her gaze as she read it.

Lucia,
I would do every second of this life again a thousand times over if you give me one second of you being my wife.
Would you give me that?
Love, Ren

She looked up from the paper to find he had kneeled down, and had his palm open for her to see the item resting there waiting for her to see.

Her *mother's* engagement ring.

Lucia blinked, and sucked in fast breath. "*Oh.*"

Renzo laughed. "That's not—"

"*Yes.*"

"Let me ask it first?"

Lucia nodded. "But you don't *have* to. I—"

"Marry me?"

"Yes, Ren. *Yes.*"

EPILOGUE

Six months later …

"Why are you looking at me like that?" Renzo asked.

Diego tried to glance away like his older brother hadn't caught him staring. Really, Renzo had been trying to ignore it for the most part. Diego had been doing this staring thing a lot more lately. Like he wanted to keep his eyes on his brother as much as he possibly could lest Renzo get out of his sights, and never come back. Or maybe it was just the fact that Diego was finally starting to believe that no, Renzo wasn't going anywhere.

Maybe he'd go off for a day or two—he still had to work, he was who he was now. And now that he was—sort of—a free agent where The League was concerned, he could be a little more choosey with his jobs. If he wanted to bind himself to a contractor, like say the Marcellos, then he could. Or, he could work for whoever the fuck he wanted to as long as their check cleared, and they were smart enough to offer him good money to do a job.

But that was it.

He wasn't going anywhere.

New York was fucking permanent, now. This was where he was going to live indefinitely. That was always the plan at the end of the day. His goal was always to come back to these goddamn streets that raised him and shaped him. This city made him into what he became … it gave him everything. The mindset he lived with every day; the go-out-and-get-it attitude that never left him; an ability to survive; the chance to become something bigger and better than he ever dreamed of … love, too. It even gave him love.

He was always coming back here.

Simple as that.

Plus, New York was Lucia's home, too. This was where her family was always going to be. She might have stayed away for a while—because she so badly needed that space—but she had closed the distance, now. Sure, there was still some work yet to go before all those burned bridges could and would be rebuilt, but it would happen.

Eventually.

"Was thinking," Diego said, shrugging his shoulders. "That's all."

"About what?" Renzo asked.

He crossed the room, and wordlessly, dropped down to one knee so that he and Diego could be on a more level playing field, so to speak. While he

206

was down there, he put his hands to work and fixed Diego's bowtie that had somehow managed to get a little twisted during the time he spent running around with the other kids in the church.

"I guess …" Diego started, his cheeks pinking as he glanced away from Renzo again, "… well, I've got the coolest big brother, right?"

Renzo's hands froze on Diego's bowtie.

He stilled all over.

His brother still wasn't looking at him when Renzo peered up at him after his statement. Diego seemed more interested in watching the cartoon playing on the television in the corner. Not like he'd just blurted something out that kind of stunned Renzo like nothing else ever had before. So was the way of kids.

In an attempt to make Diego understand where his big brother had been for the last few years, and why he hadn't been around, Renzo and Rose tried to explain without too many details. Mostly because a lot of the information wasn't kid-appropriate. Plus, he didn't think Diego would understand very much about The League. At least, not until he was older. But they did try to explain as much as they possibly could.

Renzo wondered … before all of this, how did Diego see him, then? When he was nothing more than a drug dealer trying to make do on the streets to keep them afloat, was he still the coolest?

Diego's next statement let him know. "But you always were, Ren."

Renzo chuckled. "If you say so, buddy."

"There you are!"

Rose's head popped into the doorway of the private room, and a sweet smile split her face as her gaze landed on Diego and Renzo. Standing quickly from the floor, Renzo patted Diego on the shoulder, knowing Rose was likely here just to get him to the other side of the church again with the other children, so he could get ready to take his place and walk down the aisle. If he was a little bit older, Renzo would have put his brother beside him on the altar.

But Diego wanted something else. Something that he felt was a bigger responsibility.

He wanted to carry the rings for Renzo and Lucia in their wedding. Renzo didn't know how to refuse the kid anything. Still, even after all these years apart, that hadn't changed, it seemed.

Rose took a couple of steps into the room, and even as she offered a hand out for Diego to take, her gaze drifted to Renzo. Looking him over, another one of those soft smiles curved her lips, and pride shined in her eyes. "You clean up well, huh?"

Renzo laughed, and swept his hands down the front of his tuxedo. "Thanks, I guess."

"First time I've ever seen you in a tux, Ren."

He cleared his throat, and glanced to the side where a mirror showcased his form covered in very expensive, tailored-to-fit Armani. A silk periwinkle blue tie, matching vest, and pocket square added the final touches to his shined shoes and black tux. She wasn't lying. He never did the suit or tux thing—not even now. Black leather and dark-wash jeans all the way. Preferably with a pair of combat boots that were well-worn, and scuffed all to hell.

He liked a bit of character in his clothing.

But for today ... this was good, too.

"I can't believe you're actually getting married," Rose said. Renzo opened his mouth to reply to his sister, but before he could, she glanced down at her watch, and her gaze narrowed. "Shoot—I promised to help Cella with the kids. I'll make sure to circle back around and see you before everything gets started, okay, Ren?"

That was Rose. Always looking out for everyone else and taking care of them before herself. Maybe before Renzo had caused a mess in her life, she had been able to be a little selfish. She only had to take care of herself, then. When he turned around and put the responsibility that only he had constantly carried for his siblings—in a way—on her, he kind of forced Rose to grow up quick, fast, and in a real fucking hurry.

But she did it.

Amazingly.

"No worries," he said, waving a hand. And then to Diego, he was quick to add, "You be good, huh? And don't lose those rings, right?"

Diego nodded once—firm and sure. "I won't lose 'em, Ren."

All too soon, Rose had tugged a happy Diego out of the room. Sometimes, it still stuck Renzo silent how he blinked, and his little brother went from four years old to ten, edging closer to eleven with every passing day. It felt like a blink in time even though he knew it wasn't. He knew it wasn't because he was, at the same time, all too aware of the years that he had missed out on where his brother was concerned. That, like so many other things, were still ever present in his mind.

Like something else Rose had said, too.

Aware that his sister hadn't entirely closed the door to the room, Renzo didn't bother to cross the space and shut it. Instead, he turned to face the mirror fully. His entire reflection stared back. And like usual when he stared at himself in the mirror, he found himself once again comparing the then with the now.

What he used to be ...

What he now was.

The tattoo that peeked out from under the sleeve of his tux on the back of his hand—the intricate black design that brought him peace whenever he remembered the hours sitting in the chair to get that sleeve perfect. The good twenty pounds of lean muscle he'd packed on from constant training at The League. The hard lines of his face hadn't changed, but the dimness that was ever-present in his eyes was finally gone.

Before, years ago … he'd stare in a mirror and see things he didn't want and thought he could never change. A man with no future, who came from discarded trash, and would never be more than he already was. Now, that person had been replaced by this man.

"I didn't take you as the vain type, Renzo," came a smooth, dark voice from the doorway.

Renzo spun around in just enough time to watch Lucian Marcello slip into the room. The man closed the door behind him—something Rose should have done, so then Renzo's last few private moments before his wedding wouldn't have been interrupted. Or rather, so that he wasn't caught staring at himself like a fool in the mirror.

Lucian shot him a grin. "Admiring your reflection?"

Renzo arched a brow. "No."

"No?"

"Realizing it's not the same, that's all."

Lucian nodded like he understood that, although, Renzo didn't have the first clue how the man could possibly understand. Crossing the room, Lucian took a seat on one of two high-back leather chairs, crossed his right ankle over his left knee, and rested his hands in his lap as he appraised Renzo.

He still had a way to go with this man. There were still some things that needed to be said between them at the end of the day before they were going to be one-hundred percent good again. Thing was—Renzo didn't mind putting in the effort. In a way, Lucian Marcello had been one of the only people to give a shit about Renzo. Sure, the man had a funny way of showing it by giving him to The League … the beginning had been a little rough for them.

That didn't change how this all shook out for them, though. And Renzo knew that he and Lucian were going to have the time to do that now—all Lucian's scans had come back clear. He was officially in remission from his cancer.

So, yeah, they were going to have to put in the effort together. He knew that. He was grateful for this man, too.

If not for Lucian, then Renzo wouldn't be able to look at the man he now was in the mirror. That made all the difference, didn't it? For him, it certainly did. Daily.

He was willing to mend those bridges because of it.

Lucian tipped his head to the side, and stared at Renzo's reflection. "And what do you see when you stare into the mirror, hmm?"

Renzo arched a brow. "Are you here to shrink my head, or what?"

"Just curious, actually."

Well, that told him everything, right?

"It's not what I see, but rather, what I want to see," Renzo muttered, turning back to the mirror again. In the background, Lucian's reflection stared back at him, but he was able to ignore it for the time being. Maybe if he said all this crazy shit that constantly pecked at the back of his brain like an annoying bird that wouldn't leave him alone, then he might be able to move on from it. "I've moved on from who I used to be, haven't I? I've changed."

Lucian nodded. "In a great many ways, sure."

See, even this man could see it.

"Then why do I still see the other me looking back, too? Despite the fact I'm not him now. Even though I'm entirely different. Something better. Someone more. I can be Renzo Anybody. I can change my last name three times a month, if I want to. I don't ever have to be Renzo Zulla, born and bred from the Bronx if I don't want to be. But I still see him all the fucking time."

There.

He said it.

Those words were out—there was no taking them back, now. He seriously hoped just getting them out would do the damn thing for him and make these thoughts go away for good. But it probably wouldn't. That was just his life and luck.

Lucian dragged in a quiet breath, and Renzo thought, maybe calming, too. "You know, you may not believe me when I say this, but you and I are much more alike in some ways than you can possibly know, Renzo."

"Oh, you think?"

He didn't mean for that to come out as sarcastically as it had, but it was out there now. He couldn't change it. Lucian didn't seem to mind as he waved a hand as if to brush off what Renzo said.

"We are similar in this way," Lucian said. "There was a time in my life when my name was not Lucian Marcello, you see. Instead of coming from wealth and status, I came from a man and a woman who left me with a legacy of their misdeeds. Mind you, I loved my mother and father—my biological parents, I mean. Still do today, but that doesn't change the fact that despite becoming a Marcello, being given immeasurable wealth and privilege with a simple last name, I still saw him. Luciano Grovatti, son of a murdered, shamed made man and the child of a dead woman who had been his mistress. More often than not, I thought everyone saw me that way, too, because a select few liked to remind me of exactly where I came from like it was something I could never escape."

Clearing his throat, Lucian stood from his chair and gave Renzo a kind smile before he shrugged one shoulder under his tailored suit. "My advice, not that I learned this from someone else, because I didn't, Renzo ... this was something I learned on my own time, you see. That advice from me is to stop trying to change who he used to be by replacing him with who you see in the mirror now. He and you are one in the same, young man. And you could not be you now if not for who he was then. Own it—love him, too. He's given you far more than anyone else ever has. You don't have to be proud of where you came from, if that's not what you want, but that doesn't mean you need to be ashamed of what made you, either."

Renzo blinked, unsure of what to say. Nothing felt appropriate, honestly. Lucian didn't seem to mind. He gave Renzo a pat on the shoulder as he passed him by, saying, "I thought you might appreciate someone coming in to send you off into married life ... considering you don't have your own mother or father here to do it. I wasn't sure if you would appreciate me—understandably—being the one to do it, but no one else would have been appropriate to do it, Ren."

He gave the man a look, but Lucian was already standing in the doorway, ready to leave. "Thank you, Lucian."

Lucian nodded. "It's what you deserve."

Was it?

Renzo wasn't even sure of that, considering ...

As though Lucian could read Renzo's mind, he tossed over his shoulder as he left, "But today is not the day to think about all of that, Renzo. Today is a beautiful day."

He stared back into the mirror again.

Lucian wasn't wrong.

Renzo was getting married today.

What else mattered?

• • •

Renzo had never been much for confession. In fact, he had never done confession. Not once in his entire life, despite the fact that on some Sundays, he could vividly remember his mother dressing him and Rose up and dragging them into a church.

Always a Catholic church, too, because apparently, that's just what they were. He didn't remember his First Communion but there was something about the smell of an old church that was comforting to him. Something about the hard, curved backs of the pews that felt like he was welcomed to sit there ... despite everything he was and had done.

Someone might say it was meant to be.

He didn't know if he would.

Still, as he rolled the rosary beads between his fingers, repeating his prayers for the penance from the priest who would be marrying him and

Lucia in only a half of a hour ... Renzo felt relief. As strange as it was, he embraced it. Church every Sunday had never been high on his list of priority, but it was for Lucia. And every Sunday, regardless if his ass just wanted to stay in bed or not, Lucia dragged him along with her to sit in the pew.

Renzo found he didn't mind.

Confession before the ceremony was apparently an old tradition in this church, according to the priest and every single Marcello he thought to ask. Each man nodded and grinned like they were remembering their last confession before marrying their wives when he questioned if this was necessary.

Apparently, it was.

Renzo hadn't realized he was going to need it.

Until he did.

Funny how that worked.

He had just finished repeating the last prayer when a soft knock echoed throughout the private room used for confession. Filled with rich tapestries and chairs older than fucking time, there was always something beautiful to look at, if one wanted to. But he wasn't looking at anything except the love of his life poking her head in the door with a sly smile.

Lucia.

That string of rosary beads hung limply from his suddenly still fingers as he took her in with an appreciative gaze. She was water, and he was taking a damn slow drink in that moment. Perfect makeup giving her a sexy look. Painted red lips and dark kohl lining her eyes. She had left her hair down in thick, shiny waves.

And her dress ...

Jesus, her dress.

A ballgown that filled the doorway. In soft ivory, and draped with delicate lace, she looked like every inch a queen. His queen.

Renzo blinked. "What are you doing in here?"

He could have asked a lot of things—probably should have asked anything else, too. But shit, everyone had been so damn determined to keep her away from him ... even going as far as stealing her away from him the night before after the rehearsal dinner. The Marcellos had gotten a kick out of doing that to him.

Stealing the bride-to-be from the assassin, and refusing to give her back. The bastards.

But as he was coming to learn, they were just as much his family as they were hers. Or they wanted to be. He just had to let them.

Lucia smiled, shot a look over her shoulder, and then stepped just far enough into the room to close the door behind her. He was already rising from the chair he'd been sitting in to do his penance, and crossing the room to reach for her before she was able to get a single word out of her pretty lips.

He couldn't get his arms around her fast enough—couldn't get his lips on hers hard enough to satisfy the need to touch and taste her again. All it took was being away from her for a few hours, and he was ready to burn the world down to make sure she didn't leave his side again.

It didn't have to make sense.

It just *was*.

Lucia grinned wickedly against his kiss. "See, they're not the only ones who are sneaky. Nobody can keep me away from you, Ren. I'll always find a way."

Renzo laughed. "This is bad luck."

"Nope, we've had enough of that."

God.

Wasn't that the fucking truth?

Slipping his hands under her jaw, he tipped her head back, so he could stare into her eyes. Forever stared back. That, and love. Forgiveness. Sweetness. His entire fucking life.

Everything.

She was everything for him.

He could always find it in her eyes, too.

"I love you, Lucia," he murmured.

More than she could possibly know.

For forever and a day, if God would give it to him.

Lucia stroked his lips with the pad of her thumb. "And I love you, Ren."

That's all that mattered.

The rest would never compare.

"Ready to get started on forever, then?" he asked.

Lucia laughed sweetly. "I have always been ready, Ren."

Yeah, him too.

With her … always.

ABOUT THE AUTHOR

Bethany-Kris is a Canadian author, lover of much, and mother to four sons, two cats, and three dogs. A small town in Eastern Canada where she was born and raised is where she has always called home. With her boys under her feet, a snuggling cat, barking dogs, and a spouse calling over his shoulder, she is nearly always writing something ... when she can find the time.

Find Bethany-Kris at her:

WEBSITE: www.bethanykris.com
BLOG: www.bethanykris.blogspot.ca
FACEBOOK: www.facebook.com/bethanykriswrites
TWITTER: @BethanyKris
INSTAGRAM: www.instagram.com/bethany.kris
PINTEREST: www.pinterest.com/bethanykris

Sign up to Bethany-Kris's New Release Newsletter here:
http://eepurl.com/bf9lzD.

OTHER BOOKS

Renzo + Lucia

Privilege
Harbor
Contempt

Andino + Haven

Duty
Vow

John + Siena

Loyalty
Disgrace

Cross + Catherine

Always
Revere
Unruly
The Companion
Naz & Roz

Guzzi Duet

Unraveled, Book One
Entangled, Book Two

DeLuca Duet

Waste of Worth: Part One
Worth of Waste: Part Two

Standalone Titles

Effortless
Inflict
Cozen
Captivated
Dishonored

Donati Bloodlines

Thin Lies
Thin Lines
Thin Lives
Behind the Bloodlines
The Complete Trilogy

Filthy Marcellos

Antony
Lucian
Giovanni
Dante
Legacy
A Very Marcello Christmas
The Complete Collection

Seasons of Betrayal

Where the Sun Hides
Where the Snow Falls
Where the Wind Whispers
Seasons: The Complete Seasons of Betrayal Series

Gun Moll Trilogy

Gun Moll
Gangster Moll
Madame Moll

The Chicago War

Deathless & Divided
Reckless & Ruined
Scarless & Sacred
Breathless & Bloodstained
The Complete Series
Maldives & Mistletoe

The Russian Guns

The Arrangement
The Life
The Score
Demyan & Ana
Shattered
The Jersey Vignettes

Find more on Bethany-Kris's website at www.bethanykris.com